YOUR CHANGING FACE

GUERNICA WORLD EDITIONS 67

YOUR CHANGING FACE

Gerry Sheldon

GUERNICA
World
EDITIONS

TTORONTO—CHICAGO—BUFFALO—LANCASTER (U.K.)
2023

Guernica Editions Founder: Antonio D'Alfonso

Michael Mirolla, general editor
Sonia Di Placido, editor
Cover design: Allen Jomoc Jr.
Interior design: Jill Ronsley, suneditwrite.com

Guernica Editions Inc.
287 Templemead Drive, Hamilton (ON), Canada L8W 2W4
2250 Military Road, Tonawanda, N.Y. 14150-6000 U.S.A.
www.guernicaeditions.com

Distributors:
Independent Publishers Group (IPG)
600 North Pulaski Road, Chicago IL 60624
University of Toronto Press Distribution (UTP)
5201 Dufferin Street, Toronto (ON), Canada M3H 5T8

First edition.
Printed in Canada.

Legal Deposit—Third Quarter
Library of Congress Catalog Card Number: 2023935570
Library and Archives Canada Cataloguing in Publication
Title: Your changing face / Rupert Smith.
Names: Smith, Rupert, 1958- author.
Series: Guernica world editions (Series) ; 67.
Description: Series statement: Guernica world editions ; 67
Identifiers: Canadiana (print) 20230215912 | Canadiana (ebook)
20230215955 | ISBN 9781771838313
(softcover) | ISBN 9781771838320 (EPUB)
Classification: LCC PR9369.4.S65 Y68 2023 | DDC 823/.92—dc23

1

HE WANTED TO WRITE A book, but he didn't have anything to say.

"Why, buddy?" Ozzy Man asked. "Why do you want to write a book?"

Ozzy Man shared the inside of Al's head with Doppelgänger. Only Al could hear and see them. They were his imaginary companions, the ones you are supposed to outgrow by your early teens, but he never had. They had been with him ever since he could remember. When his teacher, Mrs. Adendorf, in his first year of school, told them that an angel sits on your right shoulder and a devil on your left, Al understood: Doppelgänger on his right; Ozzy Man on his left.

"I don't know. It's my last frontier," Al said. "If I conquer this, I've done everything I wanted to."

"Crickey, Bud." Ozzy Man made big eyes. "What's going on?" He said: *gohwin awn*.

Ozzy Man, now they were in their sixties, sported swashbuckling three-musketeers looks, short salt-and-pepper beard around a crooked smile, piercing blue eyes. He delivered the iconoclasm of his commentary in a worker's accent straight from Kalgoorlie. Doppelgänger looked and sounded like Al.

"What will you say in a book?" Doppelgänger asked.

Silence echoed tellingly in response, while the Troika thought about that.

"You could spin a loose story about something that happened, and fill in the gaps with your personal theories," Doppelgänger said, always supportive.

"Hee-hee," Ozzy Man said, chuckling. "Al's personal theories. Good one, Bud."

Al never allowed Ozzy Man's running commentary to be heard by anyone; and seldom took his advice. He often did what Doppelgänger suggested: He was so reasonable, so polite, so didn't want to offend. Just like Al. Mrs. Adendorf would have approved—*always listen to the angel, never to the devil*, had been her advice.

The next day Al did no better with his sister, whose take on creative impulse and artistic pretension matched her anarchic worldview. She borrowed Buster Keaton's face to hear the plan and its obvious fatal flaw.

"You could write about the Ten Commandments. That morality crap you are always on about."

"Perhaps," he said. "You mean that slavery is okay, but adultery not?"

She nodded.

"Yeah, slavery is fine, and women's rights don't exist. There are no rules against kidnapping or insider trading or rape. But adultery is a mortal sin."

"In the top ten, no less," he said. Thinking it over, he frowned. "Sis, I can't write a whole book about that."

Crows' feet at the corners of her eyes crinkled.

"The Yin to the Yang of the greatest bestseller of all time? It should fly off the shelves."

He brooded over his salad, pushing the lettuce to one side. Meg squinted at his indecision through the smoke drifting off the end of her fag. Number sixteen for the day. She was cutting down.

"Write about the atheist on the bus," she said.

He was doing his best to be introspectively blue but couldn't get it right when she was around. He grinned at the thought. "Maybe I should—a protagonist who has no religious belief, but then the first ever fundamentalist atheist puts a bomb on a suburban bus and blows it up. The hero has to reconsider his views on religion. While he is struggling with the definition of personal morality and his obligation to society, another atheist assassinates a doctor at an abortion clinic. Our hero has a breakdown—a crisis of faith."

"Atheism is faith in the same way as abstinence is a sex position." Ozzy Man disapproved of Al's choice of words. But Al liked the idea, revelled in the thought of so many righteous toes on which he might tread.

"Imagine the outrage and indignation if anyone actually reads my story, and if, then *shares* his offence on Instagram or Facebook so others can be outraged and offended as well. His sanctimony would go viral; the political correctness would spiral exponentially with each reposting."

"Yup," Ozzy Man said. "Don't know how to make the first guy read it—but he must have thousands of followers who *like* his style and his sneakers. If he can be offended, and he says so with social-media sincerity and po-faced self-righteousness, you are set—instant infamy."

"His dissing your book will become a snippet of the early twenty-first century zeitgeist," Doppelgänger said. "Your virtual effigy would burn on a thousand sites."

"For two weeks," Ozzy Man said. "Then Camilla Cabello will have a new haircut and their attention will drift."

"You don't like the kids on Twitter and Facebook?" Meg asked, squinting, dry as Bond's martini.

Al looked sideways at her across the table. "Not so much."

The arch of her left eyebrow asked, *why not?*

"Their show is tailored for the world to notice and admire just how inclusive and accepting they are," Al said, aware how last century that made him sound. In for a penny, he elaborated: "They intuit their points of view, and think philosophy is a collection of feel-good aphorisms."

"They are Woke." Meg nodded, equally sincere.

"Completely in opposition to anything that big media advertisements might cast as social injustice or elitism. You know the look: they all drink beer together in a trendy bar, laugh a lot and do high-fives," Al said. Then sighed. "It's not enough for a whole book."

"A story, Bud," Ozzy Man said. "You got to tell a story."

"Tell a story about Sex and God and Man and Love," Meg said, adding her support for the idea.

Al nodded *yes* and shook his head *no* at the same time as if he were a wise man in India. "A story, well and good. But it can't be a brutal murder and a clever policeman. Or the plight of war orphans in South Sudan. Or a man who slept in a dumpster and now is the CEO of a listed company. I want to write an adult book about real people and actual things that happen. A book like the ones they made me read at university and write exams about."

"Yeah, Bud," Ozzy Man said. "There must be a theme and a message, and the author's deep understanding for and sensitive analysis of socially relevant and significant topics."

"The existential angst of modern man; the ennui of secular humanism," Doppelgänger said, "as evidenced by love and psychological exploitation."

"*Falling* in love," Ozzy Man said. "It's the falling part that's interesting. The part that causes all the shit. The days of love and torment."

"Certainly," Doppelgänger said. "The excitement first; the fall-out later."

"Yeah," Al said. "I don't just want to write the fast-food equivalent of a novel. I'll write about something that hurts like hell and about which you can't do a thing."

"If you get that right"—Meg blew an arrow of smoke straight at his heart—"one or two critics may be kind and you will sell three copies. I will buy two." She ground the butt end of her cigarette into the glass ashtray on the table in front of her, coughed a smoker's cough and chuckled.

He stirred sweetener into his cappuccino.

"I think," he said, "I'll write about Sex and God and Man and Love. But not so much about God and Man."

"It has worked for others." Meg watched him like a teenager watches the villain in an on-screen-shooter game. She then made big eyes that turned serious, "It's a busy street to play in, trying to break into the entertainment business like that. Fifty shades of sex, but nobody reads books anymore."

"I can't write about sex anyway," he said.

"The point, Al, is that even if you get into print, you will compete with Netflix and Apple TV. Seventeen seasons of marital infidelity and gangsterism, pretty girls, adultery, and guns. All anyone must do is sit and stare; never have to turn a page."

"Suppose …" he said, taking another good run at the blues-feeling-sorry-for-himself thing. "Somebody done somebody wrong."

Meg saw, did a Charlie Brown squiggly-mouth smile. He smiled back with a straight-mouthed emoji, accepting the solidarity. But at least his smile was from the right century.

At the car he hugged her. "You're too thin."

"You worry too much." She drew him close. "God Speed, Big Bro. Write the book."

Her car slipped into the traffic as he watched her go. On the morning he and his brother had gone with Dad to fetch Meg and Mom from the nursing home, they had left the garden in mint condition for the triumphal homecoming of the young Princess. His job had been to mow the lawn and clip the hedges. Bren had washed the windows. The Old Man was uncharacteristically joyful on the way, singing, "Clap your handies, eat your candies, there's a big feast."

That was long ago and it was far away. He didn't know if things had been any better than they are today.

2

"IN THE BEGINNING THE EARTH was without form and darkness was on the face of deep," Doppelgänger said. "Only the Spirit of God moved over the water, until He spoke. Which turned on the lights. There's also a second version: At first, the Word was on its own—It was both with and was, in itself, God."

He thought for a minute, then added: "If you can untangle that."

"Since His time over the face of the deep, the Spirit has slipped out of the popularity ratings," Ozzy Man said. "I mean, the Spirit had a bit-part as the dove for the Immaculate Conception and when John baptized JC. But after that, not much. His PR is way down."

"Yeah," Doppelgänger said, shaking his head. "Public approval can be so fickle."

"The Son is the guy now. He's the one on TV who wants you to send cash."

"His birthday party every year is the ultimate spike in public spending patterns." Doppelgänger was amused. "Christmas, day of the holy feast, difficult in theory to reconcile with that apparently peremptory rule against coveting."

"Hee-hee," Ozzy Man said, grinning. "Don't covet your neighbour's ass."

"Hawking and Dawkins have a different story," Doppelgänger said. "A long time ago, 13.8 billion years they say, there was the Singularity."

"Yeah. Sounds like a drag: No space, no time, no sex, no drugs, no wine, no women, no fun. Nothing. Nada. Bupkes. Zilch. No wonder it was dark," Ozzy Man said. "And then it exploded. Now we live in the space-time continuum. I totally get that." He said: *todally*.

Stories of where it began have ever been step one in figuring what it's for: How did the first spark jump off the finger on the chapel ceiling into Man, languid with six-pack and earthliness ever shining? How did the first chain of proteins grow a tail to wag? Where did this story, Al's story, begin? A thousand words, a million heartbeats, a sigh, a cry, the smell of coffee at a pavement café, a jingle jangle morning and that's what it is today.

"I know how it happened," Doppelgänger said. Ozzy Man looked at him expectantly. "Italo Calvino explains it. He tells the story of when Qfwfq and all of his family members coexisted before space and time. *Exist* is the wrong word, he says, but they were all there in the same place, which wasn't a place because the idea of places didn't exist yet. But they all really liked Mrs Ph(i)nk, and she liked them so much that one day—not really a day because there were no days yet—she said: *Oh, the pasta I will cook for you boys!* And when she said the words it created space and existence and time and the doing of things, and a woman's forearms white with flour in a kitchen in the late afternoon sun. The Italian food version of *Let there be light*."

Al really liked that story.

"In the beginning was the Word, and the Word was pasta," Ozzy Man said, grinning.

"In the beginning of this story, who was she? Who was Kimberley? The prophecy of aeons? A silent promise bound in sinew and ancient stone; the collision of continents; the cry of a butterfly; the shift of mid-afternoon shadow; the granite basement below vast plains; the crystal drip of a mountain stream." Doppelgänger got carried away with the lyricism of his answer. "And how did they meet? Was it destiny predetermined by great inscrutability?"

"One day they bumped into each other and said *hi*," Ozzy Man said with a shrug. "And then again, another day. And another. It was proximity that did it—same place, same time."

"Chairman Mao says," Doppelgänger, still hoping for an ontological explanation, replied, "every journey begins with a single step."

"Bud, if you go carrying pictures of him, you ain't gonna make it with anyone anyhow," Ozzy Man said, repeating Lennon and McCartney's prediction.

Al's story begins with Mrs Ph(i)nk, but fast forwards through fiery balls gradually coalescing to a stony geoid and aeons of sterility and ice; past the dinosaurs, Chicxulub, and the Summer of Love; to visiting hours on a Sunday afternoon.

"Your grandfather was a handsome man, a rake, and he liked the girls." She sits in her wheelchair in a little bedroom in the old age home, waiting for the call of her last trip. The Departure Lounge. Outside, a passage with floors of off-white linoleum and the hiss of rubber-shod wheels. In the little cells to the left and to the right, frail bags of pipes and bones with melancholy eyes have had their three score and ten—*The Days of our Lives*, without Joey Tribbiani. Most of those were labour and sorrow; and now it was time to fly.

"He had his eye on two girls. The one he liked; and the other was your grandmother." An audience is all you can ever hope for. But she is happier than that: "I have so much. They like me here. I taught Bianca, one of the senior nurses, when she was a little thing. Now she still calls me Mrs. Foster. *Mrs. Foster*, she says, *let's have a look at that blood pressure.*"

She is the only one left who remembers the small change of their lives, the passion, the smiles, the tears, the locust wind that spun the Milky Way through its spirals and curls: "He had a cleft in his chin and a look on his brow. She was a slip of a thing when he married her under the eyes of the aunties who gossiped about her swelling belly and smiled about his conquering romantic style. She had just turned sixteen."

Into each life a little rain must fall. In the one they would share it never rained. But nobody warned them—it poured. Man, it poured.

"When the War came," Doppelgänger said, taking over the story, "he knew it was his time. His nation had discovered gold and the Queen and her ministers thought it would look better in their pockets."

"In modern times," Ozzy Man said, "to do as you please with a macho army, you have to scare everyone about Weapons of Mass Destruction. But back then it was simple: *We have bigger guns, more bullets, more soldiers. You fit in with our plan or you die.*"

"Forty years later," Doppelgänger explained, "when the English Crown came under the cosh of a foreign lunatic, it was payback time. Grandfather Isaiah, with the resolve in his eye of a righteous cause, and the anger in his heart of a family mistreated by history, joined a band of young men who blew up bridges and railway lines and a post office. And were locked up. *Interned*, was the euphemism."

"They were so lucky, Bud," Ozzy Man said, "not to kick out over the crowd at the end of a rope." He fell silent, then added wistfully: "But by then crowds were no longer invited."

"When they sent him to St. Helena," Al's aunt said, "it was just her and Baby."

Al's mother, Baby; and his granny, not yet in her twenties. It's mighty hard row that their poor hands would hoe. Their deserts were hot and their mountains were cold. "It left your grandmother with Jesus as her only companion; and Baby with indefatigable *welt schmertz*." Aunt Jenny had taught literature. Her mind roamed far beyond the wheelchair in which she now rode from sunrise to sunset. "It followed her the rest of her days, and it brought her bad karma and worse luck. I was lucky. I found a man who loved me, from a really nice family. But poor Baby. She had a hard time."

Baby found Lawry, a Playboy-handsome Old-Family-wealthy man with an eye for a pretty face and unshakeable confidence in his own opinions.

"Where he walked, thorns bent double under the firmness of his tread," Doppelgänger said, having known him well. "He loved quoting from great novels and philosophy he surely hadn't read."

"Just so, Bud," Ozzy Man said, who had known him equally well. "And 87.3% of the statistics he constantly sprouted were made up."

"In his cups," Doppelgänger said, nodding thanks for the added detail, "he recited stirring lines of poetry he had learned at school; and he was never in doubt, always in charge."

When Al was a twenty-year-old socialist, as Churchill said, he should be, he wanted to restructure this sad old world where the rich stay healthy and the sick stay poor. He and Papa Lawrence couldn't see peeper to peeper. Not to speak, not to agree, not to compromise, not to see each other for a lifetime of missed opportunity; a lifetime that could have been so different.

"At thirty-five Baby was sad," Doppelgänger said. "At forty she was despondent; at forty-five she was beaten."

"Women like a man to be in charge," Lawry the Righteous would say right in front of his defeated wife, smiling at the articulacy of his own insight. "They have no sense of logic. If you put two of them together in an office, they are buddies for life. If you put three of them in there, two gang up on the third one." He shook his head in disbelief, chuckled again at the smartness of his wisdom; and bemoaned his wife's membership to such a witless clan of clowns. She borrowed an expression from the Sphinx and lit another cigarette.

"At fifty-five she was emphysemic," Ozzy Man said. "At fifty-nine she had wrapped herself in a cloud through which neither word nor prayer could pass. At sixty-two she was dead. The Lord had given, and the Lord had taken away; blessed be the name of the Lord."

Meg railed against the light that had drained so swiftly from her mother's eye. She stood in the stark hospital room, western light slanting low through slatted blinds, frowning at the bed where her mother had slipped away into the remains of the day. Al's arms around her shoulders, tears tracking to the sharp end of her chin, she sang softly: "There's one promise darling, I'll see you on God's golden shore."

Al, chained forever to the rock from which he watched but couldn't do a thing, whispered to his sister: "If she'd knowed how bad he'd treat her, Honey, she never would have come."

Dusty, who was dating Meg, and Kimberley waited in the tearoom. He tucked into a toasted sandwich with orange cheese and shiny grease; she stirred a travel size *ersatz* cappuccino. She hadn't taken a sip yet.

"Bummer, Megs," he said between the mouthfuls. He lifted a crust: "Bite?"

"No thank you." She set down her spoon. "It's hot in here. See you outside?"

Late, after midnight, when sneaky shadows slip through the cracks and torture all insomniacs with questions existential, Al nodded conspiratorially at the dark. They agreed. A great Slavic sadness ripped from a violin perfectly reproduced in high fidelity from a disc spinning on the Nakamichi. "For classics music," the young salesman had said, complete with the extra *s*, "top end Japanese decks is best mit something like Dynaudio. They is Danish." To round it out he got a Macintosh amp, so heavy it had handles on either side.

He wondered whether sad music made him miserable or whether he played miserable music when he was sad.

"Same, same," Ozzy Man said.

The violin sang bittersweet, complained in hoarse agony, yelled angry at the walls, subsided in wailing despair.

"Oh man," Doppelgänger said, deserted and empathetically appalled. "She's never coming back. What a sad and tragic mistake." The violin told the orchestra of wasted opportunity and abandoned happiness, the promise of tomorrow that never comes.

The space outside the great intersection of interest and opinion Al shared with Kimberley, held music and very few other things. She played the same disc on the Bose in the kitchen until he hid it behind a row of books on one of several shelves around the house. "Look here," he said, "turn on the Bluetooth, open Spotify, and then let them choose for you—all your favourites in playlists."

But she liked the song that was already playing: *Hey Mambo, Mambo Italiano, hey Mambo*.

She danced in front of him, pulling him by the hips.

"You're a charlatan. But in a good way." He tried to follow her easy sashay around the table. She gave him the evil eye over a half-turned shoulder. "Why, thank you," she said. A husky seductress who stepped up close.

"If you don't like the show you're watching," Meg had told him, over what was not her first Scotch, "change the channel. There isn't a pause button and for sure there is no rewind. You only get to watch it once." Baby's show had scored poorly on Rotten Tomatoes—Tomatometer and Audience Score.

It had felt like the right show when with all his worldly goods he did Kimberley endow. She promised to love, honour, but not obey him until death or entropy did them part.

"Please let me die before a fuck up." He sub-vocalised his personal mantra, panic stricken. All these people watching; all that expectation in her pretty face, from which no single person could keep her safe. In the wedding album he looks so optimistic, it had to have been a long time ago. Optimism tempered with a dose of fatalism. "If I can just get through this and not screw up, I can die in peace. Then the pressure will finally be off."

"Such morbid thoughts," Doppelgänger had said, "on your wedding day."

"He's not worried about dying, mate," Ozzy Man said. "Not being alive didn't bother him before he was born. Why should it bother him after he's dead? It's just the piece in the middle that's a bit fucking risky."

"Tsk," Doppelgänger said. "The purple headed mountains, river running by, the sunset and the morning that brightens up the sky."

"Nicely played, me old Matey." Ozzy Man acknowledged the professionally returned cross-court. "But he has legitimate concerns. The human condition is to fuck up. That's mankind's divine purpose; that's the one thing everyone does."

"It is so," Doppelgänger said. "At some point we all make mistakes because that's what humans do. What you do afterwards is what determines who you are."

"Yeah, destructive stress testing," Ozzy Man said with a drawl. He would never buy into the notion of the nobility of character building through hardship. "When it's your turn, it only hurts when you laugh."

3

HE MET HER WHEN THE last days of February carried a hint of autumn and a sprinkle of rain. Every year the country winds down over Christmas, when the boys and girls all go on a summer holiday, no more working for a week or two. But soon it was time again to roll the boulder back up the hill in daily increments of toil and administration. The metronome of Kimberley and Al's social calendar swung loose and steady, clicking through the progress of their engagements. It was Friday evening at the Wilkins' for dinner in their wine cellar and Al was seated across the table from her. The Wilkins loved that cool underground room with simple infectious enthusiasm: Lewis because it held his collection, shelf after shelf, box upon box; Margot because it looked as if the Count of Monte Cristo could spend thirteen years in captivity down there in insouciant French style.

Al told Meg later, when they met for lunch: "I hadn't spotted her in the crowd before we had come down into the cellar."

"Not unusual, Mate," Ozzy Man said, "for you not to spot somebody."

"Kimberley says it's because he doesn't pay attention," Doppelgänger explained, prissily defensive. "And she's right only in part. Al can't recognize a new face if you pay him, and has nothing to hang a name on. That's why he seems to spend his life in social quarantine."

Meg waited silently for Al to say more. Some of it she already knew: That the seasons skidded through their turns, spring summer autumn winter; that the world wobbled on its axis because the ice was melting, land masses were expanding and the viscous middle layer of the planet slowly churned; that Sirius stayed at heel behind huge Orion, as all faithful hounds should. She also knew Kimberley carried Al's heart, kept his soul, and managed his diary. "You can't go out in that shirt," Kimberley said, shaking her head, sad at his lack of David Beckham's innate metrosexual dress sense. "Don't turn on those lights." She kept the evenings romantic, forcing him to get a back-lit Kindle so he could read in the semi dark. "I wouldn't turn here." She kept him on the right road, the straight and narrow.

"It was one of those dinner parties you detest," Al told his sister. "Where people say they taste a hint of apricot in the white wine; and a delicate, yet keynote of citrus."

"If they fancy apricot so much," Ozzy Man said, "they should get juice." Thinking about it he added: "One of those little Italian glass bottles that say *Albicocca*."

The young woman seated diagonally across from Al on the other side of the table had inclined her head, listening politely to the stockbroker on her left. Al, at the same time, was hearing from his neighbour: "There's a charming little boutique in Quayside. I love it so. Their style is just, wow!" She clapped her hands together, thinking of its prêt-à-porter cornucopia. "They also had this light summer's jacket in robin-egg blue, but I prefer it in pale mauve. Isn't it gorgeous?" She held up her sleeve close to his face for inspection.

"Maybe she wants you to smell it." Ozzy Man offered his suggestion to Al's not knowing what he was expected to contribute.

The young woman on the other side of the table was doing exactly as Al, keeping her expression interested, as if absorbing every detail. She was learning of the arbitrage in that week's day trades; and while so doing, flicked her eyes around the table, hoping to find an escape. For a while Al listened to both streams of conversation: the day trader's value-added platform for synergistic interface and shareholder value accrual; and the all-consuming vortex of fashion choices with matching accessories. Both lines were abruptly cut short by a strident voice: "It's a misnomer to speak of human rights. We should speak rather of human obligations."

The retired judge, famous for being a retired judge, had leant forward into his point. "Ask who must deliver, not who must receive. That will give you a better grip. Don't say a man has the basic human right to medicine and food. Ask who has the obligation to give him medical treatment and feed him."

"Or her," Ozzy Man had suggested.

"Ask whose obligation it is to educate him and to house him."

"Or her," Ozzy Man had stuck to his guns.

"You will very soon see then who must do what; and you will also understand what can be done and what can't." The judge toasted himself with a deep slug of red wine, reward for his insight. He was entirely without humour and had an assumed self-importance that had been polished by the fawning way everyone in the courtroom behaved towards him.

"Don't forget, Bud," Ozzy Man had said, "that the pussy advocates licked his arse spotlessly clean every day for years." He said: *yee–iz*.

The judge, for no apparent reason, had looked at Al who smiled a smile of indefinite, inscrutable impenetrability. It's a fact that all muscles get stronger with exercise. Al could smile for hours without getting a sore face. He had been in training for decades.

Still smiling he turned away from the judge, and, idly looked across the table. His eyes and the dark ones there clicked together like tiny magnets. A million faces everywhere, and all he saw were dark eyes.

"Christ Buddy, she's a beauty," Ozzy Man said. He said: *beaudy*.

"And you look like her grandfather," Doppelgänger said.

"Well, how *does* she look?" Meg asked, interrupting the story.

"She's about your size; short, kinda dishevelled black hair and a hint of a dimple in both cheeks."

"Short, kinda dishevelled costs a lot," Meg said. "Black is the cheap part."

"Really cheap—I think it's still the original colour. She's twenty-three years younger than me."

"So, she's gorgeous." Meg's old habit of not using question marks.

"Yeah." He looked down at his plate, to inspect neither the *insalata verde* nor the Parmesan shavings, but to escape her scrutiny. Meg, his confessor; Meg, his interrogator. He told her almost everything; and she intuited the rest. Then she forgave him.

Back down in the wine cellar, Al and dark eyes had started chatting across the table in a private channel between the day trader and the drunken judge. Safe stuff; dinner party stuff: She freelanced as a journalist, was married to Thomas at the other end of the table. He was pushing past middle-age—fourteen years older than her; and he was blond, enthusiastically loud, soft, and plump, a banker, excited to rub shoulders with the older moneyed set.

"Thomas thinks it's ecologically irresponsible to have children," she told him. "He spent his carbon credits on a Porsche instead."

"Hee-hee," Ozzy Man had said, laughing. "I can get to like this Sheila."

She did spinning and Pilates, kept in shape. Meg didn't ask about the shape because she knew Al wouldn't say. There was another thing she wanted to ask, but kept quiet for the time being—Al would eventually have to ask himself: *Why tell Meg any of this; and revel in such detail?*

"How do you fit into this crowd?" his dark-eyed dinner companion had asked. "Are you rich and famous too?"

"No," Al said, snorting a little laugh. "I'm not important in the slightest. I am not a leader of men; the world does not depend on me for direction or stability; the economy will do just fine without me; I am not a retired premium athlete." In this room full of chiefs, he wore no feathers.

The smile reached her eyes, made them twinkle. They were just like Kimberley's.

"*Los ojos de mi princesa*," Ozzy Man had said, all correctly, with the hard-guttural -*g* for eyes; and the lisp for *printhess*.

"Thank God for an ordinary person," she said with a chuckle. "I thought I was the only one here."

"I am in the final throes of retiring from business." He painted his monochrome self-portrait. "And I'm looking forward to it.

Enjoying it already." He told her he had been married to Kimberley for thirty years. She was at the other end of the table, listening to Thomas. She tried, managed still, to look young; had always been cultured, sophisticated and articulate; was a trust baby when he had met her and now was his wealthy wife. They had one son, Jesse, married and living in Amsterdam.

By this time Al had swapped seats with the stockbroker who had discovered greater enthusiasm in a girl with a curtain of blond hair and a smile like an American gameshow host. She squealed in delight when the money man told her about his hard drive that ran on an encrypted cipher.

"I'm writing an article about offshore investment in island marinas in the Indian Ocean, but I don't understand the figures." Her voice had smoky undertones of jazz clubs and truancy. For the price of a cup of coffee, would he help?

"Thomas is a banker. He surely is better at figures," Al had tried to welsh out of it. When Meg heard that, she wasn't in the slightest bit surprised: That is predictably and naturally what Al would have tried.

The dark eyes had regarded him steadily while their owner sipped daintily from her glass. She led with a perfect *non sequitur:* "My mother liked gin and tonic, poured as they did in the finest years of the Raj: just a splash of tonic. She made that drink her own. Rafique, the charming man she lived with after my father, poured them ever so well."

"The fuck?" Ozzy Man had said.

"When I told her I am marrying Thomas, she said *Nice One.* After her next two drinks she asked me, *What will you do if you ever meet a man?*"

"Like you, Bud!" Ozzy Man had said, laughing. Al smiled without comment.

Tuesday 10:30 at Streetcar in Sandton, they had agreed. Together they would puzzle through the numbers that she thought fudged the real cost of domicile shopping on a tropical island.

"Who was the girl with the dark hair?" Kimberley asked in the car on the way home.

"Her name is Courtney. She is a journalist. Her husband, Thomas, was sitting on your end?"

"Poor girl," Kimberley had said.

Which is exactly what Al had thought when, years before, Meg had married Dusty. Although he didn't say.

"Of all the fish in the river, she chooses this guy?" Ozzy Man had given voice to his incredulity, while Al sat back, minimally shaking his head in disbelief and watching Dusty and his mates do the *haka* to entertain the wedding guests. Lined up like the All-Black rugby side before an international, they grunted and writhed and stamped their way through the intimidations of an ancient Māori war dance. One dance to get the attention of all, and in astonishment bind them.

"He misunderstands his own life's philosophy," Doppelgänger said, keeping his unwavering stare on Dusty. "He's proud of being as a rough bear's arse and insists on not being judged by standards he rejects. He lives by visceral intuition, not by any deliberate cognitive process. And he's happy that way."

"Mate, only you and Al speak like that," Ozzy Man said, shaking his head hopelessly. "Dusty wouldn't know what the fuck you just said."

"But his perfect satisfaction with his own boorishness," Doppelgänger said, taking no notice of the criticism of his choice of words, "leads him to the conclusion that if anyone speaks differently from him or has opinions that don't accord with his emotionally derivative notions, then that other person is a fool. A conclusion he came to by applying standards the fool rejects. And there you have it: The neat and complete undoing of his own life's philosophy in line two of his reasoning."

Meg, whose Quotients, both Intelligence and Emotional, kept Al forever in her shadow, answered without his having said a thing: "Dusty is kind and steady, and easy to be with and to understand."

Al looked at her without expression or comment, in his usual apparently disengaged way.

"See it for what it is," Meg said. "It's like Mum marrying Dad; and Aunt Jenny marrying Louis, the carpenter. The world sees the money and the flash and the handsome man; and thinks: Poor Jenny. But, really, it's poor Mum, poor Baby."

"Ha-ha, Mate," Ozzy Man said, giggling. "Give you odds on what's coming next."

"It's the same with us," Meg said, proving Ozzy bang on the money. "The world sees glamorous, pretty Kimberley; thinks: Lucky Al. I see kind, dependable, fun, chaotic Dusty and I think: Lucky me."

"She doesn't have your latitude of choice," Doppelgänger had told him often. "Her compromises are broader than your own."

"Yeah, Bud," Ozzy Man said, driving home the point with his usual sledgehammer. "Except she thinks you're the one with the broad compromises. Which is why she talks shit about Kimberley whenever opportunity knocks." He said: *sheet*.

"Don't confuse their standard of living with their quality of life," Doppelgänger said.

"Your wife," Meg said, dragging at the end of her fag, "keeps you in your place." No question mark at the end of that simple statement. He was a wolf, she knew it. But he wore a collar.

He wondered if she was right, but thought she wasn't. "It's not really like that," he said. But she had her views.

For the wedding Kimberley had worn a simple pale-blue cotton dress that fell straight from her shoulders to above slender calves, a little handful on each leg. She looked 1920's elegant, and in the photos the bride is dowdy by comparison. Al, next to his sister, towers over his new brother-in-law. During the first waltz, Kimberley caught his wistful stare at the buffoon who steered his bride around the floor like a bumper car at an old-fashioned funfair.

"They'll be okay," she whispered husky and confident, sliding an open palm up and over his shoulder, while they moved smoothly around the floor like a well-oiled well-tuned well-matched well-made dancing Swiss timepiece. Meg had chosen the first waltz for the combination of Cohen and Lorca. *Take this Waltz*, they offered, both from their grave: *In a cry filled with footsteps and sand*. Lorca had been shot by the Nationalists during the

Spanish civil war. Cohen was born in Canada and died in Los Angeles 82 years later.

The couple cut the cake, threw the garter, made the speeches. And much later, Al asked the bride for a dance.

"You look beautiful," he said to her as they stepped effortlessly around the floor. Doppelgänger wouldn't allow him to say, *I am so worried about this—I so hope you are doing the right thing*. Because they were only two of them left to look out for each other. Sixteen bars of a ¾-time signature later, he said: "I know you are going to be so happy. Love you, Sis. Besties forever?"

"Forever," she said.

4

"IN THE TIME OF CAESAR, all of Gaul was divided into three parts." Doppelgänger remembered Latin lessons from high school.

"*He* divided it into three parts, Mate," Ozzy Man said. "A man of action."

"He was. Modern-day Johannesburg is divided into two. The first is the old section—what used to be the CBD and neighbouring Hillbrow flatland, home of the tower that is the Golden City's icon."

"That's its purpose," Ozzy Man said. "The least imaginative artist draws a skyline of tall buildings, adds the tower icon, and *Voilà*. It's Jozi!"

The 1994 election finally ended the rule that you could live only where the Government said; and ushered in a new democracy.

"Because no man is good enough to govern another man without that other's consent," Doppelgänger said, quoting Lincoln.

"In a democracy it's your vote that counts," Ozzy Man said, exhibiting his deep understanding of politics. "In feudalism it's your Count that votes."

A flood of poor people washed into Johannesburg central, and to illustrate Newton's prediction of how actions determine reactions, money and power immediately fled several kilometres north, to Sandton. This is what became the second section.

"Before it became famous"—Doppelgänger was in the know with the local history—"Sandton was where the horsey set had kept their noses high and their small holdings exclusive."

The roaring loom of progress wove the formerly sleepy borough into central focus as the new financial capital of Africa: The technological and money muscle of an entire continent, squeezed into a semi-agricultural peri-urban district.

"*Ex Africa semper aliquid novi*," Doppelgänger said.

"You just use Latin to sound smart," Ozzy Man said. "It's your *modus operandi*."

A flood of light replaced the gentility and rural twilight in the little hollow where, until the late 1970s, there had been no streetlights. Early-morning roosters became a thing of the past—the dawn chorus had become one of internal combustion engines and people in a hurry. Al and Courtney's arrangement was to meet in a coffee shop in Sandton City, the exclusive shopping centre where money became gross expenditure.

"Why are we here, Bud?" Ozzy Man said. He didn't like any mall, let alone this one, where self-entitled housewives dressed up to compete with their neighbours. "When you've seen one shopping centre, you've seen a mall."

On the broad, high-gloss granite walkway between the jewellery stores and electronic shops on the left, and the super-exclusive boutiques on the right, a figure-hugging black mini barely covering buttocks curved into spray-on gym tights click-clacked seductively ahead of them on the six-inch heels of knee-length wet-look boots.

"If Simba had had a shaggy blond mane like that," Doppelgänger said, gazing at the petite eyeful teetering ahead of them, "he would never not have been King of the Jungle, even for a minute."

"Double negatives," Ozzy Man said, "are a big no-no."

When Al coasted past the mini, not having to take tiny steps to keep from falling over, he noticed long sleeves and flaring lacy frills at the wrist and was taken by surprise to see that she who wore the devil's seductive stilettos, was late into her sixties. Long sleeves because nothing shows up your seventh decade like liver spots and iguana skin.

Courtney was already waiting. She didn't have a handbag; she carried her stuff in a green leather rucksack. "Hey," she said, smiling. She wore her sunglasses on her head like an Alice band.

"Who is the article for?" Al asked.

"Yeah, Bud, you get on with it." Ozzy Man liked that he had come straight to the point. "We're not here to fuck spiders."

"A magazine called *Opportunity*," she said. "It's owned and edited by accomplished traders who are greatly in awe of success in commercial enterprise."

Doppelgänger smiled his approval at the description.

"They are running a comparison between countries that sell residency and citizenship?" Al asked.

"Indirectly, I suppose," she said, and told him about a marina development in tropical Mauritius, dead-centre Indian Ocean. "I've looked at it, but the pricing makes no sense—it's way expensive."

Al told her about buying your way around bothersome immigration rules; and, if you are in the Big League, other rules as well. "You can buy your way into, for example, Turks and Caicos, where you become a citizen immediately, and there is no extradition. It's a package deal and costs a fortune."

"That's for drug barons and gun runners?" She looked bemused.

"Yes. And merchant bankers and financial types who achieve beyond expectation," Al said, remembering too late what Courtney's husband did for a living. He let the apology linger in his eyes, without articulating it.

She laughed. "You need a pair before you need an island getaway."

"I've heard"—Doppelgänger looked at her steadily—"that Thomas speaks very highly of you."

"I think she's telling you, Bud," Ozzy Man said, translating for Al, "Thomas and Jason Bourne don't pee in the same pod."

"Anyway." Al pushed on ahead, heedless of the interruption. "You need to see it as a composite whole, a package deal—an apartment on the beach, a minimal tax rate, and the right not to be arrested, no matter what you did. This capitalism thing can have far-ranging benefits."

"Law is not law," Ozzy Man said, eyes sanctimoniously cast down, "if it violates the principles of eternal justice."

Courtney put her pad and pen into the green rucksack, zipped it closed, and moved on: "If I were to make it to Heaven, I will probably take against the teacher's pet angel"—she pointed to an imaginary corner, following her index finger with dark, arresting eyes—"the alto on mandolin. Because she is singing too loudly—showing the rest of Heaven just how good an angel she is."

Al tried to fit her sentence into a discussion about holiday developments in Mauritius; realised that the topic had changed; and composed his face as if he were listening.

"That's exactly how Helena irritates me." Courtney meant one of the dinner guests at the Wilkins on Saturday. "She is always perfectly friendly, perfectly polite, perfectly effusive. That's when I want to kick her in the head." She nodded, frowning slightly.

"I could like this Sheila," Ozzy Man said, grinning. He felt the same way about Helena. When Lewis had poured her a glass of wine, she had clasped her hands together in joy of the occasion and squealed like a Girl Guide who had just won a teddy bear at the tombola stand.

"Ferchrissakes, woman," Ozzy Man had said in irritation, "just say *Thanks.*"

Courtney wasn't done with Helena yet. "She told me the equilibrium of her psyche and her inherent karmic understanding allow her to be at peace with the world."

"A holy man goes to a hot dog stand," Ozzy Man said. "*Make me one with everything*, he asks the short order chef."

Courtney was a girl who didn't linger on conversational subjects. She moved on to the power of positive thought; yet was still bitching about the same woman. "She told me that Positive thinking makes her happy and pretty and smart and successful; she thinks positively, and that moulds the world to her will." Courtney sipped from her cup; a tiny bit of froth stayed on the curve of her upper lip. She shook her head. "But positive thinking is so much horse. If you are poor or have cancer or it hasn't rained in three years, you can think the prettiest, most optimistic, most invitingly aspirational thoughts ever, but that won't actually help."

"You can beseech the Lord with prayer," Ozzy Man said.

Al smiled; and Courtney was done with Helena. Rather than risk that Al would allow silence at the table, she launched into a story about a Japanese martial arts home movie on YouTube she had watched. "The Master Sensei would illustrate mind over matter."

"I don't mind," Ozzy Man said, "and he doesn't matter."

"The Master is standing next to a tree, which is being chopped down. The voice-over says the karate man is going to catch the tree on its way down, and thereby demonstrate the dominance of his mind. The tree is about thirty metres high, dense with branches and leaves. It starts to topple over and the man who has been chopping it down jumps out the way, the commentator shouts, *Here it comes!* The master braces, does an arm thrust thing and shouts the magic martial arts word. And the tree squashes him flat. You can't see any of him; he's just gone."

She evidently found that very funny. She laughed; her eyes twinkled. She shook her dark hair as she shook her head. She sat back looking happy.

"She's adorable," Doppelgänger said, sensing Al's reluctance to think it.

"God, I wish we could talk Helena into trying that," Ozzy Man said.

Courtney still wouldn't leave a gap in the conversation.

"She's just nervous." Doppelgänger defended her. "You make people nervous by always looking as if you are silently disqualifying them for their stupidity."

"Do I?" Al asked, amazed. "I never say a thing."

"That's why," Doppelgänger said.

Across the table the monologue continued: Courtney had now skipped along deftly to the package tour of Europe she and Thomas had been on. A bus with 28 other tourists, *doing* Greece. "Every morning the whole bus sang the same song, *I Got You Babe*, the special holiday song. It was sort of fun the first three mornings: The tour leader, as the bus pulled out of the parking lot, cranked up the music, and everyone belted it out. But after a week, I wanted to slip Judas Priest and satanic messages into the sound system, just to stop them being so God-damned twee. Thomas, of course, loved it—I think he liked the predictability; so that for once he felt part of a social cooperative." Outside the windows and the air-conditioning, she told Al, the Acropolis and stark hills and green valleys and nestling white harbours slid by, like the station outside Einstein's train. "It's so beautiful, but it's overrun with people."

"Mass tourism is an industry that allows people to see things that would be significant and splendid, but for the mass tourism itself." Ozzy Man had nailed down the conundrum.

Courtney insisted on getting the bill. "That was the deal."

They strolled back down the wide passage. Al half-hoped to see the mini-skirted lion mane again, but she was long gone. While they walked, Courtney carried on the one-way conversation:

"I am watching this nature programme on Netflix. It's about a mother bear and her cubs. They have been hibernating in a cave, and when they wake up, they are hungry but there is no food. She has to leave them behind to go foraging."

"These feckless animals," Ozzy Man said, shaking his head in disappointment, "never plan ahead. Nature is so disorganised and inefficient."

"The conservation team looking after them want to fit them with collars and tracking devices, so they can study them. They wait for the mother bear to come out of the cave; and shoot her with a tranquilliser."

"Home," Ozzy Man said, "is where the dart is."

"The cubs go crazy. But they are so cute."

"Nature," Ozzy Man said, "is God's gift to us all."

They had reached the B&O store, where they stopped and stared. On display stood a pair of irregularly shaped speakers, angles and planes facing off in different directions, hip high to Al and as solid as Rocky Marciano's heavy punch bag. He had been in to listen, and they were sex in high fidelity stereo. "I need those," he said, pointing them out to her.

She was interested whether they connected only on Bluetooth and Apple Play, and in their output and range. "What will you play on them?" A technical question.

"Their bass and treble response are superb. Modern music with its huge range and augmented subwoofer sound would be great. But they will be *so* good for jazz. A big saxophone." Al looked self-indulgently greedy for that treat, added: "Blowing deep inside your bones and vibrating between your shoulder blades."

"Yup," she said; could imagine it herself. "James Carter on baritone." She surprised him. Kimberley didn't know that name. "Will you get them?" she asked.

Al pointed at the price tag without saying a word.

"Oops," she said, grinning.

"She is really adorable," Doppelgänger said again.

At her car they said goodbye. She hadn't yet learned the practice of an hermetically sealed embrace and a turned cheek for the handshake equivalent of a kiss. Al smiled like a fool, bit back the corniest of questions, *when will I see you again?*

"At your age, Mate"—Ozzy Man shook his head at Al, one eyebrow raised in censure—"it's the doctor, not the police, who tells you to slow down."

"Oz," Doppelgänger said, looking patiently at his companion, "friendship is one of the hardest things in the world to explain."

"Right, me old Mate," Ozzy Man said. "You can never have too much money or too many matching accessories; and you can never have too many friends."

5

"HERE WE STAND, WE CAN do no other," Doppelgänger said. "We belong here, we belong there, we belong anywhere but in between. We pay our money, and we make our choices: Chocolate or malt? Republican or vegetarian; Manchester United or 4 x 4; country music or yoga. You are what you choose. The badge on your pocket says who you are; what club you're in."

"If you have a dog," Ozzy Man said, "I must have a dog. If you have a club, I must have a club."

Al's badge identified him as faithless, a sceptic, a nullifidian. He belonged to no society, was wary of clubs and associations, avoided fraternities, ran from charitable organisations, and was allergic to committees.

Doppelgänger explained why and how to belong: "You have to walk the walk, sing the song, do the dance, wear the hat; and you have to talk the talk, the complete liturgy: The girl, the boy, the coffin and the nail, the storm, the beard, the bonfire and the holiness."

"Christ, Bud." Ozzy Man felt tired just thinking about it. "That's just a bunch of trouble. Being secular and mundane is no trouble at all: I don't belong, and I don't believe. I can just do nothing at all."

"Yes," Doppelgänger said. "I agree it's attractive: No hushed respect; no special uniform; no meetings, speeches, sing-alongs or services; no ceremonial dignity; no names or ideas in capital letters; no need to be offended; nothing to defend both tooth and nail; and never having to shoot anyone."

"Or become a suicide bomber," Ozzy Man said.

Some believers were easier to tolerate than others. Kimberley was energetically immersed in arranging walking tours in the inner city, artistic, historical, and cultural. Their neighbour, Charlotte, babysat Labrador puppies until their first birthday, when they would start learning to be guide dogs. Hank, their friend, raised money to help underprivileged students through school. It was his thing.

"We have meetings on Tuesday evenings," he said. "My weekends are end-to-and with functions and mentoring; my free time, what was left of it, is taken up with soliciting donations."

"Yeah," Ozzy Man said. "*Soliciting donations* is better. B*egging for money* sounds so proletarian."

Once a year on a Wednesday evening, Hank was the special guest of honour who spoke at Honours Evening at St. Augustine College.

"The entry for VIP visitors is R550 a head," he said, soliciting a further donation. Al paid the entry happily enough; and had to drag Ozzy Man to the school hall, complaining and sulking.

"Rotary keeps twelve students at St. Augustine's. Full tuition and living-in support," Kimberley told Al in the car.

"We know." Ozzy Man looked at her evenly. "Hank has mentioned it. A few times."

When they got there, the hall buzzed with a mighty expectation of great things.

"Soon to be disappointed," Ozzy Man said, jealously cleaving to his solitary rebellion.

Kimberley found a program from which she learnt the school's motto: *Initium Sapientiae Timor Domini.*

"*The beginning of wisdom is fear of the Lord,*" Doppelgänger said.

"It would be more useful to tell the little snots, *Illegitimi non Carborundum,*" Ozzy Man said. *Don't let the bastards grind you down.*

The programme predicted two-and-a-half hours, but Al knew all school events start late and last longer. Teaching and logistics are not a natural mix. His best estimate was three-and-a-half.

"Rome was built quicker than that," Ozzy Man said.

All properly formal functions at school start with praise of the Lord. It follows fear of the Lord like a shadow.

"We love you, oh Lord," Ozzy Man said. "Please don't stir-fry us in a wok."

Three priests, an old guy and his two lieutenants, all three dressed like Lawrence of Arabia, made sure that the mercy of Baby Jesus was with them. They chanted mysterious Latin in whistling sibilants, did hand passes over cups of holy water, swished embroidered cloths from side to side, and swung holy smoke from incense holders on chains. When they spoke in English, it was sing-song with emphasis in odd places: "May Al-MIGHT-y God have MER-cy on us, for-GIVE our sins, and bring us to ever-LAST-ing life."

"The dyslexic, agnostic, insomniac," Ozzy Man whispered, "stayed up all night wondering if there really is a dog."

"We've heard that," Doppelgänger, impatient, said, shushing him.

The headmaster was next. He spent a full thirty-five minutes telling them that the College was the real deal: It had God on its side. He, the self-same Headmaster, had been chosen to lead it. From thousands.

"Is it solipsistic in here, or is it just me?" Ozzy Man said.

Then it was Hank's turn. Tall and bearded, he strode onto stage on confident legs, nodded to his audience. The headmaster had told them who he was and why he was there.

"I don't have many words for you tonight," he said, standing straight, without fidgeting, at the lectern. "But what I have to say is important. No matter if I use big words or quote from philosophers, or go on about it forever, there really is only one thing for you to remember. And it is just this: Be nice. Be nice to each other and to everyone you meet. Be nice to the lady at the till, be nice to your teachers, be nice to your parents, and your brothers and sisters and to your friends. Be nice to strangers, be nice to old people, be nice to children, be nice to babies. Be nice to people you don't like and be nice to people you do like. Be nice to everyone.

"It doesn't matter if you are very smart, and you can understand stuff that is a complete mystery to the rest of us. It doesn't matter if you have university degrees and have amazing skills and you become an expert in everything you do. If you aren't nice, you are missing the point.

"I am here on behalf of a charity. But let me tell you this: Giving away all your money to people who need it means nothing, if you aren't nice. If you do that, you will just be going through the motions without seeing what really matters. Being charitable must go hand in hand with being nice because that's the important part.

"Being nice means being kind. Being nice means not being jealous of each other. Being nice means not showing off, not thinking you are better than everyone, not pretending you are the bee's knees. Being nice is never being rude, never being selfish. Being nice means not getting worked up for nothing. It means not to brood about things and not to make plans for how to get even. Being nice means not enjoying it when things go badly for others, even if you don't like them. Being nice means not lying, not being dishonest. It means accepting things as they happen, believing everything that is good in the world. It means hoping that everything will go right, but not getting upset and bent out of shape if it doesn't.

"Being nice does not make you scared; it doesn't make you worry. If you are nice you don't keep score in your head of when things went wrong. Because, believe me, whatever you think you know now, and whatever you think today is important, it will go wrong at some point. You will find out that you are wrong. Whatever you think here and now the answers are, there will come a time when they stop making sense, when you won't have the answers, you thought you had any more. Because things change and get lost along the way. Even worse, you will find out that some of the things you believed were just plain wrong from the start. We live always without knowing the full picture of what is and what will be, or what might have been. So, don't think you are too special or too smart, or that you know all there is to know, because it will make you arrogant and conceited. And you can't be nice if you are either of those two things.

"I know what I am saying sounds to you like so much hooey, just an old man talking nonsense up here on the podium. When I was young, as you students are, I thought as a young person also, and puzzled things out as young persons do. Often, I came to the wrong conclusions because my priorities were wrong. I wanted to be that guy, the shining light, the person who was always right and who would always win. I thought I could choose how my life would be and change everything that wasn't to my liking. I would fight and I would never lose. But then I grew up and I grew old, and together with finding out that the world isn't here simply for my benefit, I found the one thing that is really important. All you ever have is each other. And the best thing you can ever do, is to be nice.

"Be nice. And whatever you do, don't be chop."

Ozzy Man didn't have a single thing to say.

The Führer knew to give many medals to keep his storm troopers storming enthusiastically. It's an idea he took over from the Romans who dished out crowns by the dozen, like the one on Caesar's head in Asterix. The *Corona Muralis*, for being first over the walls of a besieged city, was mostly given posthumously. But that didn't keep the legionnaires from really wanting one. St. Augustine College had a similar many-awards policy. Prizes and trophies for the fastest, smartest, most melodious, most precocious; and for every subject taken in every class in every standard.

For Science.

"Never trust an atom," Ozzy Man said. "They make up everything."

For History, Geography, Mathematics, and the new age subjects that hadn't existed when Al wore the flannels of a day scholar. For Information Technology.

"There are 10 types of people in this world," Ozzy Man whispered. "Those that know binary, and those that don't."

A floating trophy for the Exquisite Use of Colour, collected by a hapless young nerd in his final year. The Jocks, sitting together in the one section of the hall, just stared at him.

Twenty minutes after the three-hour mark, after many, plenty, lots, stacks, a multiplicity, a great number, a plenitude of awards, the last prize of the night was a silver cup, two feet tall, with eight inches of black pedestal and another six for the lid: The Spirit Trophy, to the house that consistently over the year exhibited the greatest enthusiasm in the stands, singing songs and shouting about and for themselves. Awarded this year to Ogden House. At which the auntie with big arms and heroic hair in the row ahead of them punched the air triumphantly.

"I feel a long way from the hills of San Salvador," Ozzy Man said.

On their way out of the hall, Mrs. Rogers, breathless, Head of Academics and dying to be taken seriously, stopped, and asked Kimberley: "I hope you had a good time?"

"I've had a perfectly wonderful time," Ozzy Man said. "But this wasn't it."

In the car, Kimberley was giggly with a sense of release. "What did you think?" She was smiling, to herself and at Al.

"They call their Good-Deeds Club, *Square the Circle*. Fancy that."

"What's wrong with it?" Kimberley said.

"To square the circle is literally impossible. Geometrically, mathematically, impossible. So, to say you are trying to square the circle means you are attempting the impossible. You are being foolish."

Kimberley giggled like a freshman. "Not anymore, Chump. Now it has become aspirational: If you just try hard enough, you can do anything at all."

"Except square a circle," Al said. Kimberley laughed. How he loved that sound.

"Didn't you think Hank was great? He did so well," she said. Al agreed.

"Mrs. Rogers, though, thought that he should have told the kids about *Agapé*. She said, '*Be Nice* just doesn't have the same depth of meaning.' She is an educated woman, you must know, and she deplores the shallowness of public speakers who aren't her." Kimberley laughed again. She didn't like Mrs. Rogers, right from her sensible square-toed shoes, through her miserly soul, to her unrelenting sanctimony. Kimberley was too smart to allow such a thing to be noticed, and too discreet to admit it to anyone other than Al. "And she is in a state because Hank said *Chop*." Now she really laughed, deeply amused by the preposterous woman's reaction. "I told her nobody speaks ancient Greek anymore, and she said they should learn."

"A classics professor asks a tailor to fix his trousers," Al told her. "*Euripides?* Asks the tailor. *Yes, Eumenides?* Says the professor."

Kimberley guffawed and slapped him on the shoulder. He smiled in the dark, happy to be there with her.

6

AL SAW COURTNEY AGAIN, SOONER than he had imagined. She sent him a text the next morning but one after their coffee date: *Thanks for the help—article almost done. Going Thursday morning to David Goldblatt exhibition at Convention Centre. You free?*

The hall was almost completely empty, just two of them on a slow morning in the middle of the week when everyone else was hard at work. The hall was immense, the roof high above them, echoes of soft footsteps and couples whispering quietly together. The images lining the walls were black and white, framed simply, with no commentary. Stark pictures of a divided land:

> *A young white girl in a barren garden, standing behind her black nanny who sits on a low retaining wall—she herself a young woman. Both smile shyly at the camera, the young girl with her hands on her nanny's shoulders; the nanny's long slender arm behind her with fingers curled secretly around the girl's bare left heel. Friends despite the gulf of difference.*
>
> *A working-class white family in their threadbare kitchen—a stern father seated at the head of the table, glowering at his son who stares miserably ahead, deeply upset but miles from tears: He will never cry. He will shout at his own son the same way.*
>
> *A bus crammed to overflowing with black commuters, going home in the dark, crowded beyond capacity—the lucky ones with*

seats, asleep; the others, dead on their feet, vacantly staring at their lives of quiet desperation.

A young Indian girl, a child still, behind the counter of her family's shop—her arms are improbably long and thin, her face innocent and fearful. Behind her on the wall of shelves, stuff the shop sells.

A young black man and his companion, standing close together in the raggedy clothes of poverty and neglect. She holds her dompas, her obligatory Apartheid identity document. Their eyes as empty as their lives.

The photographs ranged on, ordinary scenes and ordinary people, squashed flat between prejudice and despair. In his later life, when the focus of inequity had moved on and he had gotten old, Goldblatt photographed the country without its people. The last picture in the hall was a five-meter-wide print of a sad Karoo landscape of hills, scrub, and loneliness. Another land, so far away.

"Jesus," Al said, back in the morning air outside. "That depressed the hell out of me."

Courtney looked at him quizzically. "Let's grab a coffee," she said.

Had Al been with Kimberley, they would have lingered over what they had seen, discussed their impressions and said what they thought was good and what wasn't, discussed which images they liked, which ones had moved them most. But not Courtney: She changed gear directly for much lighter matters.

"I got a sourdough loaf at Thrupps I don't like."

Al stumbled mentally with the sudden change of pace and direction: A genius photographer; quiet, devastatingly powerful commentary, brimming with compassion and empathy—and sourdough.

"She's trying to distract you," Doppelgänger told Al. "She thinks you are upset and wants you to feel better—she thinks it's her fault for bringing you here."

"Kimberley makes her own sourdough bread," Al said. "She keeps her own yeast culture, she calls it her starter, in a bottle.

Her loaves are great—chewy and tasty. I also don't like the Thrupps loaves."

"Well done, Mate," Ozzy Man said. "You make it sound almost as if you care."

The waiter came to their table, his eyes as expressive as the buttons in old lift. When he had gone to fetch their order, Courtney asked: "What is 100% Arabica, in any event?" She had seen it on the menu.

"Arabica is a type of coffee bean that is supposed to be best for roasting and has a lower caffeine content. But that's only what I read. I'm no expert."

"I'm glad about that," Courtney said, laughing. "I'm so sick of experts."

Al felt immediately happier, inexplicably chuffed that he had made her laugh, that he had made her approve. She approved of his being self-deprecating: He liked that about her too. She didn't lecture him about self-actualisation or the need to reach for his dreams. He also liked the stability of her good mood—inclusive and infectious. While he was stirring sweetener into his cup, she hopped onto the next topic.

"You and your friends," she said, taking a bite of her Florentine, "just assume that religion is phony, don't you? I mean, you don't even consider that it could be correct. Am I right?"

"Social commentary, sourdough, coffee and God," Ozzy Man said, sighing. "Don't lose your focus here, Mate."

"Pretty much, yes," Al said.

"If it's so obvious to you that religion is nonsense, why does it exist at all?"

"Nothing is so fiercely believed," Ozzy Man said, "as that which we least know."

"Thanks for the French philosophy," Doppelgänger said, acknowledging the reference to de Montaigne.

"It's Man's desire to order and explain events beyond randomness." He looked at her, saw that he had to be less epigrammatic. "Religion is the first attempt of people to explain the world to themselves: Where the sun goes at night, where people and animals come from, what happens when you die."

"What happens?" she asked, lifting her eyebrows, and smiling her inquiry, teasing him.

"You sing the first nine million verses of a Gregorian chant, and each one takes twelve years." He kept his face serious. "If you've been good. Otherwise, you have to listen to Ozzy Osbourne for that whole time."

She laughed, resumed her interrogation. "How do you know the Bible is wrong about God?"

"Well, I don't *know*—I just strongly suspect it." Al looked at her carefully, wanted to be neither too didactic nor too provisional. "But the Bible is wrong about everything else: What the world is, where it comes from, that heaven is up and hell is down, where light comes from. It's wrong about history: For example, when Jesus was born, Nazareth didn't exist yet. It's wrong about cause and effect, about probability, about physics; and it's dead wrong about morality, except where it pinched ideas from other religions. Also, it's contradictory—in many instances you can find authority in the Bible both for and against the same thing. It's not a reliable document; and, but for portions of the New Testament, not a very tolerant one either."

Courtney looked dubious. "It's the word of God. It's supposed to be."

"You have read it?" he asked.

"Not all of it," she said.

"Nobody has." He smiled and she dipped her head in acknowledgement—she had read very little of it. "If we really thought it was the word of God, we'd persevere: Your only chance to read what the Creator of the Universe has to say. But it's just a Bronze Age text that doesn't make that much sense. So, no one bothers."

"But that's no reason not to believe in God?"

"Did this Sheila not have first-year discussions about this?" Ozzy Man said.

"She did a commerce degree," Doppelgänger said, advising patience and understanding, "and she comes from a house where they ate dinner while watching soap operas. Now she lives alone with her television set; and a fat man who loves EBITDA and the FTSE 100, and only drops in on their shared life occasionally. Can't you see, Oz, that she's a country mile away from stupid, but has never heard this kind of thing?"

"It actually *is* a reason not to believe in God," Al answered Courtney, clearly surprising her. She waited until he continued: "We know about God because the Bible tells us: He's the creator and Lord of all; all-knowing and infallible. And we know the Bible is unquestionably right about everything, because He wrote it and He is God."

Courtney grinned, not necessary for Al to expand on the circularity.

"We have only the Bible to refer to for a description of God, including whether he exists. And it is so flawed as a document as to make it thoroughly untrustworthy. In logic and reason, it's an unwarranted conclusion that the Bible, while being wrong about everything else, is right about only this one thing, the deepest conundrum of them all—that God made the universe and everything in it, and now He's in charge of our daily lives. In rationality it leads us to this inevitable conclusion: The Bible is the only proof of God's existence; and at the same time, because it is such a shoddy piece of nonsense, the best evidence *against* its own basic proposition."

"Where I come from," she said, "nobody ever thought or talked about this kind of stuff. Everyone assumed that God and the Bible were literally true, and then paid no further attention. We sort of had complete faith without ever noticing or doing anything about it. Certainly, without ever discussing it. I'm still a bit scared that you're going to be struck by lightning as soon as you step out the door." She laughed.

"I'm staying indoors from now on." He laughed too. He looked at her carefully, gauging her conversational robustness. "It's also OK to talk about things you see, even if your initial reaction is that they depress you."

Al held her eye, seeing that she got the point: She could say what she thought about David Goldblatt without tipping him into the Slough of Despond. For an instant he thought she would lean across the table and take his hand.

"Wishful, me old Matey," the realist said.

She had come in an Uber, and he gave her a lift back. She liked his car.

"My dad swore by these, he said they were the best cars in the world. He could never afford a top-of-the-range one like this, but he would have approved." She was quiet for a bit, then she said: "He was such a nice man. I miss him."

Al drove home, thinking about his morning. He was glad to have seen the exhibition, also glad to have seen Courtney. He was starting to form a view of the relative abandonment that was the basis of her life. Even though the morning hadn't gone as he was used to, with her eclectic conversational shifts, he knew he liked her—hoped he could become her friend and see her from time to time. He didn't try to put a finger on why exactly he felt that way.

"It is the indefinable that is responsible for affection and affinity," Doppelgänger said. "How we later explain our likes and dislikes to ourselves is simply a process of rationalisation. *Ex post facto* justification."

"*Nunc et in hora lapsus nostrae*," Ozzy Man said, chuffed at his own made-up liturgy. *Now and at the time of our mistakes.* "And then she had gone and made it worse, Mate, by asking whether you liked pizza."

The way to Al's heart ran through a good pizza. They would get one the next day at Conspiracy, a little hole in the wall with a woodfired oven.

7

THE DAYS STRETCHED LANGUIDLY THROUGH the gentleness of their passage. Al and Kimberley went about the details of their joint and separate lives, content and together. They shared the same bed, albeit that they defined night-time differently—Al seldom turned in before one in the morning; Kimberley seldom got up after six. At breakfast they sat together, exchanging their plans for the day; and met again at dinner to say how it had all gone. In between, their paths crossed regularly and frequently—they bumped easily and happily into each other. They were perfect companions, in a manner of perfection that is so hard to define and describe. Their coalition had long ago settled to a bedrock of unshakeable security in which constant reassurance was no longer verbal but integrated in an everyday routine of affection and care.

At twelve thirty, it was time for a light lunch under the trees at Forty-Four Stanley. Kimberley was about her own affairs, and Al had picked Courtney up on the way. The tables wobbled a rickety dance on the uneven slate paving; the waiters walked a long way from the kitchen and didn't do it quickly; and birds, Little Brown Jobs, were fussily busy in the branches over their heads.

"I hope these incontinent little fuckers can control themselves until we are done," Ozzy Man said, looking in concern up into the tree over their table: A washed-out, light-green, long-limbed wild olive.

Al ordered two glasses; and Courtney told him of a film she had seen with Ben Stiller whose kid goes to college and it causes his father to have a melt-down. She didn't skimp on the detail. "I felt so sorry for him. He wants to do well for his son and look good in his eyes. Mostly, he wants the boy to be better and happier than he himself is. But he can't pull it off; and it confirms for him that his life is a failure. The poor guy."

"When Jesse left home, I lost at least part of my sense of purpose." The sentence had just slipped out Al's mouth, without his meaning for it to have done that. Courtney listened, looking at his face as he spoke. She wore a blue light-weight North Face top, zipped to her throat.

"I had gotten so used to being a father, being his father. I knew all his stuff, I laughed when he was happy, worried when he was not. You remember the progress of your own childhood by the things that happened year on year: You played first team; you won the prize; you found a girlfriend. And then, when you're a grown-up, time becomes homogenous—every year is like every other. The only points of reference are the big things: You got married, moved to a new house, had a kid." Al had broken a lifetime's habit and had actually said this aloud. Usually, only Doppelgänger was allowed to be sentimental, strictly in the confidential confines of Al's thoughts.

"Bud, you don't want this girl to have lunch with you ever again?" Ozzy Man said, yawning his boredom and his concern. "Make 'em laugh. Make 'em laugh. Don't you know everyone wants to laugh?"

"When Jesse was growing up, I had a second chance," Al said, despite the red lights blinking in insistent warning. "He learned how to sit, how to walk, how to say Da-Da. He grew tall enough for The Temple of Courage at Sun City; he went on a date; graduated. And then he left." Al looked suddenly old and defeated. Courtney reached across the table, put her hand on his. He smiled wryly. "It's not that bad, I FaceTime him twice or three times a week, and he comes on holiday." When he heard himself and how that came out, the levee almost broke.

"Oh Lord, oh, Lord, won't you give me your hand," Ozzy Man sang.

"Oz," Doppelgänger said.

Courtney squeezed his hand, let go. Changed the topic. "Did you get the link I sent you about alien abductions? The first abduction was in the early sixties. It was quite unspectacular: A husband and wife were driving on a deserted stretch of a county two-lane when a bright light followed them all the way home."

"Like the Bethlehem star," Ozzy Man said, "but in reverse."

"Their story went viral, and from then the stories never looked back. The first story is the basic script—a bright light that follows you, and there is no way of explaining it. But the mythology grew, became more elaborate. Now the aliens catch you and take you for a ride in their spaceship. Two-and-a-half percent of the American public has had a little flip in an alien spacecraft. That's eight million people!" She laughed.

Al wondered how to describe that happy sound: Fresh as summer rain; bright as a ray of sun; shiny as the stars in a cloudless sky.

"Pay attention, Al," Doppelgänger said.

"Fewer people go on Kon-Tiki," she said, grinning. Mischievous imp; playful rapscallion, cheeky scamp, Al thought.

"Alan," Doppelgänger said again.

"Why is there such an obsession with this?" She looked at him expectantly, actually wanted his opinion.

"I think it's like the Spanish Inquisition," Al answered.

"How so?" she said, laughing, almost making him search for adjectives again.

"Well, UFO's and witchcraft are one and the same thing: They are made-up phenomena that grab the attention of an entire era, during which the convention and details of their story become ever more elaborate and generally known and accepted—it enters the social fabric of contemporary mythology. Aliens are little green men with enormous eyes. A few centuries ago, everyone knew a succubus, a she-devil, was basically tits and ass."

Courtney sat forward, leaning her chin on her fist, elbow popped on the knee of a crossed leg. Amused by the comparison.

"Both the succubus and the aliens come for you while you are asleep, to have sex with you. In different ways, which simply reflect the state of scientific and societal sophistication of the time: The succubus tempts your immortal soul; the aliens do medical experiments. But with the same result—it's your naughty bits that get all the attention."

Courtney grinned—she *had* noticed how extraordinarily interested aliens were in sex.

"Witchcraft and alien abductions are both constructs of an unfettered collective imagination and come from sublimated sexual desire," Al said in summing up. "The distinction in discourse speaks of differences in prevailing belief systems, the contemporaneously popular version of reality. Nowadays nobody, outside of the lunatic fringe, structures his life by reference to the temptations to his immortal soul; but we do believe in science and scientific advancement. Hence, the unstoppable force, the irresistible power that manipulates you is no longer the devil, but science. Of sorts."

Courtney was amused by both the analysis and the irreverence; and laughed again. Al liked that sound, hoped he could make it happen again.

"But," she said, "witches were burnt at the stake. Alien abductees tell their story to *You* magazine. That's a substantial difference."

"Sure," Al said, "but you have mixed up who is who in the story: The witch isn't the one who had sublimated sexual desire—she was the one who caused it. The priest was the one who had difficulty with his *membrum virilis*. He and the alien abductee play the same role in the story: They are both tempted by powers they can't possibly resist, powers that cause uncontrollable surges in their libido."

The waiter came to the table, took the empty plates, while Al structured his thoughts.

"The priest was tempted by agents of darkness; and he set out to find them, which wasn't difficult: The pretty girl with dark eyes and chestnut hair. It was her fault that his pecker jumped to attention every time he saw her curtsy demurely before the Madonna. These she-devils were so tricky. But he saw through the deception and set her on fire on Friday afternoon. Fast-forward a thousand years, and the priest is now the nerd in a menial job at the pensions' office, and the only attention his todger gets is when aliens have a good look at it. He also needs forgiveness, but he isn't allowed to have matches, let alone play with them. He tells his story to Jerry Springer, and his confession is recorded in front of a live audience. Same-same: The priest put his confession on display for the people to see in the village square. Both audiences forgive the protagonist his uninvited and unintended boner: The peasants at the bonfire, because it was the best entertainment in their days of mud and misery; and the viewers of tabloid nonsense because that is the five-minute thrill they seek in their fast-food and packaged-entertainment view of the world."

"But if it's such obvious rubbish, how can anyone believe it?" Courtney laughed again, sipped her espresso.

"The capacity for pathological beliefs is endemic to the human condition," Al said.

"Says Karl Jaspers," Ozzy Man said.

Courtney looked at him quietly, agreed with Meg who maintained he spoke like no one she had ever heard.

"Sometimes it's called Delusionism," Al said. "Continuing to believe the stuff of delusion and madness, notwithstanding that there is no rational or evidentiary support for them."

"I love it when you talk metaphysical," she said, chuckling.

Al smiled, lent forward on his elbows. "The wider, more fundamental implication of the difference between burning witches at the stake and believing in UFO's is one that is obvious to see, but that few people recognise. As I have said, no one nowadays truly lives in day-to-day terror for the fate of his immortal soul. What men and women of today dread is not being constantly entertained. We fear boredom as Francis of Assisi feared damnation. For which reason religion has mostly been substituted by B grade television. We used to have the Catholic Church, sin and forgiveness, fire, and brimstone. Now we have rom com and reality television. The church organ mightily ripping through the Toccata has become the electronic ringtone on your iPhone. But the melody and the chord progression are still the same."

Courtney grinned, hiding her eyes behind the palm of an open hand. "God's gonna *getcha*," she said.

No sooner was he back home than the mid-afternoon stacked clouds charcoal-grey and deep over the Kensington ridge, southeast of the city. The computer program in the sky turned the dimmer switch of the sun all the way down, as if it were three hours later, and sunset. The temperature dropped to unexpected coolness and the wind came blasting in to see what was happening. Far away against the darkened horizon, Stratocaster licks of bright-white electricity burnt snake-tail paths in the sky, looking for and finding the iron outcrop in the surrounding ridge of *koppies*, the ring of low ancient granitic rock hills encircling the city. The storm called from miles away in its deepest voice, no distortion in the million watts of amplification.

Then it was on them. The sky upended a headlong rush of fat, heavy drops, the size and weight of grapes from the Promised Land, as fast and as hard as any sky anywhere could. The old Thunder God strode mightily through the African sky, smashing down the fearsome knob on the end of his thick black fighting stick, looking hard at the land through the bemused slits of his crafty eyes and asking, just checking: *You haven't forgotten me, have you?* The trees bent first this way, then that, hissing their plea to be spared, waving supplicating hands and rustling a fearful apology. A hundred million drops crashed down, filling the air with ozone and wetness and that big-storm sound that seeped into the DNA of everyone who has lived on the Highveld for a few summers. Al watched the torrent and listened to the wild applause of the rain on the roof. It went on until there was water, water everywhere. It poured down the gutters, along the walls and through the garden, down the road and flooding the culverts, and roaring into underground pipes that couldn't keep up with the rushing mass. Then, just as Beethoven had scripted it, the deep bass lessened, the strings lightened, the volume eased up, the timpani stilled, and the afternoon returned shy and wet.

The air stayed cool with promise and the assurance that all was well; and the earth lay sighing and still. The storm lazily twitched its tail and drizzled the last few drops over their heads. The heavy sky slowly folded away its burden into cool breezes that kept the roads empty and the early evening glistening, bright and fresh. Darkness flowed in like a cool river; how could there be another day? The peace of the perfect evening rolled into night; and when the magic of its realm had come, the rain still lingered. Al spent the hours after Kimberley had gone to bed being alone and one with the steady slide to whisper-smooth midnight and then some.

"You enjoyed lunch today," Doppelgänger said. "She listens to you when you say things, and she thinks you are funny and smart. She likes you."

"Yeah, Mate," Ozzy Man said. "And for a while there you got all touch-feely." He paid Al what was not, by his definition, a compliment. A sibilant wind gusted outside. "And you wished she would stop saying cute stuff," he added, grinning and derogatory.

"Al said things that didn't need hearing; they needed saying," Doppelgänger said. "And she said some funny things, about Kon-Tiki and abductions. She is easy to be with."

"Gonna try that line on Kimberley, Bud?" Ozzy Man called the elephant in the corner by its name. Al couldn't say why he hadn't told Kimberley of their lunch. Couldn't say, because he didn't know. He would wait to see what happened.

"Yeah, me old Matey," Ozzy Man said. "Rather wait for the inevitable fuck-up."

"Oh, for God's sake, Oz," Doppelgänger answered. "She's a new friend, is all."

Ozzy Man made big eyes and said nothing.

The cat purred on Al's lap, and the night was steady and kind and near. At a shiver after one he turned out the lamp, checked the doors, started the dishwasher and carried the cat to the bedroom where she spent the rest of the night curled up against Kimberley's legs.

8

"THE DOG HAD TURNED INTO a balloon and went blowing down the road, and my telephone was ringing in my pocket. Buzzing—it was on silent. But I couldn't find it and I had to get the dog back." Courtney sat back, enjoying herself.

Indirect light streamed through clear glass panes in an old metal-framed door and swirled around their table in an eddy of mid-morning conversation. Behind the counter a barista blew a jet of steam, twisted the portafilter into the slot and flipped a switch. Life is a mix of magic and coffee.

Beyond the simple concrete floor, through the passage behind and left of Courtney's shoulder, a modern lobby with soundless lifts and disembodied objects d'art whispered of money and power. Buddha-sized Koi floated karmically through the peace of aeons in the pond into which rushed, with gentle restraint, the fall of water responsible for white-noise tranquillity that gave dignity to the multi-storied palace of capital and commerce. Only a few steps away, at the side entrance, convivial Italian simplicity with espresso, cappuccino and panini turned the morning happy and human.

"With a high degree of authenticity," Ozzy Man said, adding to the description, his cynic's eye taking in fake sacks of coffee beans and hollow plastic wheels of Parmigiano Reggiano, scattered about wooden shelves retrofitted into the building's unyielding concrete shell by an interior decorator who did a good enough job for Al to feel perfectly at ease.

"May as well be Montepulciano," Doppelgänger said, "as far as I can tell."

All things must eventually end, and so did Courtney's dream. "Do you ever dream?" she asked, looking as if she cared.

"Ah, Mate," Ozzy Man said. "Nobody can be interested in the non-sensical rambling of another person's subconscious. It is called your subconscious because it is not currently in focal awareness; and is not a solid foundation for interesting conversational interchange."

"Some people have interesting dreams," Doppelgänger said.

"No one I've ever met," Ozzy Man said.

"No, I don't dream," Al told Courtney.

"I watched a show about a man who has violent dreams he can't understand," Courtney said. "And he starts piecing the images together, searching back though his life to make sense of what is going on."

"You make us listen to this?" Ozzy Man said. "A TV show about someone's dream." He screwed one eye into a disbelieving slit.

"You did have a recurring dream," Doppelgänger said. "After Brendan."

Of course Al remembered; he just didn't want to think about it. Night after night it had drawn him in, close, personal, inescapable, all-consuming, ineluctably distressing:

> *I'm sitting on a simple wooden chair in a dark room, facing a series of panels, and I am waiting for it to start. A staccato burst of irregular drumming leads the growing sound of a brass band that appears from the left on the first canvas, and marches into and across a grey and black land of indistinct shapes and a constantly forming and reforming sky. A ragtag army of people follows a marching band of French horns, kettle drums and trumpets. Each figure is absorbed in his own purpose: Women dancing in pirouettes and twirls with sticks and flags; men with loud-hailers and carrying chairs, dragging heavy carts on ropes behind them; a division of skeletons; a world-shaped clock on legs like old-fashioned crutch-like stilts, stepping the wrong direction*

across its body; patients attached to tall drips, walking next to hos-
pital beds rolling along on metal wheels; an old enamelled-steel
bathtub walking clumsily on bowed, misshapen Dachshund legs;
a woman at her typewriter; a dancer holding a spade above her
head, another with a rifle she cradles and swings like a baby. The
broken, the beaten and the damned, marching forward through
their busy lives in time to the carnival-day Salvation-Army
tune and a chorus of voices repeating a melancholy refrain, to
the last panel where they swirl one last whirling step and disap-
pear over the edge. More sweetly play the dance while right now
they're building a coffin your size. And when it's done, and the
last player has left the world brooding and empty and deserted,
the melody fades to one last sad phrase: God bless Africa. And
then it's over and I am sitting alone again in the dark.

"Christ, Buddy, I'd hoped you'd forgotten that shit," Ozzy Man
said. He habitually said: *sheet*. Al would like nothing more than to
forget.

"Nothing fixes things so intensely in the memory as the wish to
forget it," Doppelgänger said.

They had driven East from the Cape Town airport, headed for
Worcester and Robertson, and after that to Montagu. Over the pic-
turesque bridge at the end of town and into the pass beyond they
rode, soon finding a lane of white stinkwoods beside the road, and
at the end of that a wooden sign announcing *Klein Karoo Retreat*,
as if this were a place for scones and tea and a quiet weekend. Al
turned left off the road, following a dirt track into the veldt, towards
a gap between two squat foothills curving gradually to the moun-
tainous ridge in the distance. Up a short climb the road zigged left
and zagged right, then dipped back down and evened out to the
valley floor and a group of white buildings loosely gathered around
an old-fashioned windmill and a clump of flat crowns. Bright-
eyed October had looked down from an almost cloudless sky at
the architect's sleight of hand that used the semi-circle of low hills
behind them, and the distant rise of mountains to hold the Retreat

as if in the palm of an open hand. Out of sight it stood in perfect isolation, as if the rest of the world did not exist. At night, the only light would be from a billion stars as the Milky Way cork-screwed majestically across the sky.

In several heavy wooden planters, tangled tresses of *vygies* were going crazy in a cascade of bright colours, red, purple, white, pink, and yellow. Two doves talked back and forth in rhyme: Here you could stay forever and never realise the time. A mischievous teenage wind had run around the car, kicking a face-full of dust into Al's eyes, and the morning temperature had climbed into the early twenties. He and Meg, silent and apprehensive, had crunched across the gravel to the front door.

At the doorstep, the *maître d'* waited. He nodded, smiled, shook hands with them both. Coarse, curly hair hid the power of his fore-arms and the backs of his hands, and an early hint of a five o'clock shadow coloured dimples on either side of his square chin. "Andrew Pieterse," he said, introducing himself. "Brendan is expecting you. Let me show you through."

They followed him through a spacious lounge with tables and chairs, and an upright piano in the corner, to a broad veranda with a polished red cement floor and a wide low wall around it. The arid flatness of the Klein Karoo stretched away to the protective ram-part of mountains in the blue distance. In the corner of the far wing sat Brendan in an overstuffed easy chair that had given many years of active service, and still had no complaint. His face had thinned out, and when he stood to greet them, Al saw that his body had done the same. The sadness behind his eyes was grey, his shoulders stooped, his hands looked old.

"Bren," Meg had said softly, reaching up to hug her older brother. She hadn't managed to keep a rim of tears from her eyes.

"I have this dream," Brendan said, as if it were getting late and this time he forgot to slip into his slumber. "The light is on the left side of her head; and I'm standing in the doorway. I'm mum-bling, and I can't remember the last thing that ran through my head." His eyes found the fists clenched in his lap, and he stopped talking. Nothing further to say. Whoever thought that hell would be so cold?

"Don't linger on things that have no remedy," Doppelgänger wanted Al to say. "What's done is done." But Al didn't say a word, wouldn't presume to give advice, to pretend he knew the answers.

"Bren, what happened?" Meg asked into the silence of the dry Karoo morning.

"I was in a world of hurt. Everywhere I looked, I saw her eyes. I couldn't forgive myself, and I couldn't forget, even for an instant. I wanted it to stop. I tried blotting it out with booze and pills, but it came back as my first thought every time I surfaced, no matter how far down I had been. There was no way to escape, no way to beat it, no place to hide, no way to get away from it—until I realised there *was* a way. When it came to me and I knew what I had to do, relief flooded over me. It was so obvious, so simple."

Having come to that easy but profound realisation, he moved around the house thinking only of process, what he had to do to get it done. He ran the bath, found the sharpest serrated stainless-steel blade in the drawer, balanced it on the edge next to the soap dish, and climbed in.

"The water was hot, and I put my head under, holding my breath. My thoughts were crystal-clear after being in a muddle for so long. For the first time I could think straight, and I knew this was the right thing to do. It was so simple. Just knowing the end was near, made me feel less desperate. The deep pain in my chest eased up and I felt I could breathe. I picked up the blade, held it in my left hand, with the tip against the inside of my right wrist."

With quick downward slash he had cut along the vein, blood welling up immediately from the cut. He switched the blade into his other hand, slashing his left wrist, quick and deep. "I had braced against the pain but felt almost nothing. I watched as the blood mixed with the water, swirling into clouds of pink. It looked quite beautiful. I lay back to meet the deep peace settling over me."

The walls of the world dissolved around him. Fine and thin played a flute and faraway he heard a gentle metallic touch on a cymbal as he slipped through the borders of light that unravelled and melted into muted glows of soft flowing roundness. He sank into the earth, past layers of roots and shapes of older things, to a deep bank of mossy rocks in the slow trickle of the coolest green waters. He became one with everything that was black and closed and without brightness or thought. He floated through an ancient land of tragic, deserted rock and early seas over which mighty constellations swept between cold borders of distant light.

"I watched from far in the soft dusk and heard a simple rock 'n' roll beat that closed to a touch on the foot pedal, a tap on the cymbal, a double tap of drum; and then oblivion, silent, welcoming and complete."

Brendan, beaten shape of a man, gazed quietly into the unfocussed middle-distance, wistfully remembering a lost paradise of perfect silence and peace. The sound of a car stopping outside in the car park brought him back to the present.

"I woke in a warm room where the light was soft and the silence thick. I thought I was there—where things were done, and it hurt no more. Slowly I became aware of details: Strapping on my hands and forearms and tiny noises from beyond the door. Even as I looked at it the door opened soundlessly, and a nurse came in. She walked to the edge of my bed and said my name. That is when I realised I was still here."

He looked away again, remembering those first moments of his disappointment. "And then you were there," he said, looking at Al.

A week later, Al had knocked on a door below the sign *Zalmon Behr, M.B., B.Ch., DPM Neurologist, Psychiatrist*. He had turned the handle and stepped into an enclave of peace. Against two of the walls of the tiny office were quietly patient watercolours of long deserted beaches and white-topped waves below an endless sky. If you listened carefully, you could hear the echo of a million seashells, and the rhythmic and never-ending music of the ocean. From the third wall a family of faces watched: A middle-aged woman, formally dressed and with her hair just-so; a young man smiling in a long gown with a degree certificate in his hand; a girl of six sitting straight-backed and high on a tall horse, a round, black riding hat over the seriousness in her eyes; and, in black-and-white, a stern young man with a moustache like Edgar Allan Poe and his equally unsmiling wife, watching across many decades from the early twentieth century. Behind a desk, narrower than Al's arm-span but beautifully crafted in light-brown oak, sat an old man who radiated calmness like the Eiffel-tower antenna of an R.K.O. Radio Picture. He looked to be deep into his eighties, and everything about him was as old-fashioned as Django Reinhardt on a 78 rpm Bakelite. He wore a formal white long-sleeved shirt and a striped light-blue and white tie, and a fawn waistcoat, buttoned to the top. The kindness in his eyes reached Al before the proffered handshake.

"Zalmon Behr." The old man had smiled with his eyes. Advertising executives want us to believe that good-looking people smile with their teeth—a by-product of the modern obsession with stylised personal beauty: Sleek muscles, smooth skin, flat tummies and flawless white teeth. The good doctor's smile encompassed his whole existence, as if the many lines of his wrinkled face drew the rune of perfect friendship. What he said to Al was this:

"Because a man tries to kill himself doesn't make him crazy—it just means he wants to solve his problems and he can't think of another way. There is nothing you or I can do to change his mind—only he can do that. Your brother is deeply depressed—I can prescribe medication, but that will be only as effective as he allows it to be. Now that he has seen how easy it is to get away, the invitation to try again will be even bigger. And if he tries, next time he will probably get it right."

The kindly psychiatrist had been bang on the money.

Al drifted slowly back to their table, where, in Courtney's story, the man realised that the image from his dream was the pattern of the wallpaper in the room where he had been taken by the cult members, before the exorcism.

"If you don't pay the exorcist, you will be repossessed," Ozzy Man said.

Al smiled encouragingly but didn't want to think any more about either his demons or his dreams. He was glad for the sunshine and the morning and the company.

9

"THE POPULAR MODERN IDIOM OF the world as a village," Doppelgänger said, "pretends and wants you to believe that all the people in the world are right next to each other. Neighbours, all of us. But the houses can be way far apart."

Hank, the fundraising Rotary man, thought only brothers and sisters lived in the world:

"We are all one large family. We are all related. Nobody is different from anybody else. The furthest you are from anyone ever is five degrees of separation. Five small steps between you and anyone on earth—that's the furthest you can be away. Every stranger is a friend you haven't met."

"A man was introduced to a vegetarian girl," Ozzy Man said. "*I've never met herbivore*, he said."

"It has been proved," Hank said, "that if you address a letter to anyone in the world with just his name, it gets to him after a maximum of five stops. There are only five acquaintances between you and the person on earth you think is the least known to you. We are a close-knit community, even though we don't always realise it. If everyone in the world would just realise that, we would be so much better off. A fellowship of friends; a new philosophy of Man."

"Philosophies should be obscene and not heard," Ozzy Man said.

"Yes," George said, med school professor. On his third glass of red, he had no patience for new-age sentimentality. "The loonies usually say six degrees, but let's stick with five. Point is, I addressed a letter once to Carlos Ruiz and popped it in the mail without his address. It turns out, there are seven thousand of them in Mexico City; another two-hundred-and-fifty thousand in South America. And a few in Spain. The one I had written to, with the modern diaspora and all, was living in rural Tibet. He rang me last week to say that he is still waiting."

Edward, AIDS activist, and senior advocate wouldn't stand for such cynicism: "You just don't want to acknowledge that we are all related to each other, and that although the world appears to be large, we are so very closely related. We literally are brothers and sisters on our journey."

"If a man will tell you about his *journey*," Ozzy man said, "he won't shrink from cliché."

"Edward," George said, sighing. "You have many skills, but mathematics and logic are not among them. Yes, we are all related. To be precise, most recently to Mitochondrial Eve; but that was about a hundred-and-fifty-thousand years ago. Just short of ten thousand generations. That's a fuck load of mothers and daughters. The whole of modern civilization is, max, fourteen thousand years old. From when we first moved out of a cave. We are related, sure. But we are related also to chimps and bonobos, and jelly fish and the streptococcus bacterium." He took a world-weary slug from his glass. "And you would be shocked to see what Grandmama Mitochondria looked like."

"Your ingrained cynicism predisposes you against all inclusive thinking," Edward said in his most reasonable court-room voice. "Your prejudice against altruism and social cohesion shows you up every time you try to set yourself above the rest. You lack the humility that comes from understanding equality—we are equal before the law, because we are equal in the world."

"Edward, lack of critical judgment and freedom from prejudice are not the same." George dished out an off-hand dismissal. "But to get back to Hank's dreamcatcher-and-NGO point, this world is home to one hundred and fifty million people called Mohammed."

"Fuck me drunk." Ozzy Man was amazed; and knew that, if George said a thing like that, he had checked it first.

"If you put all the Mohammeds in one place and said: *I have a letter for Mohammed*, how long to find the right one? If everybody took ten seconds to look at it, it would take about fifty years, 24/7, for the letter to get round to everybody. That's a lot of five steps."

"You are missing the point," Hank said. At which George spluttered into his red wine.

"*I* am missing the point?" His incredulity changed his question into an accusation. He glowered at Hank and Edward. "It's not just *Mohammed* that is widespread. There are also surnames." He pulled one randomly from the air. "Like Wang. Choose a first name."

"Wanting," Ozzy Man said.

"So, my letter is addressed to Li Wang; and let's assume he lives in China. But in one of the 900,000 rural villages, in none of which they speak or read English. Let's say he's in Danbazangzhai. What chance is there that a postman will pick the right place? Or would it be any easier if he is one of the 22 million people living in Beijing?"

"How Long is a Chinese man's name," Ozzy Man said.

Max Wilkins was enjoying the show. "I addressed a letter," he said, "to a man in Cape Town, with his right name and surname, precisely correct address, complete with postal code and all, and he didn't get it." He grinned, added: "Maybe he doesn't have five friends—he's an actuary."

The table laughed; and Hank stuck to his guns, "Well, it's been proved; and I believe it."

George scrunched his face to incredulity, one eye squinting towards the corner of his lop-sided grimace. "Apart from 7.8 billion people in the world being a hell of a lot of people; and despite the world being a whole lot bigger and a whole lot more impersonal than you think, the most fundamental flaw with your posting-a-letter-bullshit-story is"—he intoned his irritation—"that your *name* isn't nearly enough to accurately identify you. For that you need a social security number. If you tell me that you're never more than five steps away from the nearest bureaucrat, I am prepared to believe you. But aren't they the very antipathy to your world view of brotherhood and unicorns?"

In the early years of the 21st century, the correct way to correspond was not to. The leaders of the free world Tweet, so why can't you? If you do it right, your letter sees the light of day from the screen of your laptop, and it's addressed to *GaryStubbsFeb1955@gmail.com*. Such a complicated address because there is more than one of him on the Gmail client list.

Gary Stubbs, born in February 1955, and Al were broke young students together. Gary was as wild as the west Texas wind, compared to Al's much more measured pace. One raggedy Tuesday morning, Gary talked them both into a pilgrimage to the cinema complex in Doornfontein, instead of the lecture they were supposed to attend. They sat alone in the two-hundred-seater in the darkness and heard to the first strains of Robbie Krieger's disembodied guitar. Big-screen images coalesced from the immediate sense of foreboding and menace; and there was Martin Sheen, losing his shit in the fever of a barracks room in Saigon. *All the children are insane*, intoned Jim Morrison as a ceiling fan morphed into the blades of attack helicopters—vengeful Valkyries direct from mad strident Wagner. Robert Duvall swaggered around a burning village smelling of napalm in the morning; the primordial river oozed further and further away from reason and light; and in the centre of the jungle was Brando, as psychotically deranged as the heart of darkness, mumbling, *We are the hollow men; we are the stuffed men*. After the craziness and chaos, only Morrison's forlorn and bruised tenor floated over the fade-out of the mother of all airstrikes, sadly telling them the End: *It hurts to set you free, but you'll never follow me*.

"After graduation Gary wrote screenplays," Doppelgänger said, "getting his first mid-sized paycheque from a cigarette advertisement. In those years it was still allowed." Everyone with a radio knew that *for after action satisfaction*, you relaxed with a Lexington and that if you *light up a Life*, you said out loud: *Oh man Life is great*.

"Gary moved on to bigger and better things; and then left altogether for Los Angeles to join the rhinestone cowboys and the crush on Highway 101," Doppelgänger said. Gary and Al had in common a reverence for Tom Waits, and a dysfunctional relationship with their equally megalomaniac fathers.

The Atlantic heaved and sweated prohibitively between the shores of their two continents; their houses in the world's modern village hugged the margins of how far away it's possible to be apart in three-dimensional geography; and a human hankering for friendship and understanding kept them in contact.

This is what Al wrote to his friend:

Gary, Hi there.

I have been to Vancouver only once. It rained the whole week as if we were in the Amazon. Beautiful place though—the window in the board room, where I did financial business things, looked directly ahead at the ski slope on the edge of the city; I spent a lot of time in fascination watching seaplanes land on the water in front of us. I'd seen them in movies and photographs, but there they were in real life—landing and leaving a wake behind them just like a speedboat; and later taking off again.

Sad reason for you to be there—how old is your father now, 92? You wrote that you feel badly that he is not that important to you, even now when he is old and ill, but you should give yourself a break 'cause that's how it goes. When you're a baby, your parents are your whole life—you depend on them for everything, but it gets less and less so with every new day. Your first job in life is to develop your own ego and by the time you are seven, parents are down to way below half of our dependencies. When you turn 18, they're lucky if they feature at all—because, by then, it's voluntary as you choose whether you want them around or not. Then your table is small, nobody has a seat at it unless he deserves it. To be honest, your father hardly went out of his way to make space for himself. You feel responsible now only because you are nicer than he was (I know, because I have been down this dark and lonely road myself.) And because, astounding as you may find it, you are human. I read, just the other day, a quote from Jean-Paul

Sartre (don't worry, not in the original. I was reading Calvino who quoted him):

"In the midst of the Aeneases who carry their Anchiseses on their backs, I pass from one shore to another, alone, hating these invisible fathers astride their sons for all of their life."

When I crossed alone to the shore of my adult life and left Troy burning behind me, I thought I was gone, scot-free. Made my escape. But that old fucker stayed on my back (—he is there still, even after we put him in the cold, cold ground.) You, foot-loose and fancy free, without your own children, what you don't know is this: When my Jesse left the shore of his childhood home, it wasn't burning, and he didn't leave to get away as fast and as far as possible. But, however much I don't want to be, I am on his back even as I write this.

Oh, my Bud, this sublunary game we play hasn't been thought through carefully at all. If only Heaven had spreadsheets and Excel. We're stuck in Disney's Circle of Life: You start in nappies, and do as you are told: Mama says you can't play with your best friend, the boy next door, coz that's the way it ought to be. Then you get to set the world on fire for a while—conquer your last frontier, polish your ego, sow your wild seed. And in the end they put you back in nappies and treat you like a slightly naughty German Shepherd, coz that's the way it ought to be. Borges says, (can you stand another quote?)

"Death (or reference to death) makes men precious and pathetic; their ghostliness is touching; and any act they perform may be their last. There is no face that is not on the verge of blurring and fading away like the faces in a dream. Everything in the world of mortals has the value of the irrecoverable and contingent."

Yup, that's pretty much it. Which leaves only one conclusion: Don't be a cunt, because this is how good it gets. My Pappy, he didn't ever get that right.

'Nuff 'bout that.

I also wanted to tell you that I have a new friend, and I'm not sure what I'm doing. She is 23 years younger than me and pretty. I see her often, for tea, for lunch, for coffee. We chat. Well, mostly she chats. She tells me the details of her life and of the lives of the Soapy characters she watches for hours every day. That last bit sounds horrible, I know, but it's light and easy. There's no dissemblance and no posturing. What you see is what you get. And there's this: She doesn't tell me what to do, how to do it, and when to do it; and I can say what I like and how I like. That's not my usual dispensation. I know (to stray into euphemism) you and Kimberley see the world from a different point of view; so, you know what I mean, it's tangled up in blue.

I really enjoy our conversations and spending time with her—but here's the problem: Kimberley is upset that I like this girl, Courtney. She hasn't said so yet, but it's obvious. She doesn't think I'm having an affair. No, it's worse than that. She is upset because she is my best friend, and she thinks her rank is in danger. You know that Hollywood cliché: "It didn't mean a thing," which means outside of American cinema, "Yeah, we screwed like minks, but please don't divorce me—alimony is karmically so negative." The fundamental distinction is between, on the one hand, adultery (which the Good Lord frowns on); and, on the other hand, loss of Philia (which is how the old Greeks thought of love for your wife—I looked it up) which goes hand in hand with the loss of dependability, companionship and trust (which the Good Lord also doesn't go for so much because your woman must love, honour and obey you.) Well, I've done neither of those two things, ever. And I'm not doing them now. But I know Kimberley is upset and, at the same time, it's the first easy friendship I have had in many years. Some of my easy friends buggered off to Los Angeles, can you believe that? Anyhow, I will have to do something about Courtney soon. I'm just not sure what as I don't want Kimberley to be unhappy; but equally, I don't want to give up my friendship with Courtney because I'm not actually doing anything wrong, and because I like the company.

What do you say, Big Spirit of many moving images and speaking shadows? Commune with me now in the wisdom of your shaman ancestors—What can a poor boy do?

Let me know when you're back from Vancouver. I hope this thing with your dad is as painless as it can be (for both of you).

Chat soon,

Al

10

DOPPELGÄNGER TOLD THEM A STORY.

"A man is driving along an endless unchanging road. Hour after hour he drives on, but the road and the plain through which it stretches stay the same. He can't remember how long he has been going, but he isn't tired. The country around him is vast, flat, and open, and nothing moves in the shimmering heat. Secrets of recent rain lay hidden in hints of green in the fields undulating to a broken line of distant hills. The sky sighs piles of soft white cloud into the endless blue. The man tries to remember where he is, where he is going. He sees a big bird, a raptor circling in the lazy high thermals out near the horizon. The man speeds on, reassured by the hush of rushing wheels on the road. The miles drink time like a slow faucet leak. Time stretches out, slows down."

"Time flies like an arrow," Ozzy Man said. "Fruit flies like a banana."

Doppelgänger was used to his interruptions and Al wouldn't interfere. He pushed on with his story: "As the car speeds on, the man thinks of a farewell on a night when the world was so quiet. *When was that?* He tries to remember. Dark eyes and a brush of freckles across softly rounded cheeks; a dimple; a dark fringe."

"Maybe it wasn't you." Ozzy Man meant Al.

"Let me tell the story anyway," Doppelgänger said looking less dreamy. "She was almost young, and they walked along black sand in the icy spray of a troubled sea. Her hands were cold in his when she turned to face him, fully a head shorter than him, a box full of years younger."

"A *box* full?" Ozzy Man said, grinning. "How many years in a box, Bud?"

"At least six," Doppelgänger said without missing a beat.

"Good one, Mate. When were you ever on a beach like that?"

"Okay then, it was still warm on a subtropical East coast beach after the mid-day silence had scorched the sand in blinding whiteness, and shadows slid from the dunes in expectation of the clamour of night. The ocean sighed, slowly welcoming evening, and the sun had sloped Westward, turning the sand caramel brown. Shy, almost translucent crabs scuttled in the wet mirror pull-back of the waves."

"Christ, mate! If you had a guitar, you would be Rod fucking McKuen." Ozzy Man rolled his eyes like a West Coast miner.

"Anyway, this isn't about me," Doppelgänger said.

"*Sitz im Leben*. Giving context to your creative text." Ozzy Man said: *condext*, lifting his eyebrows in mock approval.

"His chest was brown and bare; he carried his shirt rolled up like a bandage around his right fist. She filled the curves of a light-blue long-sleeved rash vest. She loved him; thought she knew he loved her. Didn't want him to say."

"Why on a beach, mate?"

"They have to be somewhere." Doppelgänger lost the dreamy tone. "Do you want to hear or not?"

Ozzy Man gestured open hands like a henpecked Jewish husband.

"'I leave tomorrow,' he said, keeping his face neutral. 'Here we are, Pierrot and Columbine.'"

"Christ Bud, nobody speaks like that!" Ozzy Man said. "She wouldn't know what the fuck he was saying." If Doppelgänger was put out by the outburst, it was impossible to tell.

"The man dropped his eyes to the instruments on the dashboard. No change—still going 120, fuel and temperature fine. Fixing his eyes on the horizon where the ribbon of road cut through the haze, he forgot about saying goodbye—maybe it was still in the future;

maybe he knew he had to do it but hadn't yet. Perhaps he made all of it up; perhaps there was no girl, no reason to say goodbye. He thought instead of the lovers who had passed through his room. The ones he had lost his heart to; and the ones who had done the same for him. His mind's eye saw the picture on the wall, drawn by a man who loved that girl—she looks back at him, deep hazel eyes ever shining, caught forever in a sad African landscape of thorn trees, brown thatch, and bush; of wide-open sky and solitude."

"In the land of Uz lived a blameless and upright man," Ozzy Man said. "He feared God and shunned evil. But he lost it all on a bet: his children, his camels, his goats. His wives. A bet between God and the Devil—he didn't even get to the casino."

"Exactly," Doppelgänger said. "The man worried, saying to himself: *I don't want to end up like the righteous man of Uz.* But what did he want, what did he dream of in his loneliness? He dreamed only of the girl, wanted it all back again. His thoughts were simple, yet complicated: They walked hand-in-hand on the fine wet sand of a snow-white beach, squinting against the setting sun, with the icy water playing catch with their bare toes. Only the two of them— she stopping to look for cowry shells and he happy just to be there. The sand crunched under their feet at every step and scrubbed away the last shred of everything that was to blame. At the rocks they had chosen to be the end of the never-ending beach, they turned and followed the riverbank back up to their little white house where they sat on a wide wooden deck, wrapped up against the early evening chill. They watched the wind sweep a curtain of sand sharply over the edge of the dunes, while the sun slipped slowly over the horizon behind them, leaving a glove of shadow and the silent touch of darkness."

"They stayed up all night, wondering where the sun had gone." Ozzy Man spoke in the same reverential tones as his companion. "Then it dawned on them."

"He stood at the edge of the rocky drop of a deep mountain with the freezing wind in his face and his arms wrapped around her." Doppelgänger carried on as if Ozzy hadn't said a thing. "Her head leaned back against his chest; her hands deep in the pockets of a blue-and-black padded windbreaker. She stood alone even though he was there, the deep blue mountains in the distance watching her think fragile thoughts. When they turned to make their way back across the barren plateau, down the ladder and the winding mountain path to their little red car far below, only the eternal silence reverberated from the tall cliffs, and only the patient song of slow aeons guided them through the wide and desperate land."

"Is the man in the car still driving?" Ozzy Man asked, feeling confused.

"Yes. The road brought him to a series of bending uphill rises, slowly climbing away from the flat floor of a plain, the bottom of an ancient inland sea. Over the crest of the last hill the road fell back down to the plain stretching wordlessly across the emptiness to a distant ring of mountains and their foothills, so far from here, in another time, in another world."

"Christ, where *are* they, Bud?" He said: *aah*, stretching the long vowel into incredulity.

"You may be missing the point." Doppelgänger raised his eyebrows at his companion, who nodded in agreement. "The man remembered another time: They held hands underwater as they snorkelled in shallow pools along the reef where tiny black tropical fish no bigger than your thumb cheekily sneak up and nip you in the leg; and where a big old moray waited patiently through the seasons, toothy and stupid in his cave at the back of a rocky overhang. Later, they sat at high tide in the shallows behind Splash Rock where sinister black crabs cling skittish and oblique to the far wall, washed by cascades of retreating waves. He laughed with her when waves galloped noisily across the open sea and smashed over the top of the massive fortress behind which was their hidey hole, pouring a torrent of warm foamy white water over them."

"Yeah, I remember that," Ozzy Man said, dreamily nostalgic.

"The car was whisper-quiet, followed the road on its own, taking him to a place from which there is no return. Had he been here before?" Doppelgänger asked dramatically, rhetorically. "The faster you go, the more time slows down; the further you get away, the closer to home you think you are. The man remembers another moment: She stood at the railing on the veranda in a rest camp in the dry wilderness far up North, near the Limpopo. Around her the tawny bush, the faded brown veldt, the isolation of being away from cities and rushing and noise. She wore khaki shorts, button down shirt and a wide-brimmed hat loosely tied under her chin. The rangers were getting ready to take them bouncing on the back of an open Jeep into the hot afternoon of thicket and tangled undergrowth, where the endless loop of life and death had held inexorable sway since an unreachably distant dawn. On the way back they saw the thoughtful round eyes of an enormous owl picked out in rapier beam of the tracker's lamp. The eyes that were there and gone in a quiet instant."

Doppelgänger paused, thinking of their life and its precious, precious things. Then he continued: "He followed the trail blazoned by her strong calves as she strode out in such small boots through the damp towering forests where sticky creepers had caught silence in a tangled ancient web and kept it safe for them to hear. They listened to the stillness and power of the trees; and they were alone and close with the slowness of forever. The morning was patient and wise and consoled without presuming to advise. Later, they waited on a massive boulder near the point for the sun to slip under the horizon behind them; and watched the ocean charge green and violent up the narrow gulley, crashing high and wild against the black granite cliff. She leaned back against him, and he kissed the top of her head. Just the two of them, safe above the untamed water."

"All the stuff you remember, Dobby," Ozzy Man said, impressed. "I also have a photographic memory, but it hasn't developed yet."

Doppelgänger paid no attention, got back to his story: "The man wonders when last he saw another vehicle. At the bridge he crossed there had been a caravan, the type in which roadworkers lived when they were on site. But he hadn't seen anybody. They probably had the day off. He stretched his neck, sighed, concentrated on the shimmering road ahead, and remembered: In the burning furnace of midday in the Richtersveldt they rested hip-to-hip in the shade of an overhang with their backs against an ancient rock face, together always in this sliver of eternity. The gnarled hands of time had bent into crooked patterns and swirls, craggy layers of weathered sedimentary rock in the side of the canyon through which the river slowly found its way. He looked at the side of her sun-red face under the brim of an Indiana Jones hat and saw the beauty. He wanted to scoop her up in a butterfly net, keep her in a locket next to his heart, never leave this moment."

"I heard National Geographic is looking for feature writers who pack adjectives like six-guns," Ozzy Man said. "You interested?"

Of course, Doppelgänger paid him no mind, carried on with what he was saying: "He flashed by a sign that told him there was a dust road to the left at a T-junction ahead, to a place he hadn't heard of. He sped on, forgetting the name; he wouldn't be turning. His thoughts drifted back to where he was going. Then he remembered why he was here: He wanted her to share the long, unchanging road along which they drove through loneliness and flat desolation, with the sun slipping slowly over the lonely blue ridge of the far horizon. In a quiet moment he would notice in the soft green glow of evening that she was asleep and right there with him. She trusted him; she loved him. She knew he would never allow anything to harm her; he would hold her and keep her. Forever. This long road would never change. They would ride it together, for all time, till the very end. He would always have her with him. Nothing would ever change."

"You *are* talking about Kimberley here, Mate," Ozzy Man said. "Like Christina Rosetti's road that winds up-hill all the way and to travel takes the whole long day? You do mean the road with her from back when they met to when Al one day slips over his own last horizon, don't you?"

"Ha, I am a modern troubadour: I sing the song and it's up to you to unravel what it means," Doppelgänger said. "Maybe it's her. But maybe it's an archetype—the distillate of all women; a conglomerate of all personalities and characteristics. All of them and all his memories rolled into one: A composite, irreducible ideal. Maybe she doesn't exist; maybe she can't."

"Okay, Buddy." Ozzy Man blew a round-cheeked breath. "But this car and the long road, it's not about arriving: it's about how he gets there?"

Doppelgänger, having said so much, now kept quiet.

"Dobby, you know him best." Ozzy man stated the simple fact. "For all intents and purposes, you are identical. So, tell me: Why is she not in the fucking car?" Ozzy Man's inflection emphasised and drew the word into astonished bewilderment: *Kaah*. "Where you goin' with this, Bud?"

"The man doesn't know," Doppelgänger answered. "The miles slipped by outside, endless, and unending, the unchanging road. Day after day he drove on, but the road and the plain stayed the same. He didn't know where he was going, hoped the car did. What he did know was that he couldn't do it alone. If she wasn't with him, he wouldn't make it."

11

LATE AFTERNOON SHADE WHISPERED THROUGH the trees and silence echoed around the garden. Streaks of soft gold slanted in from the rim where the sun slowly settled to a Western horizon, blurring fragile edges, and politely waking an indolent young breeze from its nap. It alone stirred, deferentially cooling the torpor that had settled over Al in the heat after lunch. A distant thoughtfulness had colonised his diffuse attention, planted its flag and allowed only fuzzy abstractions to form and fade in the newly conquered territory. Unfocussed and vacant, he slouched in his big chair, subliminally speculative and distantly doleful. From what Lobsang Rampa may have called an astral remove, he watched the afternoon slide silently away on a peaceful ebb towards the quiet cove of evening.

"Sometimes you sits and thinks." Ozzy Man described Al's reverie. "And sometimes you just sits."

"Melancholy longing and unfathomable sadness for an unidentifiable loss puts you closer to the essence of things, makes you more introspectively human," Doppelgänger said.

"Mellon Collie and the Infinite Sadness," Ozzy Man said in mock moodfullness. "And Lobsang Rampa was a plumber from Devon before he found his third eye and became a best-selling mystic."

Doppelgänger looked at Ozzy sideways, ignoring his habitual cynicism. "There was a time and a place where heavy red drapes perfectly framed the light in a bay window, and dark ball-and-claw furniture stood in dignified stillness around the edges of a fading Persian rug. There we were secure in the afternoon that had dug its foundation deep into the basalt basement of safety and belonging. It was *Home*. It was where we belonged."

"Wherever the fuck that was." Ozzy Man blew a long breath from ballooning cheeks, like Dizzy Gillespie on trumpet.

"It was *Home*," Doppelgänger repeated, surfing high on a rippling crest of nostalgia. "As I said. You know where it was."

Al couldn't figure why he remembered that—nothing had actually happened; it was just a still life picture in his head from before his world had known controversy. Against the wall closest to the kitchen, the gramophone cabinet gaped open. A pile of vinyl records on the left; the turntable and heavy black-armed stylus in the middle; and the dials and glass-fronted panel of the radio on the right—FM at the top, AM at the bottom, and a vertical red stylus that moved from side to side with the turning of the tuning knob.

"*Home* is like the holy river," Ozzy Man said. "Once it flows under the bridge it won't ever be the same again. You can only hear it say *Om* once. The next time is not the same moment, not the same water, not the same river."

"Gee, Oz, you're becoming such a thinker," Doppelgänger said. "And so original. Haven't heard that one before. On top of which you may actually be right." Doppelgänger made flat frog lips of equivocation, continued with his description. "Once you're gone, once you leave the shores of youth, there's no going back. *Home* can only mean something real, can only exist while you are a child. Having your life's anchor in one place is what *Home* is. It's not only the centre of your world, it's the whole of it. It's the place where you belong because that's where your life is: your parents, your bedroom, your things, your games, your thoughts—the whole of your existence. All your changes are there. When you have grown up, you don't have a *Home* anymore, except the original one you never can get back to. All you have is a place where you stay. You may coincidentally like it and may be happy there. Look at us: We stayed at *Home* until we were 18 and left for Uni. Since then, we have lived in different places, some of which we were fond of, like this beautiful house and garden. But this is just where we sleep and eat. It ain't *Home* no more."

"Almost to quote the Diamond," Ozzy Man said, keeping it commercially accessible. "Just one tiny lil' thing though, Bud. You're feeling nostalgic for a time and a place where there was ongoing, unrelenting war. Sniping from the trenches during the day; active open engagement every dinnertime. We were in the front line— the bombardment and hand-to-hand of the time you now so badly miss led to *No Speaks* for how long? Seventeen years?" He said: *sivineen yee-iz.*

"Zackly." Doppelgänger borrowed an expression straight back. "That's why it's so hard to understand, so difficult to rationalise. It feels like football and marbles and thick red crackers at Guy Fawkes; and smiles and Family. But it was never completely happy or together. Hence the feeling of deep loss for something that never was. Nostalgia QED."

"Home is made for coming from, for dreams of going to," Ozzy Man said, quoting from the spiritual teaching of the Swami Lee Marvin.

Doppelgänger heard a rustling wind blow away the ashes of summer. "The older I get," he said, "the better it used to be: When the sun shone kindly all day, and they loved us; when the night was dark and quiet, and they kept us safe. All of us—Al and Bren; and later Meg as well."

"Crickey, Bud, what's come over you? Check out all the flowers over here." Ozzy Man gestured at garden.

"I'll tell you now of some that I know." Doppelgänger dropped his depressing train of thought like a dumbbell after fifteen heavy reps,

"Moon Flowers, Cape Myrtle, red Bottlebrush,
Peony, Day Lily, Jasmine, Watsonia,
Clivia, Gazania,

Angel Wings, Strelizia,
Inca Lilies, Marigolds, Gardenia,
Liquidambar, Silver Birches, Avocado trees."

"And those you missed, I'll surely pardon," Ozzy Man said, grinning.

Kimberley appeared from the direction of the house. "Remember we are going to the Linder tonight," she said. "Concert starts at seven-thirty."

Appropriate dress is a wide concept. At the fountain outside the auditorium the Van den Bergs held court. Raymond wore the uniform of a Wild West cardsharp: Dark suit, ruffled silk shirt with embroidered lace, and a string tie—the bolo of which was a cabochon opal, the size of a walnut, set in a rim of gold; and ends of the laces were the same, but smaller. Elsobe's ankle-length shimmering gown cupped her shape closely and reflected the light in a shifting rainbow spectrum, like the back of a CD in the sun. Its tightness of hem allowed her high heels to click behind her in only the shortest of steps. Her fur stole was authentic—the shrivelled head of some poor dead thing over her shoulder stared lugubriously from empty eye sockets, keeping watch for the Anti-Fur Coalition.

"Don't you love Handel?" she said, gushing.

"Absolutely," Al said.

"Tonight's programme is Haydn, silly-assed woman." Ozzy Man tried to correct her expectation. But Al wouldn't say. She probably couldn't tell the difference anyway.

"Haydn, Handel, Hubble, Himmler, who cares?" Doppelgänger was amused.

"Ooh, I'm so excited!" Elsobe trilled like a novitiate Franciscan at a lake-side picnic with boat rides and ponies. She crooked her arm proprietorially around Raymond's manly elbow. He puffed away on the end of a stogie the size and calibre of an Italian sausage, not noticing his anachronistically anti-social habit had cleared a five-meter radius no-go zone around them.

"A woman is an occasional pleasure." Ozzy Man eyed the dead badger around Elsobe's neck. "But a cigar is always a smoke."

"Hey there!" somebody said in Courtney's voice, causing an automatic happy smile to break over Al's face. Kimberley noticed. Not so much the smile, but the spontaneity of it. The person using Courtney's voice was Courtney. Dark eyes, standing elegant and lithe next to podgy, florid Thomas, who explained the commercial aspects of their mid-week adventure: "We are doing a deal for Bigbux Bank and they sponsor the orchestra." *We* didn't mean him and Courtney. "They gave us tickets, in the circle. Do you come here often? Do you like the classics? What are they playing? Where are you sitting? Do you play any instrument? Do you know the CEO of Bigbux?" A silent look passed between Courtney and Al.

The gong sounded, calling them to sit down; and they weren't anywhere near each other—the circle was for money and privilege, and was discreetly placed so that no-one would notice if you dozed through the difficult bits. The conductor had a neat comb-over and a double chin, and when he had been sweating under the lights for no more than a few minutes, the thin streaks he had plastered down across his pate with such care became unstuck—they resumed their natural curl, sticking straight up in the air like a pig-tail antenna on the roof of a patrol car.

In the half hour interval, Al got himself and Kimberley each a mass-produced thick-lipped caterer's glass of white wine, made the previous week in the industrial area south of the airport. Kimberley had found Ronald Khan, the emeritus professor who used to be the head of the Faculty of Fine Arts at Uni. Like many mature gentlemen who met her, the old prof was trying to charm Kimberley. He did this by showing her how smart and knowledgeable about music he was. He had, after all, been head of that department.

"Something in her style encourages pomposity," Doppelgänger said.

"Music evolved in conjunction with and as support to our facility for speech." Prof Khan's lecturing style and accent were pretentiously fake British upper-class. "We know this because capacity for music is functionally and neurologically distributed throughout the brain, exactly as with speech. And they have the same mellifluous lilt, inflection, and cadence."

Kimberley watched with apparently her entire attention. Al looked at the old guy's scraggly beard.

"He didn't like that beard at first," Ozzy Man said. "But then it grew on him."

"The spandrel theory of music postulates that music is an adjunct to speech, and became highly decorated, just as a spandrel in a cathedral," the prof said.

"A spandrel is the decorated bit between the arches that support the dome and roof of the building," a bystander said. Al nodded gratefully.

"I don't agree with that theory, though. I think music served more of a social function, in choosing a life's partner, and in religious observance. That's why so much music is devoted to love and religion." The prof grinned, well pleased with the peacock display of his own suitability for being a life's partner. He chugged back half a glass and kept a leery eye on Kimberley to see if she shared his pleasure.

"Why are there fashions in music?" she asked. Al was nonplussed; couldn't work out why she would ask such a boring man such a banal question.

"She wants to be the best student, Mate," Ozzy Man said. "She wants the teacher to know she's most attentive girl in class."

"Music reflects not only the ethos of the people and the time, but also every part of your personal history has a different sound. For me, my father's generation sounded like Gigli singing *The Pearl Fishers*. My own generation sounds like John Surman's big saxophone playing *Nestor's Saga*. The current generation like Dubstep on an out-of-control subway. Some people can hear the notes; others not."

"You can tune a piano," Ozzy Man said. "But you can't tuna fish."

The bell saved them, calling them to get back to their seats. The self-satisfied professor, preening and plummy, said to his wife,

"Shall we go, my dear?" And led her away. She wore a floral dress and much make up; and her hair was Mercurochrome red.

"When she saw the first strands of grey," Ozzy Man said, pointing at her, "she thought she would dye."

They didn't see Courtney and Thomas again, but in the car, Kimberley was uncharacteristically quiet. Halfway home she asked Al: "Why do you like Courtney?"

He thought that a pin-point accurate answer was beyond the scope of her tone of voice. "I like her company," he said, shrugging.

"Enough to see her every day?"

He didn't ask why she had flirted with the hapless professor. Although he had to admit, the professor looked like a whole box of frogs, and Courtney didn't.

Doppelgänger, though, answered for him: "Attraction is subliminally ineffable. You have no control over your response to that set of indefinable attributes that determine like or dislike, love, or indifference."

"Yeah, Sheila," Ozzy Man said. "It grabs you or it doesn't."

12

"WHEN THE GODS AT THE beginning of the world made the valleys and green hills sloping to the emerald-green waters of a subtropical ocean," Doppelgänger said, sitting back like a Skaldic poet at a feast in Thor's great hall, "they paved the sandy brown beach with cracked paths of pitch-black volcanic rock, and circled the land with an impenetrable granite girdle, buttressed and foreboding, close to the sun lonely lands. They propped the highest support pillar of their vast heavenly domain on top of the cruellest craggy spire and bade the sun every morning to peer, imperious and demanding, over the salty rim at the far side of the world. From the first mirror streaks on the flat primordial pond under its convex horizon, over the edge where wave after wave galloped to shore and gradually lapped into seahorses, to the furthest high extremity of the land, the master of the vast airy realm climbed to the crest of the sky-blue sky. *I am the ruler*, said he, *of all that I see*."

"Cue dramatic advertising type music." Ozzy Man helped with the stage direction. "Carmina Burana and Nescafé: *O fortuna* instant coffee."

"They put milk in it," Doppelgänger said, pulling a face.

"Carmina Burana and Old Spice aftershave," Ozzy Man said, "the mark of a man."

"Better," Dobby said. "*The Barrier of Spears*, the first men and women said, going about their daily business of quietly getting on with it in the lee of those tremendous, unreachable peaks."

Doppelgänger struck a pose like the Fiddler on the Roof, remembering that, so far, he had described only the one hand. "On the other side, pioneers with Western Europe in their veins and ink in their pens, looked up at the monolithic reaches, rocky spike after rocky spike, and thought of dragons. The *Dragon Mountains*, they wrote on everlasting paper; and that's still the name today. The Dragon liked the name; ruffled his razor-studded back, hissed the mountain wind through his teeth: *Don't mess with me*, he sighed, closed one golden eye, and went to sleep."

The Western plateau flattened into a slow spread of summers, reaching an undulating savannah to the far cities and the world of men. Across the Dragon's everlasting shoulder, between the sheer black armour plates and rough shards of his scales, a busy man scraped a dusty ribbon through a high and lonely pass, to the pocket of peach trees inside a hedge of brambles, next to a patch of shadow under the thick arms of a walnut tree. In that shadow stood a little house where Al's Grampa lived with his gentle God-fearing wife.

"Poplars tall and thoughtful waved goodbye to Summer, hello to Autumn, softly rustling yellow and burnt orange in lemon-blond lakes of shoulder-high thatch grass," Doppelgänger said. "The morning smelled of blue gum and silence, and in the lane a single dove, melancholy and alone, called over and over: C*oo–Coohwer-Coo. Let this be forever*, she sang."

"A Dragon is forever," Ozzy Man said, "but not so little doves."

Meg held the reins, Grampa walked next to the buggy. Handmade, light blue and a few winters past its showroom best, it had only two wheels—from an old car, silver hubcaps neatly in place. Gideon was in the lead, pulling steadily in a slow stiff-limbed amble. An old fella now, he loved to be tickled behind his enormous ears, his fur so soft and silky and his head so bony and huge. He was too old to graze, yet stood all day in the paddock pretending to do so, blowing softly at the grass between his neat front hooves. Grampa knew it was just a show and fed him special donkey food every morning and evening. This morning Gideon rolled back the years, buckling down like in his younger days, and pulled the city kids across the dusty track. A row of tall weeds grew in the middle between the twin paths where the wheels went.

"Yah! Yah!" Meg shouted, flicking the reins.

"He's an old chap, Meg," Grampa said gently, his voice dark brown bass. Grampa's doing days were also done: His wars fought, his battles lost. He'd fought the Law, and the Law won.

On the veranda Dad stood, watching his father-in-law with his kids. He never could figure out why they liked the old guy so; how Grampa could make them do what they wouldn't dream of doing if he suggested it. Al saw him and waved. Brendan, serious and protective of his younger brother and much younger sister, sat facing backwards, dangling his legs over the tailgate. He also did a little wave, but cautiously—exuberance was not something to be taken lightly.

"Do you remember that, Meg?" Al asked.

"I remember the sound of the wheels rolling over the grass. That was the only noise. How far did we go?"

"We went down to the gate and back. Maybe 300 yards altogether."

"It felt like forever. He was a nice man."

"Yes, he was. To us."

That's all that ever counts: *He was nice to us.* There were stories and there were hard times; and he had put his wife through her paces properly. He was a rebel and a hard man with a stubborn head and principles. The softest part of him was his front teeth. But he loved us and he was nice to us. Can't fault that part of it. Got to hold onto that.

"They've knocked down the house. The walnut tree is still there, but it is in the courtyard of a boutique hotel, as if it was planted there by the landscaper after the architect and interior decorators were done. The whole place is chic modern make-believe-old, cutting-edge electronics in an artfully weathered box with a decal that says 1922. Authentically ersatz." Al had spent a weekend there, fussed over by the well-trained staff. *We go the extra mile*, their mission statement and promotional literature proclaimed. *We aim to please*, the sign said on the reception desk.

"Sounds horrible."

"It isn't. Apart from that I was looking for half a century ago and it wasn't there anymore. The little town is Hollywood perfect, and the hotel really tries to make it look real. But if you remember: *Actual real* was candles, a coal stove, and a long drop on the other side of the chicken run. Wi-Fi and underfloor heating with muted lighting in the cocktail bar doesn't seem so bad. If Gideon was still around, they would have built him a special donkey house with fresh straw every day and a bell to ring for room service."

"I suppose," Meg said. "The longer ago it was, the closer to heaven it seems to have been." She dragged on the end of her cigarette, and screwed up her eyes. "That was the weekend Dad shouted at Mum in the car and she cried all the way home?"

Al stared away into the distance of a different life. "Not only that weekend," he said eventually, remembering soft lullabies and sweet dreams that gave way, year after year, to resignation and withdrawal. Later, she had no more tears. No more smiles either.

"Why are you so blue?" she asked into his silence.

"I don't want to make the same mistakes as he did. I don't want to be him."

"The chances aren't big," she said, looking to see if his eyes gave anything away.

"But they are."

Meg shook her head tiredly. "You're exactly like the sons of German High Command who didn't have children because they thought that if they had parental authority, any authority, they may turn into Heydrich or von Ribbentrop. You are convinced that your unfulfilled potential, the unstoppable tide just waiting to break through, is for you to be abrasive, uncaring, and boorish. Selfish and cruel."

Al sighed. The weight of the world.

"What?" she asked, suddenly impatient.

"Kimberley is wonderful. She is beautiful, clever, kind, well-informed, energetic, resourceful."

"Is there a *but* hiding in there somewhere, Bud?" Ozzy Man asked.

"But?" Meg matched the antipodean reprobate as if she had heard his question.

"But we are at loggerheads. I have a friend she doesn't want me to have; and I don't think I am disloyal to her for having that friend."

"And she thinks you are?" Meg asked.

"It's not as simple as you try to make it, Bud," Ozzy Man said, interrupting Al's self-pity. "And you know it. Her complaint lies in the detail: *Friend*, she doesn't mind; Courtney, she definitely minds. Courtney, the person, is the problem."

"She does, Meg." Al took Ozzy's point on board at least in part. "She wants to be my One-and-Only. She doesn't mind my having friends who are no threat to that; but when she feels threatened, she minds." Looking miserable he added: "I see her point; but at the same time, it's a tall order."

"And that's what's bugging you?" she asked.

"As surely as night follows day."

"Sunday's on the phone to Monday. Tuesday's on the phone to me," Ozzy Man said.

"Why would you even care? You're an adult; you can have friends." Meg clung steadfastly to her antipathy for Kimberley. When Kimberley was interested, Meg thought she was nosy, prying. Kimberley's enthusiastic arrangements were proof to Meg of an overweening bossiness. Kimberley's intelligence and insight smacked to Meg of a superiority complex. Kimberley's generosity, to Meg felt like charity, like being patronised.

"And your sister doesn't like it much that Kimberley is a dish," Ozzy Man said.

"Because she is perfect for me; and devoted to our being together," Al answered. "She accepts as axiomatic that she is for me and I'm for her. Top priority 1A. And if I have a friendship that is inimical to that, of course it matters. It matters a great deal."

"But I thought you said she *is* all of that; you *aren't* untrue to even that unrealistic standard?" His sister pulled a face. "What has she to be concerned about?"

"She *is* all of that, Meg. My point is that I don't think her exclusivity and special status are in any way in danger. But she doesn't see it that way." Al frowned.

"Don't be so easy on yourself, Bud," Ozzy Man said. "Her concern is one friend; one Sheila; one Bestie: Courtney."

"Al has been married for almost thirty-five years," Doppelgänger said. "It's no wonder that his life has expanded to include other people as well."

"The thrill is gone." Ozzy Man sang a line from BB King, specifically to get under Dobby's skin. He managed too.

"That's bullshit, Oz," Doppelgänger said, "and you know it."

"And this loss of exclusivity you worry about," Meg asked, having not heard Ozzy Man say it loud and clear, "that's Courtney?" Meg looked down at the table, didn't want him thinking this was an interrogation. "Are you in love with her?"

"This could be the right time to say it out loud, Mate," Ozzy Man said. "Surprise us all, including yourself."

Al sighed. The weight of Jupiter. "I don't know. I don't think so."

"Are you having an affair?" She looked at him speculatively under crinkly forehead.

"No. I'm not. I'm twenty-three years older than her. She thinks I'm her uncle. She has a boring husband and an empty life. She likes talking to me and I like listening. And, more and more, her opinions are becoming the same as mine. She is smart, but somehow missed the developmental steps to adulthood."

Meg didn't even ask, just tilted her head, and lifted her eyebrows.

"No. I don't think I'm in love; I'm not in lust; and I'm certainly not having an affair—it doesn't work that way. I like her and I like spending time with her. I like the sound of her voice and how she laughs. But I don't think I'm in love with her."

"Really?" Ozzy Man said, his eyebrows flying high.

"Yeah, really," Doppelgänger said. "Kimberley is the one. You know that."

"So, she's basically good company?" Meg asked.

"She is. We don't have the same congruency of priority, understanding and interest as, for instance, Kimberley and I have. She often tells me what she watches on TV. Tells me the *plot*."

"Must be fascinating," Meg said.

"She also tells me what article she's working on and what she has read and finds either interesting or stupid." Thinking about how his conversations with her go, Al added: "And she is still working out what her views are on the big-ticket items; and she discusses those with me as well."

Meg made a face that said *that* doesn't sound spellbinding.

"Here's the thing," Al said. "While she is telling me all her stuff, I sometimes think: *This is tedious.* And then, as soon as our lunch is over, I hope I can see her again the next day." He thought in silence for a heartbeat. "It also helps that she listens, actually listens, when I say things. There are no proscribed topics—I can talk about what I like." Al warmed to his subject. "She is interested in what I say and listens and understands. I think she has never been in the company of someone who has actual views and can express them concisely. So far, her life has been determined by popular mass culture. She likes and is attracted by what lies beyond that; she feels a natural affinity for a more cerebral approach than simply Twitter and YouTube; a less unquestioning acceptance of the mundane. But she hasn't ever brushed up against it before, has never seen it in action, so to speak. To a large extent I am her guide and her catalyst for an expanding horizon."

"And you don't have sex?" Brass tacks question to which Ozzy Man made big eyes again, even though he knew the answer.

"We don't, Meg. She just doesn't think of me as an actual man; and I am with Kimberley. I'm like a devoted old bullmastiff, basically—I like eating and having naps and going for walks. And I have only one mistress."

"You're responsible," she said.

"Yes. I am plagued with responsibility; it follows me like a bad penny; won't let me go. I was born that way—if you need someone to rely on, and to behave like the Pope, no matter what yummy things are just over there, I am that feeble grey little man: It is in my cells and in my stars. How I would have loved to trip the light fantastic, fly with the dragon, drink an abandoned toast to wild good fortune and smash the glass in the fireplace. But no, The Universe, which is a capricious bastard, to be sure, decreed that I should tread life's pathway in moderation and prudent common sense. I am the little man forever on the Clapham omnibus; I am always reasonable, always responsible, never thoughtless of consequence." Feeling as if he had been self-indulgent, Al added: "And, it's the only one little life I had."

"I know. And to make it worse, you're honest," Meg said, not as a compliment.

"The secret to life is honesty," Ozzy Man said. "If you can fake that, you've got it made."

"Yes, I am. Meg, I'm certainly not *dishonest* with Kimberley. There is nothing to be dishonest about. I don't do anything with Courtney, other than chat over lunch. I don't plan to do anything. I don't fantasize about anything. I just like listening to her, and spending time with her."

"And yet you feel as guilty as sin?" Doppelgänger said, prodding the raw nerve.

"Maybe she is not in charge," Meg said, getting onto her favourite pick of the twenty-five reasons not to like Kimberley. "Maybe she doesn't tell you what to think and what not to do, and what you're allowed to say. Maybe you can just relax a bit and not do performing-seal tricks. Get the beachball off your nose."

Al sat at the table in his usual pose, turned away to the right, left leg crossed over right, knee eight inches higher than the tabletop. He inspected his shoe, thought about what his sister had said. "You're being unkind to Kimberley," he said, looking quietly distant.

"Only you will know if that's so," she said, reaching for her car keys.

"And me," Doppelgänger said.

"Don't get all pissy with her, Bud," Ozzy Man said, surprising them both. "Having the shits with Kimberley is just her fucked-up way of defending you."

13

"*I* *AM THE RULER*, Zeus said, *of all that I see.*"

"Like Yertle the Turtle," Ozzy Man said.

Doppelgänger sniggered. "A bit; but he was the sky and thunder god and ruled as king of the gods on Mount Olympus. They called him Allfather."

"Olympus?"

"Yep. Olympus was the stately pleasure-dome Zeus decreed for him and the other gods after they killed the Titans in battle and became sole rulers of the universe. Their palace was twice five miles of fertile ground, with walls and towers girdled round; and there were gardens bright with sinuous rills."

"What's a rill?" Ozzy Man asked.

"It's what Coleridge called a little river. The twelve gods lived together in splendour and magnificence."

"Like the Ewings at Southfork," Ozzy Man said.

"Again, a bit," Doppelgänger said. "But only some of them were brothers and sisters. There was much jiggery pokery, and only the most astute knew who begat whom."

"Yeah. Exactly like the Ewings."

"Zeus outdid even prime time American television drama with how, where and who he had sex with," Doppelgänger said.

"I heard the lad had a hard time with his wallaporoon," Ozzy Man said, waggling his eyebrows. "Why you telling me, Bud?"

"I've been thinking about soulmates," Doppelgänger said, frowning. "The idea that somewhere, somehow, there is somebody who is the light to your shadow; the *anima* to your *animus*; the song to your silence."

"The drake to your duck," Ozzy Man said. "The hart to your roe."

"Zackly," Doppelgänger said. "When the two of you meet, you click together like two halves of a whole that have been separated since time immemorial, and together you become one complete being. That which was ripped apart is reunited at a stroke. *One & One is One*, as Medicine Head sang for us."

"And this makes you think of the randy fuckers on an ancient Greek mountain?" Ozzy Man asked.

"Sure does. In ancient Greek times, Plato says, humans had four arms and four legs, one head but two faces. They weren't scared of anything and were openly defiant of the bunch on Olympus."

"Like Australians," Ozzy Man said.

"The gods had already had one war, in which they killed, not to put it too delicately, their parents; and they thought to do the same for the humans." Doppelgänger pursed his lips, a thin line, thinking of the problem. "But then there is the old chestnut: If all the humans are dead and gone, who would worship the gods? And who would be left for Zeus to seduce? It's like the tree falling in the forest—if you do godly things, but there is no one to see and be impressed and intimidated, have you made a ripple in the space-time continuum?"

"A live audience is best, with a canned laughter track," Ozzy Man said.

"The elegant solution Zeus found," Doppelgänger said, "was to rip all the humans in half, one by one; so that they became the reduced things we are used to seeing now, with two arms and two legs and only one face. Elegant, because they were less powerful and no match for Zeus and his pals. And there were *twice* as many of them to tell the gods how smart they are. That's why there are men and women."

"I pronouns you he and she," Ozzy Man said, blessing the imaginary couple with a semaphored cross.

"If ever two humans who had been halves of the same prototype before, met up, they would be in ecstasy: Reunited and made whole again as the original. And religion teaches that the animating force, the essence of the being, is a soul. Hence the two separated halves, reunited, are soulmates; together they are one complete composite soul."

"Are you suggesting though, Mate, that some cynical bastards wonder if soulmates are a real thing?"

"Just so," the all-purpose expert said. "Modern neurology teaches many incomprehensible things, among them that there just ain't no thing as a soul."

"Bang goes Heaven?" Ozzy Man said, pulling a face.

"Bang goes Hell," Doppelgänger said.

"But what's with the Greek bullshit today, Bud? One little mistake and the Big Black Book of Hebrew and Aramaic Mythology isn't good enough for you anymore? Many is the person tortured to death to make its wisdom available to you."

"Well," Doppelgänger said, "it's just that, if Al can't have a soulmate because he doesn't have a soul, the real explanation must be Greek: That Zeus ripped him in half and he now spends his days forlornly hoping to find his complement confrère."

"His consummate companion," Ozzy said, making big eyes.

"His abiding associate."

"His kindred consort. His perpetual playmate. His comrade confidante," Ozzy Man said.

"His apodictic paramour."

Ozzy Man thought for a minute; couldn't do better than that. "Sounds right," he said. "Because the dumb-arse is doing something stupid."

"Don't mind me," Al said.

"What's happening with Al is not deliberate. The degree of disorder and randomness in a system always increases with time," Doppelgänger said.

"Entropy isn't what it used to be," Ozzy Man said.

"Nothing is happening with me," Al said, irritated with the conversation in his head. "I have a new friend, and I like spending time with her. There is no randomness, no disorder; certainly, no search for a different soulmate. There is just Kimberley. If you would allow me a soul, she would be its mate. And, Ozzy, your jokes can become tedious."

Ozzy Man looked hurt, shook his head in disappointment. "I told my friend jokes to get him to laugh. Sadly, no pun in ten did."

"You're an idiot," Al said, aware of who he was saying it to, and the inherent implications. If he was at war with himself, he realised, it was time to think about what do.

They sat quietly, watching the mid-afternoon sun slip through the sky without fuss. On Olympus he wasn't such a big deal. Zeus killed his son; and later there was a debate whether he was Helios or Apollo. This afternoon, though, he was doing all right, all but completely closing Al's drooping eyelids.

"There are," Ozzy Man said just before Al could manage to slip the knots of his dilemma, "two kinds of people—those who demand closure."

14

ABOVE THE FRONT ENTRANCE THE sign read: *Wits Art Museum*. A handmade poster Sellotaped to the outside of the glass, left of the door, said: *White Loins of Timbavati— Photo Exhibition. 29 Oct—7 Nov.*

"A dyslexic man walked into a bra," Ozzy Man said.

In the entrance, the harassed woman behind the trestle table had laid out the name badges for invitees in a rectangle, with A top left and Z right bottom: new age arty, therefore arranged by first name, not surname. The PR company had got maybe half of those right. All the guests seemed to have come through the door at the same time, looking to find their ID for the night as if in a bargain bin on Black Friday. The theme font added to the confusion, indeterminate Greco-Sumerian-Cuneiform, printed in faded green. The woman was HR, wherefore her smiled hadn't slipped, yet had elements of both rictus and moue.

Over the racket, he told her: "Al. Al is my name."

"El Alamein?" She looked puzzled.

He leant over and tapped his card, raising an eyebrow to ask if he could take it.

Ozzy Man had a good look. "In hieroglyphs," he said, "its eye before flea, except after sea."

It was opening night of Atma Yemaya's exhibition. Man of the Moment stood a few paces into the gallery, smiling and greeting.

The beading on the turn-up toes of his Aladdin slippers matched the turmeric pyjamas and tasselled fez.

"Dahling!" he gushed at Kimberley, ignoring Al.

A man in Don Quixote pantaloons leant on Jeeves' umbrella, talking at Mama Cass in a flowing kaftan. "Biomorphic juxtaposition," he said. She nodded solemnly. A couple dressed in short sixties Wimbledon whites held hands, listening to the tall man with the ascetic profile and the austere winter's coat. Nefertiti in a black mini and heels withstood the clumsy advances of a teenager in his late sixties, squashed into torn-at-the-knees denim and a bondage T-shirt. In fingerless weightlifting gloves, he held a mobile phone instead of a skateboard. Over in the corner, a circle of men in black business suits discussed interest rate swaps and inter-creditor arrangements. Thomas detached himself from that knot, headed directly for Al, smiling like an estate agent on show day.

"Al!" he said, beaming from halfway across the room. "You're an Art lover."

"Well, Kimberley is," Al said, smiling.

"Mate," Ozzy Man said, "you being here is a bit odd. But what the fuck is Numb Nuts doing here?"

Thomas didn't keep them in suspense: "We are doing an ADR offering for Multizillion Inc, and they are the sponsors tonight. Have you got a drink? Have you met the CEO? Have you seen the installation pieces? Do you think this is a good investment? Do you think there are liquidity issues in Art? Can you introduce me to Francesco Manzella, he's just over there?"

Al stood over to have a look at a three-dimensional piece—he hesitated to think of it as statuary. A window dummy with only one arm, wearing swirls of many-coloured fabric, way more flamboyant than Joseph's. Her eyes had been blacked out, her mouth a dripping red scar; and her head under the diamond tiara, temple to temple, had been pierced by an arrow. A green stuffed parrot sat proprietorially on top her unpainted bald head.

"Less is bore," Ozzy Man remarked.

"Rational Ignorance is the way to go here," Doppelgänger said, shaking his head. "The effort to try to understand what this is, exceeds the benefit of finding out."

On a wall behind the arrow lady, a vast canvass, easily five meters wide, as tall as Al, showed, in the middle, a tree; on the left, an unidentifiable animal with fangs jumping up to bite at fruit hanging from that tree; and on the right, a man with a bowser of a penis, weeing a flood against the trunk. The whole of the astonishing scene was coloured in broad streaks of red, orange, and yellow.

"He's an artist," Ozzy Man said. "He knows where to draw the line."

Al turned away and saw Cliffy Sutton. "Kimberley drag you here?" the man said. "Let's get a drink." Business at the bar table was brisk. Free booze brings people together, releases an innate gregariousness. Cliffy held up two fingers at the young man in a tuxedo who was pouring bubbles into flutes.

"A Roman centurion walks into a bar, holds up two fingers," Ozzy Man said. "He says: *Five beers, please.*"

"Did you watch the golf last night?" Cliffy asked. Together they ambled around the hall, came to the entrance of a darkened room behind a curtain, music drifting out. Around the frame, somebody, presumably Atma Yemaya, had drawn life size images of miniature mass-produced plastic soldiers in action poses: Waving their comrades on; holding rifles; flinging grenades; their feet melded to rounded rectangles on which they stood. War as a game. A description of what was inside the room in 18-point old-fashioned typeface, as if from a 1940's Olivetti:

The Music of War

Lale Andersen recorded, in 1942, the song that stands as the reminder of the heartbreak of a generation. The recording, made in Berlin, fell out of favour because Lale wasn't married and her partner had been Jewish; and German High Command thought *the song was too sad—Patriots were required to be military and up-beat about the War Effort. But then the song became the call signal for radio Belgrade, from where German radio broadcast to the Eastern front, and soldiers on both sides of the fight tuned in every night to hear it—Lili Marlene.*

Take three minutes out of your day to listen to it—listen to the original, 1942, version. DON'T listen to Vera Lynn; don't listen to Marlene Dietrich; and certainly, don't listen to Connie Francis. And, don't listen to the later recordings, when the yearning and hope of youth had been scrubbed from Lale's voice.

Al and Cliffy took their champagne flutes inside. On the screen, flickering black-and-white images of soldiers in trench coats, helmets, boots, charged across a battlefield erupting with explosions. Tanks rushed on skiddy tracks, belching silent plumes from their gun turrets. A soldier fell, holding on to his rifle as he hit the ground. Scratchy and hissing with static, Lale sang, hoarse and sorrowful: *Wie einst, Lili Marlene; Wie einst, Lili Marlene.*

"Did you see his putt on the 17th?" Cliffy asked. "Twenty-six meters downhill and the green breaking left to right, then levelling off."

In the main gallery, guests in groups of two or three wandered from work to work, paying spiritual attention: A decapitated body, blood spurting from the neck, upwards into the shape of a phoenix; a toddler's broad watercolour brush strokes in primary colours, with a photo of decaying teeth in the middle; two arms coming out the wall and holding a long-bladed knife, about to commit hara-kiri.

"Youth and beauty." Ozzy Man said. "Gone after summer's all too short a lease."

"Have you seen this?" Cliffy asked, pointing at two bald, snow-white plaster of paris heads, kissing with tongues. Eighteen- inch long, both of them, plaited together like a tow rope.

"Am I ambivalent about this?" Ozzy Man asked. "Well, yes and no."

"I hate it," Doppelgänger said.

They drifted into the next room and heard George, Med school professor, drink in hand, holding forth to an audience of five perfectly ordinary looking men and women.

"I love this artist," he said, waving his glass enthusiastically. "He pulls the piss with everyone in the room, and he gets away with it; they beg for more. Take, for instance, his name: Atma Yemaya. I had to Google it: I love his chutzpah. *Atma* is Sanskrit for *Inner Self.* Yemaya is the Ocean Mother Goddess in Santería, which is an Afro-Caribbean religion. How perfect is that? The subtlety of it—if anyone actually looked it up, like me, he would say, *It's the inner fulfilment and liberation of my anima in its role as Artist, to disseminate the ancient wisdom of the Ocean.* Brilliant, isn't it? And he gets the whole of Johannesburg's intellectual and moneyed aristocracy to throw a party for him, and to buy the stuff he scatters around the room." He indicated the four walls with a circular motion of his glass. "The man is a genius!"

Ozzy Man grinned. "I love this guy," he said, meaning George.

The lecture group broke up and George replaced Cliffy at Al's side. "Look here," he said, pointing at a life size picture of Il Duce, looking ridiculously camp: Fist on a cocked hip, profile turned and lifted heavenwards in defiance of the rules that bind ordinary men. Atma the Mother Goddess had painted frilly pink shorty pyjamas over the General's uniform, but the megalomania remained indomitable.

"All power corrupts," George said, taking another sip, "and absolute power is pretty neat."

Into the next room they sauntered, and in the far corner, Kimberley and Courtney laughed together like old mates. Even as he watched, Courtney said something and, across the room over the hubbub, Al heard Kimberley's explosive laugh. The sound he loved best. Al gazed at them, heard Doppelgänger murmur: "Leave them, Al. Just let them be."

"Look at these," George said, laughing. "My admiration for this guy just grows and grows."

Inside a glass display case, lined in white samite, the definitive collection of butt plugs invited inspection: Plastic; metal; glass; straight; bent; big; medium; small; with fluffy tails attached; and with Donald Trump's face on the biggest one.

"To what end, Mate?" Ozzy Man asked.

Behind the display, in curly mauve script on a light-peach background, George's favourite Artist had written:

We shall not cease from exploration
and the end of all our exploring
will be to arrive where we started
and know the place for the first time.

No acknowledgment to T.S. Eliot—just the greeting-card look to made it seem like spiritual advice.

Al heard Kimberley laugh again, and, looking across to where they stood, saw Courtney holding a hand over her mouth and nose, in stitches too.

"Let's see what else this lad has put out for us to look at." George said, grinning, and setting off to the second darkened chamber, this one labelled: *Jewish Tombstone.* The legend at the door appeared to be in Hebrew, in Jewish script, except when you looked closely it resolved into English. It was a story:

> *Sunday morning was the unveiling of a tombstone in West*
> *Park—under it lies Avi Dobrow, my dearest GP for our all*
> *twenty-eight of my twenty-eight years. The rabbi wore a hat*
> *made for Kirk Douglas as Cactus Jack; and had a beard like*
> *Hagrid. I wore a yarmulke, borrowed from a box in the side*
> *office. The wind licked at my cold ankles; people stood around,*
> *waiting for the show to be over so that they could go back home*
> *for tea and croissants. Before the service, temple admin handed*
> *round prayer books that open in the wrong direction and had the*
> *ancient alphabet on the right-hand page and a translation on the*

left, in English. The prayer for the day asked: "Who will abide in thy tent, oh Lord?"

George's eyes were sparkling. "Let's go in," he said, directing more than suggesting.

Another black-and-white film: A dusty, barren hilltop, and a rabbi rocking back and forth, back and forth, intoning a prayer in what used to be music when Moses and the Tribe cruised the desert with the Holy Ark: Monotonous rapid polysyllabic chanting, all on the same note but with each phrase ending one note up, two down and back to the same place: The secret chord that pleased the Lord. The congregation mumbled its response. Connected by tendrils of ancient tribal commonality to when Yahweh was planning His extended vacation on a tropical beach and Cain was finding out about duplicity.

They watched for a while, Al slightly non-plussed by both the lack of action, and the lack of rational explanation why *this* piece of social history. Al also puzzled that nobody else was puzzled—as if this is what you get in your car for on a Wednesday evening to come see in an Art gallery.

George was suddenly philosophical: "What strikes me is that after fourteen-thousand years of organised sentience and attempted civilisation, people gather round a grave and say: *What the Fuck?* Some say it in Hebrew, some in Sanskrit and some, we, the enlightened New Atheists, say it in modern English with correct modulation and articulation. But the fundamental question stays the same: *Who will abide in thy tent, oh Lord?*"

Al said *hi* to Courtney and not much else; and in the car on the way home Kimberley was in high spirits. She had loved some of those pieces; some were weird. She and Courtney had laughed together so. The radio played softly. Jazz from long ago.

15

Lunch on Tuesday found them in Just Eddy's, a trendy coffee shop that specialised in vegan and vegetarian food. Before sitting down, you placed your order at a wide, wooden bar counter behind which a shiny-chrome old-fashioned coffee machine blew steam like the dragon Orm Embar of Earthsea.

"A termite walks into a bar," Ozzy Man said, "and asks, *Is the bar tender here?*"

Cappuccino was on the menu with ordinary milk—full fat, low fat, skim or fat-free; or with almond, soy, rice, or oat milk. Grampa Isaiah wouldn't have found a thing to eat, but Courtney was pumped about the Kale fries and Quinoa pilaf.

At the table, Courtney immediately started talking about what was on her mind.

"Persian carpets are a huge business that depends on an exploited work force, much like the sweat shops of the clothing industry."

"There's no filter," Doppelgänger said, shaking his head, "between her brain and her mouth. As soon as an idea forms in her head, she says it out loud."

Al listened, as usual hearing a bunch of stuff he hadn't known before. Because she talked a lot didn't mean she wasn't invariably well-informed—she read and heard things, and repeated them accurately, albeit sometimes in overly generous detail. Soon she had moved forward while sticking with basically the same issue.

"Upholstery for new motorcars, especially the more expensive ones, is similar: Masses of underpaid workers from which the corporations turn a profit."

"A man fell into an upholstery machine," Ozzy Man said. "He's recovered now."

Then she started on the soapy she had watched all afternoon the day before.

"A beautiful flirtatious girl, Juliette du Toit, does her best to interfere with down-to-earth honest and kind Sonya's attempt to get Armand to like her."

"Obedient Martha worked hard to please the Lord," Ozzy Man said, "but her sister, Mate. Now, she didn't just know what he needed; she knew what he wanted."

"Oz," Doppelgänger muttered, trying to put a lid on it.

Meanwhile the story rolled on: "Armand is the handsome heir all the girls are after for his good looks and inheritance prospects. Meanwhile Jacques, his kind and artistic brother, leaves the farm because he doesn't care who it will ever belong to."

"The secret of being a bore," Doppelgänger said, rolling his eyes, "is to tell everything."

Their food arrived at the moment when Schalk Brinkman, Al's friend and doctor, strolled into the restaurant.

"Hey there," Al said, happy to see the sawbones; and introduced him and Courtney, seeing the roguish respect in Schalk's eye—he had told his doctor about Courtney and Schalk had immediately assumed she was more than the lunch buddy of Al's description. What Schalk hadn't guessed, because Al hadn't said, was how gorgeous she was—this afternoon in jeans and her favourite lightweight blue North Face top. She was delighted to meet him, in that remnant of our peasant heritage ways that made us respectful of the shaman and now makes us want to be friends with an actual doctor.

"Join us?" Al said—and Schalk did.

"I watched a programme about a homeopath," Courtney said, upping her game for the medical man. Al could almost see her thought process: *Doctor. Hmnn. What to say to a doctor? I Know: Homeopathy!*

Schalk's face didn't show what he might think of her intro.

"This woman comes to see him. She has swollen legs and says she has seen many doctors and they couldn't help her. He asks her lots of questions about whether she likes hot or cold drinks, and what her favourite colour is, and whether she gets on well with her father. He doesn't do blood tests or anything, doesn't even really examine her—he just looks at her legs and says, *Very swollen*, looking worried. Then he makes medicine for her—they show how he does it; and he explains along the way what he is doing and why."

Doppelgänger and Ozzy Man both worried that she would come to the point within Schalk's tolerance for trivia.

"He took a dead *bee* and dried it out"—Courtney invested the word with the full spectrum of her incredulity—"and ground it into powder. He said that a bee sting makes you swell up and if your body recognises a bee in small doses, its natural defences would kick in, and reduce the woman's swelling in her legs."

Schalk smiled, enjoying her description, pleased by her scepticism.

"He put the powdered bee into a big bottle of water and shook it up, and then he threw out almost all of it—he said he kept a hundredth part, which he filled up again to the original amount. And then he did the same dilution again, 30 times over. It took him ages. And then he gives it to the woman as a remedy. The programme never showed if her legs got better."

Schalk guffawed, sipped from his cup, looked at Courtney in amusement and pleasure. "That *is* what they do," he said, shaking his head. "That's the basis of all Homeopathy."

"It just doesn't seem likely that his medicine would do anything." Courtney also shook her head; and, glancing over at Al, caught him looking fondly at her. She gave him a little crinkle-eyed smile and turned her attention back to the doctor.

"No," Schalk said, chuckling. "You are spot on: It's quackery and nonsense. Its implausible and doesn't work."

"And other alternative remedies?" Courtney asked. "The ones I read about in the magazines?"

"You mean chiropractic medicine, osteopathy, herbal remedies, naturopathy, acupuncture, Qi gong, reflexology, Reiki, Tai Chi, aromatherapy, Ayurvedic medicine, herbalism, hypnosis, meditation, and naturopathy?" Schalk was enjoying himself.

"And faith healing," Ozzy Man said.

"Those," she said.

"They're bullshit." Schalk pursed his lips. "All of them."

"Except faith healing," Ozzy Man said. "That works."

Courtney laughed, looking at Al. "Thomas believes it," she said.

"Stupid is," Ozzy Man said, "as stupid does."

"Strangely intelligent people *say* they believe this stuff." Al smiled at her. "But I bet when he's sick, he goes to see a doctor, doesn't he?"

She giggled. "He does."

"Faith healing, though," Ozzy Man said, persisting, "is a real thing. It can make you speak in tongues and lame people throw away their crutches on stage and run down the aisle."

"Oz," Doppelgänger said, trying to shut him out.

"Except for amputees," Ozzy Man answered his would-be silencer. "God hates amputees—won't allow them to grow new legs and arms."

In the car on the way back home, Courtney chatted about her garden and the service that came twice a week to keep it spick and span. When Al took his eyes off the road for a second and glanced at her, he caught her looking fondly at him; and gave her a little crinkle-eyed smile.

"Bye, have a good afternoon," they both said when he stopped in front of her apartment complex. She hopped out the car and they went back to their separate lives.

16

"A MAN WAKES UP TO THE sound of rain," Doppelgänger said. "Christ, Mate," Ozzy Man said, rolling his eyes. As always, he said: *Chroist*. "Is this another one of your stories?"

"He reached for, tried to hold onto, thin wisps of a dream slipping away into nothingness," Doppelgänger said. "A dream about a lover with whom he had been, in a room he knew well, where he was at home, where they were used to being together. Perhaps where he now lay half asleep under the covers. But he couldn't catch it, couldn't get there in time. It was like trying to catch smoke drifting from the end of a cigarette. Then even those threads were gone—he didn't know whether he had dreamed at all."

"He tried to catch the fog," Ozzy Man said, "but he mist."

"As he wakes, he realises he doesn't recognise the room: It is featureless, a modern hotel. Square walls, anonymous configuration. He saw himself darkly reflected in the black screen of a silent TV at the foot of his bed. To his left, heavy light-blocking drapes, keeping the world outside. He doesn't know what time it is."

"Outside the sky is black to East; purple over the West," Ozzy Man said.

"No, it's morning—he knows he has been there all night."

"A slate-grey morning smudged the Eastern horizon," Ozzy Man said, adjusting his prose. "Grey mist on the sea's face, turbulent waves crashing onto a hostile shore."

"He's in the middle of a city—sometimes, as if he is on an upper floor of a tall building, he can hear sounds as from faraway, of traffic, a siren, the crash of glass breaking in a dumpster. He doesn't know the time—he is inside the room, but can't remember why, doesn't know where he is. He could be anywhere. Rain touches faintly on the window. On the bedside table the phone, the hotel's landline, is ringing. Perhaps that, not the rain or his dream, woke him up."

"Well, well, is he ringing your bell?" Ozzy Man said, humming.

"The man reaches for the receiver, picks it up. *Hullo*, he says, surprised at the sound of his own voice. Over heavy static of the line a distant voice speaks—a male voice, treble and drumroll-quick—a long sentence in a language the man doesn't recognise, maybe Japanese. The voice gets fainter and fainter, then disappears. Only the static crackles still. *Hullo*, the man says again."

"If at first you don't succeed, try and try again."

"The man puts the receiver back in its cradle and relaxes against the pillows. Something nags at the back of his mind; something he can't bring into focus. He thinks about the voice on the phone—was it trying to tell him something? The memory slips away from him: Already he can't remember its sound, wasn't sure how it happened, did it happen at all? He is awake now; looks around the room. Mass-produced, modern, hard-edged furniture, chrome frames and dark veneer, monochrome spill-proof upholstery and bedding, piles of white pillows. There is nothing in the room that belongs to him, nothing to remind him why he is there or where he is. The space in the bed next to him hasn't been slept in—he is in bed and in the room alone."

"Sleep on, sleep on, with hope in your heart, and you'll never sleep alone."

"The man tries to remember the previous day, maybe the evening, how he got here," Doppelgänger said. "If he can remember that, he thinks, then he will remember why he is here; where here is. He remembers autumn grey of lonely rain, the quiet hush of a masked day, the emptiness of his solitude. He feels disengaged, as if he is everywhere and nowhere; he senses no boundary in the haze. The focus of his attention blurs further; he drifts into drowsy murkiness; he closes his eyes."

"Like truthless dreams, so are my joys expired," Ozzy Man said. "And past return are all my dandled days."

Doppelgänger paid no attention: "Then an image comes to him, coalescing from the tendrils of his thoughts: Eyes of polished obsidian sparkled behind the dancing flame of a single candle on the table between them. Her eyes held the only innocence in an otherwise impishly complicit face, as if the way the world works and what it demands, not her own choosing, forced her to be forthright and stubborn. Her face said she could look after herself, yet needed him to stand beside and protect her, keep her safe. She was grown-up, but still a child." Doppelgänger paused, remembering a time long ago. He carried on:

"He adored her smile that was there often and sincere; was beguiled by her laugh that was spontaneous and without limit; was smitten by the way she clicked her tongue against her palate when she was happy. She had broken through his implacable reserve and managed to make him talk about himself, by asking blunt questions and ignoring the evasions and platitudes behind which he usually took cover. She was straightforward, frank and disconcertingly direct, insisting on equality and reciprocity; all the while keeping her secrets close and putting things only in her own terms. The mystery of her attraction lay equally in her unwavering honesty and her deception. She presented as a well-practised novice, disarmingly naive and expertly accomplished. The sum of her contradictions far exceeded their individual parts."

"She slipped into his jeans pocket along with his keys."

"The man reaches across the bed, switches on the bedside lamp. He looks for the remote to open the drapes, finds the TV controller which he tosses aside. He remembers her direct, open honesty—she cannot tell a lie. And when events conspired to push her into a corner not of her choosing, she cannot surrender to the banal truth."

"Yeah," Ozzy Man said. "She never overlooks the truth. Properly handled it can be so effective in a fight."

"So, you know this Sheila, then?" Doppelgänger looked at him, deliberately using one of Ozzy's expressions. Getting only a wry shrug in response, he continues: "The man hears voices outside in the passage, indistinct, on their way to the lift lobby. Strangers from a place beyond windows and walls. He settles his head comfortably amongst the pillows, closes his eyes again. Drifts back to a provincial hospital in the dry rustling of a summer morning.

"She stands beside the bed, reaching through the metal support sides. *Mum*, she whispers. Eyelids flicker open; the older woman reaches out a hand. *Mum*, she says louder, leaning forward as if to envelop the frailty under the sheets. But the doctors have said she is broken; be careful. The sadness of millennia lies shallow under the varnish of a happy life—scratch through the transparent membrane and uncover the collective sorrow of mankind, the wretched tide held back for an instant by the pleasures of a sunny day. The patient is bandaged, bruised and silent, only her eyes finding her daughter. *Mum*, the young woman sobs, gently laying her hand on the other's forehead, stroking strands of hair back into place."

"Of all which past," Ozzy Man said quietly, "the sorrow only stays."

"The man had seen it all long before, in the faces of the Tarot deck and the wrinkled hands of the old gypsy lady in her painted trailer. She had turned over, one by one, the Hanged Man, the Devil, and then the Trickster. In a soft Spanish whisper, she told him that his heart was a prison, and he could not forget what he would always remember. He listened carefully, heard the notes of another day.

"Hers was a pale, shift dress that fell straight from the shoulders to below her knee, with darts around the bust and a square collar trimmed in simple white lace. As uncomplicated as any in the room. She moved with grace and gentle self-assurance and wore the easy confidence of a bride who knows that Love is not love which alters when things are not the same. She wasn't there for someone who would ever let her down; she was doing a sure thing—betting on a certainty. But just for an instant the confidence slipped, and a shadow of doubt dipped into her eye. He saw, reached for her hand, promised wordlessly that his love waited for her inside the rainbow, beside the sun, between the rain, beyond the stars; he stood so tall above her and his axe was made of gold. She promised until death does them part; and the locker of his willing heart clicked shut for eternity. The pulse in her throat believed him; the helpless beauty of her vulnerability took his breath away."

"It was a day," Ozzy Man said, "made from the footsteps of a cat and the roots of a mountain."

Doppelgänger looked evenly at his co-traveller, impressed. Then carried on speaking: "The man sits up to turn off the lamp; lies back down. A rim of light from outside faintly outlines the window. He closes his eyes and remembers again:

"The young lad waits for his dad to start speaking. *The day you were born*, the attentive little face hears, *all the nurses were there and Mom and I, and Dr. Copenhagen. We were all waiting for you, and you decided it's time to come say Hi. One moment we were all alone; and then, there you were! You were so cold, the nurses wrapped you up tight and gave you to Mom.* She was crazy in love right away. What has been joined together into one family, let no man put asunder."

"Memories are made of this," Ozzy Man crooned in his best imitation of Dean Martin.

"Drowsiness slowly steals over the man." Doppelgänger wasn't done yet. "Slipping closer to the edge of slumber, he hums quietly under his breath his personal mantra, repeating it over and over: *Loyalty, Honesty, Kindness, Compassion.* Behind his whispered words he hears the voice of an operatic soprano, singing cadences of angelic beauty."

"The aspects of things that are most important to us are hidden because of their simplicity and familiarity."

Doppelgänger didn't seem to hear the philosophical interjection. "Images appear to him, as if in a dream, one after another. She sits at the kitchen table, her elbows on the red-print cloth, her eyes bemused, a half-smile on her lips. She lies on a couch, reading, her dark fringe falling away from the uncertainty and determination inextricably intertwined on her cheek. She wears a sweatshirt, not hers, the sleeves rolled into soft woolly tubes over her wrists, the body like a bag around her and the hem halfway to her knee. She with her son on her lap, his cheeks dabbed in irregular chocolate strokes and laughing like a pirate. She, asleep on a winter Sunday afternoon, snuggled into soft folds of a patchwork quilt, the peace of her expression framed in exquisite fragility."

Doppelgänger frowned into the middle distance, stuck to a steady hypnotic tone:

"The man's eyes are closed; he slips quietly over the brim into sleep. He dreams of silver bracelets and red-wine bottles, sandy floors, and college rock echoing from an old boathouse on the shore; and an on old woman with gypsy eyes turning over cards one after another. *The world stretches ever wider when you are cold and alone*, she says."

"Christ, Bud," Ozzy Man said, heaving a ragged breath, "you tell really shitty stories."

"For an anarchic old cynic, you scare easily," Doppelgänger said, squinting at him.

"Not so easily, Mate. But she's not in the room. He slept the whole night alone. She's not in the fucking room."

"Yeah, right. It's not good." Doppelgänger looked at Al, sitting quietly on his own. "It *is* concerning."

Al didn't say a word. If you had pressed him to say why he loved her, he could say no more than because she was she, and he was he.

17

"THE BOSS IS COMING ON tour," Al told the other two.

In 1976, when he was a freshman and the country was tearing itself apart, Al stayed in a single room in a rent-controlled building a few blocks from Uni. Only two students lived there—he and Rory Grace. In the other 38 rooms was a sorry tribe of ancients who had in common that they were hopeless losers on State pension. Rory was a slovenly engineering student who thought only about internal combustion and torque, and walked his motorcycle, a roaring sin-black 600cc Honda without crash bars, into his room on the second floor every night. Up the narrow stairs, while the moribund occupants of Harcourt Mansions feebly protested, unheard and ineffectual beside the unbaffled bat out of hell riding its clutch upward in the narrow stairwell.

Doppelgänger remembered. "They liked you, but hated Disgrace." Their neighbour, who lived entirely on chocolate and beer.

"He was addicted to drinking brake fluid," Ozzy Man said. "He said he could stop any time."

Al was respectfully quiet always. If he was home after eight thirty at night, he listened to his radio on a single plug earphone on the end of a thin yellow wire. "Remember how scratchy the signal was, and how it would disappear and come back." Doppelgänger became dewy-eyed with nostalgia. "Through the earpiece it sounded like a chorus of spiders."

"Yup," Ozzy Man said. "Nostalgia was so much better back then."

The only progressive rock was on Radio 604, broadcasting on AM from Port St Johns, famous for fecklessness and Sweet Mary Jane. That's where Al first heard The Man Who Would Be Boss, sweating it out on the streets of a runaway American dream. When the Soweto riots kept uniformed patrols on the street and him in his little room, Al heard the complex lyrics of urban desperation and abandonment overlain on an alternately compelling or quietly in-sidious rock beat: The songs of rasping desolation, forsaken-in-love. 'Whoa-oh, she's the one,' the young singer exulted the lamentation.

"You were often forsaken in love yourself," Doppelgänger said. "In touch with your sensitive inner-self."

"He was a slave to his donger," Ozzy Man said.

Courtney had also heard about the concert, from Thomas. "He is doing something or other for Megabux Co, and he tells me about their EBITDA. They have given him four tickets in the Golden Circle. Will you and Kimberley come with us?"

"Nils Lofgren and Little Steven are both on tour with him," Al told the face completely devoid of interest. Her look *Don't, please, turn into an enthusiast*. For which reason he didn't say: Dan Patlansky, the local guitar hero, was the supporting act; and big-man Clarence was blowing tenor riffs in the fields of Elysium.

All four of them wore jeans and T-shirts, because that's what you wear to a rock concert. Thomas also wore a cardigan, which annihilated his coolness factor. They threaded their careful way to directly in front of the stage and were immersed in the buzz of excitement that can be made only by sixty-five thousand people in a stadium: The lights; the people; the bass from the stack of speak-ers thumping in your chest; the close presence of the evening; the damp grass under your feet; the untamed animal voice of so many cheering throats. And then, there he was: Dark shirt and sweatlets on his wrists, holding that guitar, that self-same one—straight off the cover of *Born To Run*.

"Don't, for fuck sake's, Bud," Ozzy Man said, "be that guy who tells everybody."

They were in that zone where the irresistible wall of sound from the E-Street Band met the unstoppable wall of sound from the crowd. "This is why there are humans. This is why we are here," Doppelgänger said. "The Universe exists, was created for this moment, this bright instant when all sorrow and happiness, all bitterness and joy coalesce. This magic moment."

Al knew not to tell the others.

"The world used to be magic," Doppelgänger said. "Dragons and wizards; and demons bound in shackles of lightning. When we lost that, we got Stratocasters, big speaker stacks and Springsteen."

The concert started in a frenzy, and never looked back. The Boss swung into *No Surrender*, loved his audience, treating them like a handful of friends around a campfire. In the circle everyone sang the chorus, most of the revellers sang the whole song. When Springsteen got to the end, wild cheering started, but not to be— the band ripped straight back into the refrain, drowning out the applause. The Man loved that joke, laughing like an adolescent, well pleased with his prank. At the end of the chorus, the cheering was twice as loud—and the laughing Superman at the mic stand did it again: Ripped through the refrain one more time: *No retreat, Baby; No surrender*. Lord, how they loved him.

"This is fantastic," Courtney said, laughing, out of breath from dancing. Kimberley, laughing too, had been singing as well—she knew the words—and Thomas, podgy and flushed, looked as if he wanted to check his emails.

The Singerman spotted a sign he loved, motioned it to be handed up, and held it for the camera to show the rest of the stadium on the massive screen behind the stage: *We love you Burt Springsteen.* During an instrumental extension in the middle of *Cadillac Ranch*, the Man pulled a dumpy, bald, fifty-something old guy in jeans and a biker's jacket onto stage and gave him his guitar—that guitar: The biker struck the right chords, almost sounded as if he could be one of the heroes; and still tells everyone he meets that he, briefly, was in the E Street Band. Kimberley and Courtney danced together, laughing and singing, two free spirits on an enchanted evening.

Hungry Heart took no less energy, and at its end, Bruce—because by now he and the sixty-five thousand were on first name terms—pulled up onto stage a beautiful young lass in tight jeans to dance with him. Kimberley and Courtney both wished it was them. Then, magician that he was, with a wave of his hand dimmed the lights and listened while so many South African voices sang, *I'm on Fire*, doing the modern-day equivalent of the sea of lighters: Holding up thousands of cell phone torches.

"Jay Zeus, Buddy," Ozzy Man said, "this is fucking marvellous." He said: *maah-vlis*.

Right then it started raining. Not little sissy drops like they have in London—a proper drenching, pissing-down as only the Highveld can produce. The Man joked about the rain and said: "It's good for you." And: "Maybe it will stop." And, seeing the funny side, added: "But maybe it won't." He came to the edge of the stage and stood out in the rain with the crowd, and held his arms open to the sky, welcoming the water; and he played and he laughed and he danced. He did his best to stop the rain; yet revelled in its torrent, as if this were the most auspicious portent the gods could have sent to a Saturday evening shindig.

All the efforts of the band, the leader, the crowd and the night couldn't get through to the empty, shrivelled soul of the dumpy merchant banker, who had never voluntarily listened to rock music in his life. "It's wet. I'm getting out of here," he told Courtney in sulky tones. She seemed not to hear; definitely didn't care.

Kimberley, who had been having a great time till then, wasn't a big fan of being wet and cold while standing in an ever-more-muddy patch. "I'm cold. I'm going with him, if you don't mind?" Al definitely heard, definitely cared; was immediately torn in two: This was Kimberley, his first responsibility, his soulmate, even if Ozzy Man and Doppelgänger thought differently. But. But; but, this was *Springsteen*. Al had waited for thirty-five years to see him; knew all the words to all his songs; had fallen in and out of love to the soundtrack this man had written; laughed his joy with the spinning of the black circle on happy songs; cried his grief on the sad ones.

And here He was, right there: Bigger and better and more immediate than any ordinary human would dare try.

"Can I stay?" he asked, despite Responsibility, despite Duty, despite being sorry that she was leaving. Of course he could, she said; kissed him goodbye in the rain, and left with Stick-in-the-Mud to call an Uber. Al felt bad, seeing her go, but if Courtney noticed, she didn't say. While Al was still of two minds, the Wizard up on stage changed the pace, doing a ten-minute version of *Tom Joad*, dark, moody and finger-snapping. Courtney caught the change in mood, listened carefully, and leaned back close to Al—while the rain kept falling down.

Two and a half hours after his magnificent entrance, the Boss looked set to wind down, starting with what could only be his final encore—reeling off a fast-paced medley, with never a break, never a stammer in the driving rhythm. Song after song that lives in the cells of every twentieth century person: *Born in the USA; Dancing in the Dark; Born to Run*. The crowd had woken up again, and, sensing the end was near, was in a final frenzy of adrenaline and dopamine. And still the rain poured down.

Just about then, Springsteen turned off all the lights, letting the first silence of the evening fall: Only a heartbeat of bass and a darkly lit stage, rain pouring from a wounded sky. And *then* he spoke to the crowd; not for the first time, but serious as he hadn't been before. What he said was this:

"You don't know how lucky you were. In the States we had the Reverend Martin Luther King. He was assassinated, and he was *never* replaced. You had Nelson Mandela for a lifetime. You *just* don't know how lucky you were."

The heartbeat of bass changed into *Who'll stop the Rain*, the old Credence number. Even Ozzy Man didn't mind the lump in Al's throat. The rasping sincerity of that voice Al loved so well turned on the sad, introspective refrain: *And I wonder, still I wonder, who'll stop the rain?* The crowd went crazy, mad, properly snot-flying Hooligan berserk.

And then the rain stopped.

"Fuck it, Bud, this guy can do anything." Ozzy Man spoke for all of them. Courtney was laughing, along with every member of the crowd around her, and exultation was on the face of the deep. She leant further back against Al, and from somewhere, his arms found their way around her. She snuggled in, resting her head on his chest; and then he let go again.

Together they watched the band leave the stage; the end of a hell of a night. Yet the lights stayed off; and then He was back on stage, just him and an acoustic guitar and his sixty-five thousand new friends. Just him: Sang *Thunder Road*; and when it was done, he said: *Good night South Africa, I'll be back soon.*

If you are scared and thinking that maybe we aren't that young anymore, show a little faith. Sometimes there is magic in the night.

18

"**M**ONOGAMY IS A SOCIAL CONSTRUCT, not an evolutionary or biological impulse." George would know—he was a professor; he taught at Med School.

"And he follows his dick around town," Ozzy Man said.

"If Man actually were monogamous, there would be no adultery. You don't see the stud oystercatcher ducking in behind a big rock for a quickie with the new gal on the beach. Because he is monogamous. He just doesn't do it. One girl, one boy, some grief, some joy. But never the cutie in Accounts." He grinned, happy to be controversial. Again.

Roguish looks and a convincing manner are what got George into trouble serially. That and a raging libido. At 57 he supported three ex-wives, a girlfriend and four children.

"Is that why you are such a lone wolf?" Max Wilkins asked, jokey, tall-stemmed glass in hand.

"Case in point," George said. "Wolves are monogamous. A lone wolf is one who has lost a partner and is lonely because of his fundamental nature that keeps him from getting another. When human males lose a partner, they get another as soon as possible." He smiled at Max. "Some of us don't wait that long." He winked his complicity.

"No, you're so wrong!" Outraged sensibility had driven colour into Tessa's cheeks. She had been trying not to disagree with George because she knew from years of seeing him in action, how he dealt with his opponents in argument. But this was too much. Her expression was stern and her shoulders tense, her voice just a tad squeaky with emotion.

"And her chest heaved most attractively," Ozzy Man said, completing the description.

"You only say that because of your own disreputable habits. You can't control yourself, so you say it is natural to behave that way. You should be ashamed, not proud. You pretend you have a superior intellectual point of view, but all it is, is that you lack decency. That you have no restraint; you are outrageous. You have no decency." Her clumsy repetition should have alerted her to the growing possibility that she wouldn't come out of this well.

George crowed, revelling in having reeled a moral matron into his debate. Not that she looked like a matron: She was a gym Baby Boomer who kept her hair stylish and shiny, like Mireille Mathieu; her waist trim; her complexion clear; and her décolletage on the borderline of conservative permissibility. She didn't look like Mother Grundy—just sounded and behaved that way.

"Decency!" George said, guffawing. "What a quaint notion. We should get Petula Clark to sing a song about it. Who says what it is even? The church aunties?"

"No, the whole of Society." Edward, the AIDS activist, not only wanted to help Tessa, he also agreed with her, when it concerned other people. He presented with inescapable pomposity that showed the world just how seriously he took himself; and he was a senior advocate: Therefore, felt up to the task.

"Anyone who speaks for Society is a bullshitter." George looked at both his accusers, suddenly serious. "You are just saying what you think and attributing it the everyone. Next thing you will be telling me about Right-Minded People."

"There are social *mores* that define what is acceptable conduct and what is not." Pompous Edward in full courtroom flow. He was very sure of the strict limits that defined how other people should behave. He knew he would soon be a judge, and then his convictions would have the force of law. He already looked the part with horn-rimmed spectacles and an aquiline profile.

"Absolutely. And it's always more convincing in Latin. But tell me, do these *mores* permit little dalliances with pubescent boys?" Even George knew that he had struck way below the belt.

"A belt frequently unbuckled." Ozzy Man felt compelled to support his team captain in debate.

Edward blanched; Tessa's jaw dropped an inch, the tips of upraised fingers reaching for her face that reflected a blend of shock and deep appreciation for a bitchy comment.

"That's a bit heavy, George," Sy said. "We are all entertained by you as the perpetual iconoclast, and your anti-establishment sentiments have a certain naïve charm. But don't be insulting. Play nice." He nodded in George's direction, lifted a glass to toast his well-rounded reprimand.

"Okay. Sorry," George replied, looking not sorry in the slightest. Edward's penchant for employing young boys from poor families and demanding of them a wider bouquet of services than was traditionally expected wasn't exactly a secret. But it didn't affect his conviction about what was proper for all the other, ordinary people and how they should behave.

"I think your emphasis is wrong, George," Kimberley said. "The determining issue is not what primal urges you have. It's how you control them. If you get really angry with somebody, the issue is not that Homo Erectus would have killed him with a stone, but that you, as a civilised human being, would deal with your anger within acceptable societal structures."

"Good point, Sheila," Ozzy Man said. "Pity you said *Erectus*."

"You are such a child," Doppelgänger said.

"Yes." Edward stepped back into the fray. "Imagine if we went around indiscriminately killing each other."

"Imagine," George said. Silence settled at the table as everyone tried to imagine what the world would be if people behaved violently: Guns in private possession; the murder rate as an actual statistic; formal armies with inspired notions of and methods for killing by the thousand.

"But how wrong you are to equate killing and sex," George said after his measured pause. Timing is the essence of both comedy and debate. "Not only is your Freudian slip showing, you also missed the point entirely. In evolutionary terms, not killing leads to a desirable outcome: A society where the members don't slaughter each other will do better than one where they do. A simple numbers game that leads to an evolutionary impulse not to kill. On the other hand, producing as many copies as possible of your genes is exactly what biology wants you to do. The most successful fornicator is rewarded by evolution—his family and his nation prosper. Special albeit sad exception in your case, Edward; but well done for going through the motions so enthusiastically in any event," George slipped the ropes of his recent apology; wrapped up for the rest of the table: "So, the hippies are literally correct when they tell you to make love, not war."

"Hee-hee," Ozzy Man, who really couldn't stand Edward, said chuckling. But Al refused always to say.

"Nothing in your argument talks to your position in a civilised and interactive society," Kimberley said. "Maybe you have a point if you are a troglodyte. But we are much better than that now. We do all sorts of things that are not simply a biological impulse. We live in houses, we cook with butter and cream, we smoke cigars. We have literature and art and music. We live in a Welfare State; our best, most admirable people are philanthropists."

"Philanthropy comes directly from social evolution," George said. "Same issue as not killing your fellow citizens—keeping them alive does the same trick. Picasso's and Debussy's contribution to overall happiness is less clear; and Picasso, from what I read, wasn't exactly a one-filly jockey. But the relative importance of fine arts isn't what we are talking about: It's our socialisation that tries to convince us that *monogamy* is a good idea. In modern times that socialisation is taking a step away from dogma in the direction of pragmatism: There is nothing in the teaching of Gordon Ramsey in favour of having only one life's partner. The argument in favour comes from, traditionally, the old religions and their obsession with pussy and its preservation for men to conserve and use at their exclusive pleasure, so to speak. Latterly and more rationally, the support for the position has to do with matrimonial proprietary rights and the duty to support your children. But it's not inherent to our nature, it is a bolt-on. It may well have societal benefits and may accord with a perceived religious morality. But it stays a bolt-on."

"I agree with George," Charles said. It was his table they sat at. He had a nose like champagne cork and was the editor of the *Florestan*, known for its liberal views. Charles' views, mostly. "Strict monogamy is virtually non-existent: Sex with only one person, ever, has so few supporters as to be vanishingly irrelevant."

"Well, I am in favour of it," Tessa said. Everyone tried not to stare at her. "It's one of the Ten Commandments," she said into an uncomfortable silence that followed her outburst.

"Sure, sweetie," George said, pissing off every woman in the room. "But there are a few exceptions to that bronze-age dictate. You excluded, I'm sure, nobody in this room has only ever slept with one person. Nobody raises an eyebrow if you have sex when you are not married. Nobody cares if you get remarried and sleep with your new wife. It's kinda expected. It's not the multiplicity of lovers that is the issue, it's the rule about timing that bugs you. It's not whether, but w*hen* you have sex."

"I'm talking about adultery," Tessa said, emphasising the second syllable: A*dul*tery.

"Yes." George looked at her steadily. "That's the social construct."

Meg listened to the story with half a smile, poured her sparkling water into a glass, lit a cigarette. "What was his actual point? That he should be allowed to screw around, and no one must care?"

Al grinned. "No. He knows why there are rules. It's good that children have someone identifiable who is obliged to care for them and pay for their orthodontist. And also, it's a good thing to remember that we are sexually jealous. If the milkman has sex with your wife, it's a good thing for him to know that you aren't that likely to tip him at the end of the month." He sipped his ristretto, perfectly bitter, pitch black and thick with flavour. "His point is that perpetual monogamy is foisted on us by social expectation; that to disappoint that expectation is easy because our selfish genes wish to make as many copies of themselves as possible. Our biological selves conflict with the creatures we would like to be. Our fundamental biology puts us in unresolvable conflict with our moral aspiration. And you see the evidence of that conflict everywhere."

She squinted at him. "Is it a rule you are having difficulty with?" An arrow straight to his heart. How did she do it so unerringly?

"Gee, Sis." He looked at his fingernails, taken aback by the directness of the assault. "I have never been unfaithful to Kimberley."

"Not exactly what I asked."

"*Si, correcto*," Ozzy Man said.

"You have to be the Thought Police to ask anything more." Although his tone remained mild, this was as close to scolding as Al ever came when talking to Meg.

She reached across the table, put her hand on his. "I'm not criticising."

He knew she wasn't. Courtney occupied a bigger part of his thoughts than he wanted her to. Despite his stern and regular lectures to himself, he knew perfectly well that he thought of her too often. He remembered the cuddle at the concert too well. He hoped she wouldn't text him and was stupidly eager that she should. He tried to convince himself that she was a nuisance but agreed with a song in his heart to meet for coffee or lunch. Most of all, he knew that she thought of him only as a kindly old gent, and he tried to keep their conversation light. Courtney, he knew, could do no other.

"We watched a series on Netflix called *Ozark*," she told him on the Monday after the concert, with never a mention of his arms around her in the stadium. All she spoke about was that she and Thomas had watched TV.

"She doesn't tell you the good bits, Bud," Ozzy Man said.

"She doesn't want to make it more difficult for you than she knows it is," Doppelgänger said. "She knows about Kimberley and Responsibility. And her mother did ask what she would do if ever she met a man."

Al sat listening and thought of her TV-watching and how different that made them: He watched the news when something in particular was brewing; and sometimes he watched sport. But sitcoms, dramas, murders, romances, reality shows and almost-history held for him no appeal. Still, she prattled on. "It's about this guy who launders money for a Mexican drug cartel, but his partner steals from them and they kill him. They come into his office one night and just shoot him dead. They almost kill the guy as well, but he talks them into allowing him to launder their money from a lake district where very little happens." She laughed happily. "Nothing in his life after that is ever so bad that it can't get worse."

Al wasn't at all interested; except that he loved how she told him, wanted to hear her speak, was captivated by the sound of her voice. He wasn't alone. The manager of the restaurant had had her in his sights since they came in and chose that moment to oil his way across the floor. Oozing charm from every pore, he leaned over the table, delivering his best combination of manliness and charm in Courtney's direction.

"Did you enjoy your meal?"

"Thanks." She smiled prettily.

"Very nice to see you here. Hope to see you soon again."

"Ha ha," she said.

"Can I get you anything else?"

"No, I'm fine thanks." She still smiled.

"It would be only a pleasure. I could get the kitchen on it right away."

She smiled and said nothing.

"Right, right," Ozzy Man said. "Now off you fuck."

Al told Kimberley about their lunch. "What did you talk about?" she asked.

"She told me about the series she watched on Netflix."

"Oh," Kimberley said, surprised that he would voluntarily subject himself to that. "Do you want us to have them over for dinner?"

"No. I don't think it would be much fun," he said truthfully, thinking of the merchant banking component of the guest couple.

"That's not all of it, is it, Mate?" Ozzy Man looked sidelong at Al, censure in his tone.

It wasn't; but what it was, wasn't easy to put a finger on. Thomas was as interesting as the dance of rotisserie chickens at the delicatessen. To be brutally honest, some of Courtney's conversation could be as flat as the test wicket at the Wanderers; except that she often told him interesting, wholly diverse, factoids; and he found it endearing that she had no filters, told him all her stuff: What her sister said; how her latest piece was getting on; why her father should have stopped working and spent more time at home; what new laptop she was thinking of getting; the specs of a camera she saw in the shop or on line; why she preferred Helly Hansen to North Face. None of it earth-shattering, but taken as a whole, somehow engaging. She also listened without interrupting and didn't have any suggestion about what he should and shouldn't say. He found, more and more, that his opinions and theories influenced her way of thinking: He told her his views, mostly because she asked him specifically what he thought; and in later discussions he found that she had understood and adopted his often esoteric take on things. She was becoming libertarian. And perhaps the clincher—she thought he was funny, laughed at his jokes.

"But that's still not all of it, is it, Mate?" Ozzy Man looked at him knowingly.

Maybe. Al wasn't sure.

19

"FANCY A CUP OF TEA?" Al asked Kimberley.

"She drinks Earl Grey, because she is a socialist," Ozzy Man said. "All proper tea is theft."

"Yes please," she answered, not looking up from the newspaper. Al boiled the kettle, put loose leaves in the pot.

"When Moses makes tea," Ozzy Man said, "Hebrews it."

Kimberley looked up from the paper, laughed; the sound Al liked best. "What?" he asked.

"I'm reading Ben Travis' column." She giggled. "He says there is a general perception that comes from being politically correct, that all people were created interesting." She chuckled. "Oh, he *is* funny."

"Did you read him a few weeks ago," Al said, smiling, "about the man who said to him: *If I've told you before, don't stop me. I'd like to hear it again.*"

Kimberley snorted another laugh. "And the man who told him: *Before I start talking, I have something to say.*"

The tea added the seal to the morning: Chatting and chuckling, they wove breakfast into the frame of their day. "What are you up to later?" she asked.

"I have to write to Gary. His dad died last week. Me, amateur psychologist, thinks he is somewhere in process along DABDA—Denial Anger Bargaining Depression Acceptance."

"President Mubarak was in denial," Ozzy Man said.

"How so?" Kimberley wanted to know.

"You know he and his father didn't get on. Now the old guy is finally gone, Gary is blue as October skies, and doesn't know why. He is at Depression, I think—sad for the friendship they could have had. Before that he was angry that he got such a bum deal; then he tried to negotiate for a better one. Soon he will get to Acceptance, and then he'll feel better. A few more pages in the calendar."

"The calendar's days are numbered," Ozzy Man said.

Al opened his laptop and wrote:

Hi there Bossman,

 How inadequate to say, but sorry. To use the language of our youth, it's a bummer.

 On the morning my father rasped his last few breaths through a respirator that inflated and deflated a red balloon in front of his face, it was more difficult for me than I thought it would be. For years I had said that when he dies, I will find his grave and dance on it in a wild thunderstorm with hail and sheets of rain. But there I was, disheartened, again, by the lifetime of missed opportunity between us. I'm sure you feel the same.

 I also thought this: When you die, you die alone. There may be other people in the room, but it's just you: You are the only one who is dying, and you do so on your own. That's why Blind Willie says, You gonna need (Ah-ha) somebody on your bond. These old Mississippi bluesmen knew their stuff.

 My conclusion? All you can do is don't be a chop, make the best of what you've got; laugh a bit; Keep on chooglin'.

 I think you have made the right choice avoiding the funerals industry. Their front of house is a skilful combination of professional mournfulness and hard selling. Their sales office is softly sad, edged in purple and black; hush-hush quiet, and organ dirges piped surreptitiously from somewhere, perhaps from behind the red velvet drapes. Their colour scheme assumes you are blind. The man who meets you unhappily at the door is dressed for heartbreak, his hair combed and cut as neatly as a blow-up sex doll, and he says, "I'm sorry for your loss," and "These are your days of sadness and sorrow." Then he leans on you, edging you in the direction of a feeding frenzy of acquisition: You can rent or buy—depending on your preference, but mostly on your budget—casks, plastic flowers in bubbles, invitation cards, programs with or without photos, purple ribbon, piped music, organists, pallbearers, and preachers. If you say you want the cheapest box, because, hey, tomorrow it goes into the furnace, he somehow conveys, without saying or doing anything you can put a finger on, that if this is how you want to treat your loved one in the last thing you will ever do for him, well, he has heard of people like you. And I don't lie about the preacher—you can choose the denomination, age, and gender of your priest; and you can choose the service—the longer one with three hymns is, of course, a little more expensive. "But this is your FATHER. So, sorry for your loss," says the slimy little turd.

I wanted to ask about a wooden pyre on the tempestuous hilltop at midnight, with flames licking at God's feet and sparks flying up into His eyes, but it wasn't on the price list. So, I told him, when with softly wringing hands he frowned at not being able to charge for a bit of religious fakery, that there is only one sensible religious question: "Do geese see God"?

I am glad I kept it as simple as possible: For I have seen the absence of simplicity, my son. A few months ago, Kimberley's grandfather's cousin's son died (I think that was it), leaving me without a close familial connection, but nevertheless at his funeral. The priest had a short, trimmed beard like Jesus after the PR consultants edited him, and a serene expression like Barry Gibb; and an Afrikaans accent that accentuates all the wrong syllables and replaces every "d" at the end of a word with a "t". [Remember that in the vernacular of the Old Country we write "curd"; but you say "curt".]

"Wiyah gethert toogether inde missy ofde Awlmarty Gort," he welcomed us to his/His house. After reading from his thick book that has caused all those wars, about the tent peg from Gilgamesh and the ram's horn shackled like a rich man unto the

eye of a camel, he laid aside academic things, fixed us in his kind-est all-embracing focus, and told us that life is like marmalade. You see, Bossy, without the bitter, the sweet would not be the same. Jung had more or less the same idea when he said that you cannot know beauty without having experienced its absence. But the marmalade thing works better.

Unfortunately, he then went on and on about it: The warm toast at the breakfast of our youth, the smattering of bitterness on the cheese of our lunch, the sharp bite of our dinnertime; the acrid foretaste of a final snack at a shiver before midnight. Personally, I preferred the bit later, when he said that Shehbui, god of the South Wind, would cherish and keep all her children from their first laughter in the cradle through summer's golden glow, from the tears of love's frustration through winter's icy blow.

Ok, he didn't say that, but he might have. He said instead: There is a Skipper in charge of the boat—your boat and mine, everyone's boat. Sometimes He allows us to sail on a pleasant, mirror-smooth sea; sometimes He sends us where the fishing is good; and sometimes He sends us into the storm.

OK, he didn't say that either. But if you want your nonde-nominational profit centre to stay in business, you have to move with the times: What he did say is that his congregation now has an App you can download to stay in touch with your salvation 24/7. Repent on line.

After the service one of Kimberley's far distant several times removed cousins, who had driven all the way from Bloemfontein for the service, walked with us; then said to me: "More core's porked year." And sure, there was his car, parked right next to mine.

Gary, I'm trying to distract myself with the idiocy of the ones who are left behind. My own father, in whose house there were many mansions, in none of which I was welcome, had many expressions. One was "That explains it" (despite that he was Afrikaans.) Over the years it contracted to "Splainzit." Another was that he waved with both hands, lifting the palms in your direction, at mid-chest level, a bit like the smiley-faced icon who waves with both hands. After you pare it down, that's all that was left to us in the end. When it was half after midnight on the long day that was his second to last, and it was time for me to go home because the doing was done, I patted his hand and said Bye. He hadn't known all night whether it was teatime or Florence's Sunday hat. Suddenly he saw me and there was a question in his eye: Where the fuck am I? I told him quietly and he frowned and said, "Splainzit." Then, as I turned at the door, he waved at me with both palms turned up.

I drove home on the highway that you see better at night: an endless row of yellow lights, the road empty as you never see it during the day. And I tried to think of when he had been nice. All I could think of was when he'd been really dreadful. And all the while my treacherously contradictory heart kept hearing him say "Splainzit" and I kept seeing him wave both palms at me. Ah Christ me old matey!

Whatever other gross deficiencies of that particular chapter of my earthly progress, I have come to the unshakeable conclusion that we need a red switch, so that one day when you stand at my bedside and I'm 5% human, you can nod at me and flip that switch. And I will wave and say: Splainzit.

Because if you aren't part of the solution, you are part of the precipitate.

Oh my Matey, I am sorry he made you miserable, both in living and in dying. But hey fuck, keep on chooglin'.

I am planning a trip to the Land of the Free/Home of the Brave. I will see you soon, and we will write sorrow on the bosom of the earth and tell stories of the death of kings. And we'll drink too much scotch.

Until then
Al.

He pressed *Send* and found he had depressed himself with his letter.

"No matter, Bud," Ozzy Man said. "I'm sure Gary will be happy as Larry when he reads it. It's very uplifting."

Al's phone buzzed in his pocket, and immediately he felt the thrill of his mood shifting. Courtney on the line.

"Pizza?" she asked.

In the car on the way to pick her up, Doppelgänger said, "Such a good suggestion and she doesn't even have an alligator purse."

She shifted into the passenger seat, dark hair and eyes, smiling a burst of sunshine. Her jeans were crisp from the laundry and her shirt button-down and pearly white.

"I'm thinking of getting a Canon," she said. "It has a 30.3 Megapixel full-frame, and an EF-EOS-R Mount Adapter; and EF and EF-S Lens compatibility. What do you think?"

"I'm thinking, *I hope she's talking about a camera*," he answered, keeping his eyes on the road. She laughed a bright fountain spilling into his cup.

"You don't know about cameras?" Her eyes sparkled.

"I do. It's a dark chamber with a little hole called an aperture, and a lens in front of it that focuses light onto a surface where images are captured. Some people even have them on their phones, but I have no idea how that's possible."

She laughed again; the cup overflowed.

"I'm sure goodness and mercy will follow this arrangement, Bud," Ozzy Man said. "It's likely, though, that you are headed for the valley of shadows. But fear no evil."

"They are just friends; it's just pizza," Doppelgänger said.

"The road to hell is paved with pizza," Ozzy Man said. Getting no answer, he added: "Take my advice—I'm not using it."

Al and Courtney ordered, and their conversation moved on, skipping lightly.

"Thomas says socialism is what holds the world back from achieving its potential," she told Al. "When the masses say they have the right to work, he says, it's just a way to muscle in on the effort of others."

"But he can afford to be a socialist, Mate," Ozzy Man said. "He has the bucks; the Live-and-Let-Live patter can easily fit into his budget. Will go nicely with the Porsche."

Courtney waited for Al to respond, and he settled for: "Capital makes such a mockery of earning capacity. The discussion about the right to work takes your eye off the ball."

"I don't get it?" Courtney frowned.

"A person who gets a wage can work 24/7 for his whole life without any hope of smelling the old boots of someone with a bundle; someone who does nothing at all. Living on interest and dividends from a big pile will keep you way out ahead of the chasing pack of everyone who works, no matter how hard or how much."

"From San Diego up to Maine, in every mine and mill," Ozzy Man sang.

"Where working men defend their rights." Doppelgänger joined in the duet.

"It's there you find Joe Hill." Ozzy completed the anthem.

"But isn't it the intellectual class that creates the opportunity?" Courtney asked. "Without factories and corporations there would be no place to work?"

"I think we are hearing straight from the double-chinned wanker here, Buddy," Ozzy Man said.

"Sure," Al said. "The chosen few, with money and skills, have always been able to decide how it will be. It's a complicated inter-relation of moving parts that ultimately depends on how important you think you are. If you think you deserve Beluga and Cristal and your workers must have half a spoon of boiled rice, you will feel they hold you back. If you think chicken and ciabatta is enough for you, you will allow them fried onions and cabbage with their noodles."

Courtney looked at him slowly, savouring the juxtaposition. "Thomas is way more important than you?" she asked and smiled.

Al nodded, just once, a tiny inclination of his head.

Ozzy Man watched how that exchange had gone down and how badly the podgy husband had come out of it. "I think sex is better than logic," he said, "but I can't prove it."

"Oz," Doppelgänger said, sighing. "Sometimes you are relentless."

20

THE NAME PLATE, FADED FROM original copper to tarnished brass, was partly hidden behind an enthusiastic Virginia creeper that had conquered the entire front wall of the property. *Melissa Rogers, Consulting Psychologist,* Al read. He pushed the button for the bell and was buzzed into an enclave of peace, paved in raw red-orange brick, uneven and mossy with age; overrun with an explosion of carefully curated bushes, shrubs, trees and potted flowers; and with a shy fountain unobtrusively singing a quiet watery cascade from deep inside the thick entanglement. Unkempt perfection under the hand of a master gardener who advised but did not insist.

The consultation room was to the right of the house, at the back of the garden—white walls and many colonial-style panes in grid patterns, letting in all the light in the world. Inside there was enough room to swing a medium sized cat. Against two of the walls, where the windows allowed, traditional Chinese landscapes stretched out in infinite perspective, indefinite in retreat and exquisite in detail. The room was neither empty nor crowded, but just as Goldilocks liked. Framed degree certificates, a few photos, an old-fashioned tapestry, flowers in a bowl, a tribal woodcut of an unidentifiable animal.

In an easy chair with armrests, and with a tray of tea things on a side table at her elbow, sat a woman who was in between thirty and fifty, an indeterminable age. Her short bob was flecked with grey;

she wore no make-up; and she had dressed for the dual purpose of maintaining the gravity of her professional image, and of allowing her patients to see her as an actual human. Goldilocks outfit to go with the room and its appointment.

"Melissa Rogers," she said, smiling, not offering to shake his hand. "Why are you here?" the doc asked; and, despite the abrupt directness of the question, somehow managed not to sound pushy.

"To get right straight to the point here, Mrs. Rogers," Al said, a little surprised and a lot relieved to have missed out several minutes about the weather and mutual acquaintances, "it's because I'm an idiot."

"Nah, Mate." Ozzy Man was disappointed. "Tell her your life has been full of terrible misfortunes, most of which never happened."

The analyst inclined her head. "Missy," she said. Al, who specialised in not hearing what people said, looked non-plussed. "Call me Missy," she repeated.

"Missy is short for Melissa," Doppelgänger explained, somewhat exasperated. He wanted Al to be on his A game.

"Oh," Al sub-vocalised. Out loud, he said: "I'm an idiot, Missy."

The two stared at each other quietly across the desk, Al in a comfortable leather recliner that had a lever to pop up a footrest.

"Do you mind if," Al asked, pointed at it. The psychologist gave permission with a wave of her hand.

"Schalk Brinkman sent you?" the doc checked her writing pad. "Yup."

"Does he know you're an idiot?"

"He knows, to my discredit, that I am not terribly patient with new-age touch-feely talk; and he knows I told him I need to speak to someone who has greater insight than I do. He sent me here. Apart from that, I'm sure he knows I'm an idiot—we have known each other for decades."

"Nicely put, Bud." Ozzy Man complimented him. "Now's the time to tell her you have a shrinking feeling. Then she can tell you to be a little patient."

"Well, I'm not new-age." Missy chuckled.

"I can tell." Ozzy Man looked at her sensible, square-toed leather shoes. Lace-ups.

"I like your garden," Al said.

"Thanks. Benign neglect, that's the secret." Silence settled across the desk, stayed there until the doctor smiled again. "I see I can't just keep quiet and let you fill the awkward silence by telling me your innermost secrets?"

"Oh, sorry," Al said. "Is that what you were waiting for?"

"Pay attention, Al," Doppelgänger said. "Tell her why you are here."

"Missy, it's like this, I have been married to a wonderful woman, Kimberley, for three decades and a few years. She is lovely; she is devoted to our life together, as am I. We share the same opinions with very few exceptions, and we like each other, enjoy being together, live together successfully. No. More than that—Happily."

"But?"

"But I have befriended a young woman, Courtney, with whom I don't have as much in common as I have with Kimberley, but I like spending time with her."

"Are you sleeping with her?" Missy's voice was non-committal, her face neutral.

"I'm not," Al answered with such lack of passion, the doctor believed him implicitly.

"Then what's the problem?"

"It's substantial. My wife, Kimberley, is upset that I see Courtney and that I like her. She hasn't said, but I know it makes her feel sad and displaced. And I feel guilty that I am friends with someone other than Kimberley."

"*That's* the problem?" The doctor looked a little bemused.

"Yes. A very serious problem. Bigger than any I have had in my married life."

"That makes you sound like such a pussy." Ozzy Man gave his take on it.

"Does she think you are having an affair?" Missy asked, frowning slightly.

"Doc, it's worse than that. She knows I'm not having sex with Courtney. We have known each other for a lifetime, and she knows that's just not how I roll. But she is deeply compromised. She feels her position in my affection has diminished. It's not as if she has dropped into second place. That she also knows. She just feels she has lost the exclusivity of the One-and-Only status she has had for thirty-five years. If I had sex with someone, casually, she would be hurt, but I'm sure she would say sex is just sex. My forming an attachment to someone, that's much worse: That is a betrayal."

"*Do* you have casual sex?" Again, no judgment—simply asking for details.

"No. I don't."

Missy looked him over slowly, sizing him up. Spreading the fingers of her right hand like a Chinese bamboo fan to semaphore *what-if*, she asked: "Why don't you stop seeing Courtney?"

"That's complicated too. I like her, and I like spending time with her. She's my friend, and she needs a companion; she isn't in a happy position in her life and is best in a one-on-one friendship. She is, in my unqualified opinion, emotionally compromised; and depends heavily on me, just to talk things through and to have access to an uncritical ear, one who is prepared to listen. She thrives on the company; suffers without it. She somehow missed out on an important developmental step, and is sorting the world into categories, trying to understand things, trying to decide what's important and what not. She asks me my views and listens carefully to what I say. I know it sounds dorky, but she respects my opinion and adopts much of it. Simply put, I like her. She feels like an intimate companion. I owe her an obligation and I don't want her to get hurt."

"And," Ozzy Man said, "she feels like his friend, not his handler." Doppelgänger frowned at him, disapproving of such an unflattering description of Kimberley.

"Do you love her?" Missy stared across the table as Al battled with his question.

"I don't know." Al shook his head miserably. "I think not. My sister, in whom I confide, thinks I do. In fact, she says it's obvious. I was hoping you would tell me."

"If it's obvious, that would be what makes Kimberley unhappy, don't you think?"

"Yes, I think so. For sure."

"How often do you see her?"

"During the week, every day. We have lunch together. Seldom at the weekend."

Missy raised her eyebrows and said nothing.

"Yeah, Mate," Ozzy Man said. "Look at those eyebrows. Listen." He said: *Leesin.*

"It's an hour's arrangement," Al said, "often less. We eat, we chat, we laugh, then we and get back to our respective days."

"So, Al, do you love her? Don't tell me you are too old—the fact that you are in your sixties doesn't give you a free pass to avoid falling in love." Missy looked steadily across the table at Al.

"Hell, doc. I don't know. I don't know exactly what that means. I don't know what is encompassed by it."

"Yes. I think I may agree with you. I think you may really be an idiot."

"I knew you'd see it my way," Al said drily.

The psychologist smiled again. "Shall we unpack why you're an idiot? Let's start with terminology. What is love?"

"Love is a morning sunrise, love is the rain that falls," Ozzy Man sang in Australian imitation of Roger Whittaker.

Al had no answer, gestured silently with empty hands, squiggly non-plussed smile.

"Love is both having hairy forearms," Ozzy Man said.

"You must have some idea," the psychologist insisted.

"You mean *Agapé, Philia, Eros,* that jazz?" Al asked.

"No, not that."

"Romance is the icing, but love is the cake?" Ozzy Man said.

"Doc, pardon me, but the terminology won't help with the substance. Call it whatever you like best. I need to know how not to hurt either Kimberley or Courtney. If push comes to shove, I will throw Courtney over, because my first obligation is to Kimberley. But I would do that at a cost to my soul, and I would feel that I have betrayed a friend of whom I'm truly fond, and who only ever was kind to me. Her crime would be that she wanted to be and was my companion, and she trusted me to treat her well and with consideration."

Missy waited for him to carry on. "To make things worse, Courtney really likes Kimberley; she thinks they are friends. She said to me the other day that Kimberley and I are like her family, her only relations in Johannesburg. On top of which she doesn't think of me as a potential partner. For me to say to her that I'm not going to see her again requires an explanation. If I were to say Kimberley is jealous of her or she thinks Courtney may be screwing me, it would be a bolt out of the blue. She just doesn't function on that wavelength, at least not with me."

"You are sure about that? "Missy asked.

"Absolutely," Al said.

"I'm not," Doppelgänger said.

"Wishful thinking," Ozzy Man answered Dobby drily while Al was still trying to work out what his double had said. "What could she get from an old guy like him? An old guy with commitment issues?"

Yeah, what? Al thought.

Missy thought about Al's answer to her question, then asked: "Do you think it's possible to love more than one person?"

"If he doesn't know what love is," Ozzy Man said, "how the fuck should he know?"

"I don't think it's possible to have more than one closest friend. I also don't think it's possible for me to have more than one lover. And for me, both those categories are filled by Kimberley. Immutably. Unquestionably."

"Not gonna say *irrefrangibly*, Mate?" Ozzy Man mocked him.

"But that's not what I asked," Missy replied. "Can you be very fond of more than one person, to use your avoidance speak?"

"Yes, I think so. I'm very fond of both of them, but not in the same way. Kimberley is my heart, my soul, my wife."

"Your soulmate?" Ozzy Man kept up his torture.

"My reason to live." Al got carried away trying to shut him up.

"All I own I would give," Ozzy wailed like Tom Jones, "just to have you adore me."

"Courtney is a friend." Al concentrated on Missy's question. "I like her very much, but don't want to substitute Courtney for Kimberley in any way. I am very fond of both of them, but in different ways, fundamentally. Because I like them both doesn't mean I'm doing anything wrong. Nor am I doing anything deliberately. It just is what it is."

"All this talk of guilt and wrongdoing. You are religious?" she asked.

"On the contrary."

"Your position is one of remarkable strictness; and, may I say, of unusual morality." Missy looked at him quietly for a beat, then said: "You don't know how many people sit where you now are right now and try to convince themselves and me that several lovers is the way to go."

"She didn't think that sentence through properly," Ozzy Man said, sniggering behind his hand.

"You are such a child," Doppelgänger said.

"Doc, it may work for them, but it doesn't work for me. We all have obligations and responsibilities, and I take mine seriously. I don't want or choose to be like that—it's just how I am and what I do. It's not possible for me to separate what I do from the effect it will have on the people I owe an obligation to."

"You see this thing in terms of obligation and responsibility, guilt and innocence." Missy shook her head slowly. "You owe these two women a duty or several duties, and that is what determines how you will behave, and whether you are, in your parlance, guilty or not. But at the same time, you say if you broke off your friendship with Courtney, you will do it at a cost to your soul. What do you mean by that? Where do you fit in in all of this? Where is the space for you? What do you want out of it?"

"What I want out of it is no different to what I want from the whole of my life: I want to make it to the end without doing that which can't be undone. I want to die before I fuck up; that would be my finest achievement." Doppelgänger just looked sad, listening to him. "It doesn't mean I want to die soon; it just means I want to pass the exam at the end. And that's the Biggy: *Did I disappoint the ones who were entitled not to be disappointed?*"

"That's such a negative way of looking at things: What you want is not relevant?" Missy asked softly, keeping her eyes down.

"I've just told you what I want." Al gestured incredulity with open fingers. "I want to get out of this mess, but I don't know how. I don't know how I got myself into it in the first place. I didn't actually do anything. I didn't have intentions, or plans, or devious schemes. It just happened on its own. By the time I realised what was happening with Courtney, it was already too late. What I want right now seems like an impossibility to me."

"How so?"

"I want to keep and protect Kimberley with everything possible and make her happy and never give her cause to think badly of me, until I snuff it. And I want Courtney to be my friend, not to be unhappy, and particularly not to have to hear from me that I don't want to see her again. But I can't see my way clear to doing both things. I am going to be a dick to somebody." Al looked out the window into the garden where a tabby cat sat gracefully self-contained on a low retaining wall, licking the inside of her paw and rubbing it over her face. Then he added quietly: "That somebody is Courtney. I'm going to be a douche to Courtney. But I really don't want to be."

Doppelgänger had known this for several weeks already. He said nothing, felt sorry for Al.

"Alan, you are very hard on yourself. What is it that would make *you* happy? What do you want, for yourself?"

"Hee-hee." Ozzy Man chuckled thinly. "She's going to say you must be happy too, and if that takes a roll in the hay, you owe it to yourself to have a go. If you'll pardon the double-entendre."

"She is so not," Doppelgänger said.

Al ignored the interjection: "But I've told you, Missy. I don't want to hurt anybody; I don't want to disappoint anybody. I want to check out of here before I offend anyone who has been foolish enough to trust me."

"I asked what *you* want. Not what other people want from you."

"It's the same thing, doc. It's the same thing. I have obligations and responsibilities to both of them. To Kimberley more so than to Courtney. Infinitely more. But what I want for myself is that both of them think well of me; that neither of them thinks I have treated them badly, that I don't disappoint either of them. I can't stand the thought of either of them being unhappy because of me. I'm not entitled to cause that."

Al sat crumpled in misery at the implication of what he had said to the therapist, who listened intently as he spoke. He imagined and cringed at the thought of the hurt in Kimberley's eye if he were ever to say he loved Courtney—the reprobation, the accusation of betrayal. Equally he imagined and shied away from the disappointment in Courtney's face if he were to say *Farewell, enjoy the rest of your life.*

"If I understand you right," Missy said, "Your own happiness is derivative such that it depends entirely on the happiness of others?"

"Yes. But not just any old body, only the ones I care for and who depend on me. In this case, Kimberley and Courtney." He paused; added: "And Jesse." His boy had a dog in this fight as well.

Doppelgänger had known this about Al since he was a teenager. Since he tried to stand up for his mother; since he couldn't save Bren from his desperate downward spiral; since he saw the casual cruelty of the world to its people, the sad and the lonely, the forgotten and the oppressed, the broken-hearted many, the ones who are lost and lost again.

"The last thing Al wants to do," Ozzy Man said, "is to hurt either of them. But it's still on his list."

"Jesus, Oz," Doppelgänger said, exasperated. "Just stop."

"Al, I think we have several things to talk about." Missy looked professionally mournful.

"Well, this *is* a day for firm decisions," Ozzy Man said. "Or is it?"

"I think you should come back in a few days so that we can make a start to getting a clearer understanding of what goes on in that head of yours," she said, reaching for her diary.

"Definitely not new age—keeping a paper diary like that," Ozzy Man said.

21

"Popcorn and movies go together," Doppelgänger said, "like salt and pepper." Feeling exuberant he added: "Like body and soul. Like bride and groom. Can't have one without the other."

"Like birds and bees," Ozzy Man said. "Like prim and proper. Like nice and easy."

Doppelgänger nodded.

"Like null and void; like cloak and dagger."

Doppelgänger looked sideways at his travelling companion.

"Like forgive and forget; like wait and see; like down and out; like slip and slide."

"Oz, we get it," Doppelgänger said.

"Like touch and go," Ozzy Man said.

Two red buckets of popcorn and two bottles of water cost more than the tickets, making Al wonder about principals and accessories. They were almost alone in the theatre, five-thirty on a Thursday afternoon when only the indolent and the old thought of moving pictures in darkened cinemas. They were, fortunately, in a city surrounded by unseen thousands who kept the economy going.

"What are we seeing?" Al asked.

"*A Slow Wager.* The director used to be in advertising, and the lead man got an Oscar nomination for Best Actor." Kimberley knew all the info; had read the reviews and had heard from her friends who had already seen it.

In the dark they sat with their red buckets, watching slow motion shots of tight, naked, young male buttocks in a swimming pool. An unhappy man, himself a chiselled Adonis, sees those buttocks over and over, always in slow motion while he thinks of suicide. He practices, in stylised artistry, putting the barrel of a gun into his mouth.

"Pull the fucking trigger, Mate," Ozzy Man said.

On screen, the tortured man finds love and dies of a heart attack.

"God, this is so sad," Doppelgänger said, appalled and shocked.

"What did you think?" Kimberley asked, sitting down to grab a quick bite before going home. Outside it would still be early evening, inside the mall it was indeterminate neon-lit daytime.

Al tried to steer a course halfway between his two advisers. "I'm interested in the fact that watching tight, naked, young male buttocks, if you are a man, makes you sensitive—a good person, in touch with your emotions. If you are a woman, it makes you strong and liberated, in control of yourself and your destiny. But if you are man, watching tight, naked, young female buttocks makes you a pervert and a dirty old goat."

"*That's* what you got out of the movie?" She shook her head incredulously.

"Yes, and that the film portrayed loss and desperation with great sensitivity and understanding. And the fact of his unwanted death in juxtaposition to his plans of suicide is the ultimate irony and most damning reproval of the human condition: As soon as you find happiness, there is always a bullet to take it away again. Calvinism in a nutshell. But with a surprising subject for explaining an essentially spiritual concept."

"Yeah," Ozzy Man said. "Life's a bitch. Then you hop on the last rattler."

Kimberley shook her head, trying to disapprove, but smiling at the corners of her eyes. Looking at him steadily, she asked: "But did you *like* it?"

"It's not the kind of film anyone can *like*, is it? You'd have to be mentally ill to enjoy watching so much unhappiness right in front of your nose and say, '*I liked that.*' And I feel, at some level, that I have been manipulated as I was set up to be emotionally vulnerable so that the director could pull the trigger and kill the main character and me at the same time. But there is this: I definitely was very skilfully emotionally manipulated, as he set out to do. The scenes and camera angles were masterful; and he knows about clothes and interior decorating because everything was stylish and picture perfect—not a t-shirt or a pair of slops or a beige couch in sight. And the lead actor was very good. He didn't get the Oscar, though, did he?"

"You can't just say you thought it was good?" Kimberley looked for a simple acknowledgement, bemused despite her impatience with his contrariness.

"I can—it was good. But also made up. If someone is going to make up shit to make me feel bad, and make me pay money and time to see it, has he done me a favour? It's why I read non-fiction."

"You read non-fiction because you're a *man*," Kimberley said, neither as a compliment, nor as criticism. This wasn't the first time she had heard him take against the deep and melancholy sadness of stories made up specifically to be deeply and melancholically sad.

"What you thinking of?" Al changed the topic, pointing at the menu with a look.

Before the waiter came over to their table, Nate and Tracy Moore found them. Tracy had a voice like Sybil Fawlty, and Nate reminded Al of a housetrained bear.

"Hi there," Nate said. "Been to the movies?"

Al nodded. "*And you?*" Smiling with the front of his face.

"We saw the thing about that dog. What's it called?" Nate asked his wife. But she had struck up a monologue with Kimberley,

"Chantal is back at the salon. It's amazing! I have an appointment with her tomorrow afternoon. I'm going with Suzy. We decided to treat ourselves. Chantal is so amazing," she said, deeply into talking mode inside three seconds, while Kimberley smiled warily.

"Fuck me drunk," Ozzy Man said.

"Join us?" Al said.

"Mate!" Ozzy Man held up supplicating hands in poignant combination with his appalled, wide-open eyes.

"He lives with his partner in this amazing space in an old fire station," Tracy told Kimberley. "It's so amazing how they did it up! And he curated the collection. Such sensitivity; and these stunning bold designs and hectic combination of primary colours. It's amazing!"

Ozzy Man pretended to stagger, having become dizzy by how amazing it was.

"They got their licence and opened their doors full-on last month. Their stock has shot up; trading at a P/E of nine," Nate said, letting Al in on a big secret—pity he had missed the part of who *they* were: He had been listening to Tracy's amazement.

"Do you think that loss of global biodiversity is more concerning than deforestation?" Ozzy Man asked. But Al wouldn't allow the question out loud.

"He turned around and he said, he said to me, he said." Nate got ready to tell them what the man had said.

"Smoked salmon salad?" the waiter asked appearing between Nate and a part of his audience. Three more dishes and wine glasses were topped up.

"Enjoy your meal," he said in the tone of voice and accompanying facial expression that wished them apathy all the way to anonymous oblivion.

"I hate it when they do that," Nate said. "Bloody rude. It's a lack of training, I always say. These people should be trained."

"Are you a betting man?" Ozzy Man asked Doppelgänger. "Ten to one against, I offer you: he isn't so annoyed that he won't tell us what the man turned around and said."

"Well, he must put down the plates, and if he waits for the end of your story, the food will be cold," Tracy said, no doubt having previously heard what the man had said.

Nate glowered, forked a mouthful off his plate, started chewing and continued around his mastication. "Anyway, so he turns around and he says, he says to me, he says."

"You've told us that bit already," Ozzy Man said.

"She has this great new homeopath," Tracy said. "The doctors couldn't do a thing for her for years, and in three treatments he has cured her headaches."

"There was this suicidal homeopath," Ozzy Man said, "who took a millionth of a lethal dose."

They finished their meal, mentioned how nice it had been to catch up. "Spontaneous is always the best," Nate said, then said good night. While in the car, Kimberley burst into giggles—the sound Al liked best.

"Are they not simply the most boring people you have ever met?"

"He told me, actually said, *I avoid clichés like the plague.*" Kimberley guffawed.

"And that long story about how he couldn't learn things because, growing up, he had suffered greatly, like David Copperfield, although not with money and hardship and stuff. To paraphrase, he said: *If I was smarter, I would know so much more.*" Kimberley slid down in her seat, laughing without restraint—what Al loved the very most. Bestest.

"Oh dear," Kimberley said, out of breath, wiping a tear from the corner of her eye. "They *are* funny."

They drove home, holding hands in the dark like young ones in love.

"That's the thing," he told Meg over lunch. "She and I see things the same way, we find the same things funny, we are irritated by the same things. When we differ, it is in the nuance of something we are broadly in agreement about. She and I think and do stuff in much the same way, and we don't disagree on any fundamental issue."

"Except jazz," his sister said, dragging on the end of her cigarette.

"Except jazz. Kimberley is nicer and more accommodating than me, and she is truly interested in the minutiae of other peoples' lives. And she cares more deeply, and people like her better than they like me."

"Subject to some exception."

"But we are the same: We aren't deliberately rude to anyone, we don't want to be leaders of men, we aren't overly pleased with ourselves, we are both relatively kind, and neither of us wants to offend." Meg didn't demur, because what he said was broadly true. "She is the girl for me and I am the boy for her."

"A sixty-year-old teenager," she said. "In love."

"Ooh I love to kiss her, love to hold her, love to miss her." Ozzy Man imitated the 60's pop band. "Love to scold her, love to love her like I do."

"And set against that panoply of synonymity and compatibility," Al said, "that long history of togetherness and complicity, there is a young woman with dark eyes and hair who likes me, and I like her. But we don't have a fraction of what Kimberley and I have."

Meg said nothing.

"What the fuck is wrong with me?" he said.

"Oh, for God's sake, Alan." Meg screwed her cigarette butt into the ashtray. "See it for what it is. You didn't expect to have a young, pretty girl befriend you, and you are flattered. Flattered that she wants to be friends; flattered that she asks your opinion and, as you have said, adopts it; flattered that she laughs at your jokes; flattered that she chooses you to spend her time with. And, if you weren't so bound up with responsibility and tied down by duty and obligation, you would admit to yourself that you want to sleep with her. But that, you would never admit, even to yourself. Forget the chance that you would actually *do* it. But because the possibility may, just may exist, you think there's something fundamentally wrong with you. You think, deep down in your soul, that you are just like your father: You are selfish; you think only of yourself; and you treat your wife like shit. That's what you plead guilty to when you prosecute yourself. That's what you convict yourself of as the judge. And really, you've told me so many times it's what you *do*, not what you *think*, that determines whether you have done wrong. What you may or may not have *thought* about Courtney, is irrelevant. It's what you *do* that counts."

Al sighed, felt that his guilt had been confirmed, his doom sealed and delivered. "I *do* do things, Meg. I like being with her, I like chatting to her, I like hearing her laugh. Those are things I should do with Kimberley alone."

"You are a basket case." His sister shook her head helplessly. "What makes you think you can and should feel all of that about only one person? What makes you think you can avoid those feelings and emotions even if you try? Why do you think you can dictate to yourself who you will like, at that most basic of emotional levels where all real affection comes from? The level everybody but you would call love."

"Yeah, Mate," Ozzy man said. "A touch of love, and you will become a poet."

"Have you ever even heard," Meg said, "anybody seriously suggest that you can choose your girl on objective criteria first, and *then* like her, *then* fall in love with her? Like from a shopping list or a menu?"

"That's right, Bud." Ozzy Man agreed with Meg. "Women are meant to be loved, not understood."

"You aren't in charge here, Alan," Meg said. "Nor is anybody else. You did literature courses all through university and you have read and read and read. *You* have told *me* about behavioural psychology, I don't know how many times. How we are predictably irrational. Do you really think you will decide when and how your emotional attachments are formed? Who and in what sequence of events you will get to like someone, and to what extent? You really think that's how it goes? You tell yourself when and when not, and how and how not to fall in love?"

"I'm not in love," Al said.

"So much the better. Even less reason to feel so cut up. And then there is this tiny little thing: Does Courtney tell you what you may and may not do? Who it's OK to see and who not? What you should like and what not? And what you are allowed to wear, and where you should and shouldn't go to fit in with her and her circle of friends?"

"Kimberley is not like that," Al answered, down in the dumps.
"Sure," Meg said.

"Well, that was uplifting," Ozzy Man said in the car on the way home.

"Meg can be so forthright," Doppelgänger said. "And so didactic. She is wrong about Kimberley."

"Yeah, she is. And she's wrong about you too, Buddy." Ozzy Man meant Al. Being who he was, of course he wouldn't let up. "You're as guilty as sin." He said: *gildy as seen.* "Kimberley isn't arse over tits about anyone. That would be you, me old codger."

Doppelgänger made a dismissive hand action, irritated by the charge. Al crumpled further into his culpability.

22

JACARANDAS LINE THE STREETS OF old Northern Johannesburg. In spring they pitch a purple carnival tent over the suburbs, before dropping flowers in their millions, carpeting the avenues and popping under passing wheels like strips of bubble wrap. The people of Johannesburg are proud of the weather. The best in the world, they say. Because it never gets cold, June and July take them by surprise every year. Rather than prepare for the crystal nights that dress every droplet of dew in every fold of grass in a coat of frost, they hang out for spring. When it finally comes, they say to each other: *Gee, that was an unusually cold winter. But look how lovely it is now.* August brings a few weeks when the wind blows you upside down, but if you live in Jozi, you don't remember that either.

Early Friday evening was straight from meteorological heaven: The gentlest breeze, unobtrusive and fresh as from a Bentley's AC, and the digital mercury of the weather App on Al's phone back down into the early twenties. The wispy streaks of a candyfloss-pink sunset had faded to deep cobalt dusk, the moon had risen over the gloaming, and lambent green suburban big-city night had fallen, cosseting the folk who dallied in the slow beginning of another weekend. The table was set outside, on the veranda—ten places with wine- and water-glasses, and matching kenti cloth serviettes.

George, Med School professor, louche and deeply into the welcome of the Cabernet Sauvignon proudly produced by Max Wilkins from his cellar, talked about expectation:

"When a review says you will roll in the aisles, you know that now that you have braced yourself, nothing short of an earthquake will make you roll anywhere. Your level of expectation determines how you will enjoy anything, whether it's a holiday or one of the wonders of the world; or a meal or wine or a cup of coffee; or a film or a TV show or a play."

"Oh, tosh," Leo Lipinski, a flamboyant gay English lecturer and critic, widely recognised for his laborious, self-absorbed conceit, said. His views were expressed as the Voice of Culture, instructive and pedagogic. His tendency was to lecture rather than converse, and he closed his eyes while he did, as if his audience wasn't worth seeing. "The better informed you are, the greater enjoyment you will derive situationally."

"Situationally?" Ozzy Man rolled his eyes. George looked over the rim of his fine crystal glass.

"We think we are objective, but our judgement depends on what we hope to find," George answered, apparently mildly. "The films I've loved most, and the ones I've hated most, are the ones I've known nothing about before the time. When I'm told before the time what to expect, my experience inevitably tends to the average. It can never be as good as an exuberant review; it's seldom as bad as the reviewer says. Especially if he sets himself up as a connoisseur, leader of the exalted elite of refined taste."

Across the table, Leo blanched visibly. Certainly, an animated start to the evening. Max and Tessa, the hosts, looked apprehensive. Edward, senior counsel, and AIDS activist, sat quietly beside Musi, his date for the night. Musi was a novice advocate, a stranger to the group around the table, a pretty young man in an effete sort of way and didn't say boo to a goose all evening. Edward had suffered cruelly at the end of George's tongue over the years, and was anxious to avoid another laceration, particularly if opportunity at the evening's finale might closely follow his conversational performance at its beginning.

"Meaning derives entirely from context," Leo answered, his accent tailored to culture and its preservation. *En-táh-ly*, he said.

"Context is informed by intelligent comment. Opinion of an audience is shaped and refined by that comment."

"Christ, mate," Ozzy Man said. "Spit the dummy."

Kimberley watched, bemusement in her eye; and the final couple, Courtney and Thomas, not knowing what to expect, were out of their depth and quiet as a pair of mice.

George made a so-so face and said: "It's impossible for a film to be brilliant if you have listened to a sermon on its brilliance before you see it. You go with an expectation that it will transcend its medium, somehow will be more than just a film. Even if that's impossible. You expect to find a film with free peanuts and beer, perhaps; or with tips for syncing your camera to your iPhone."

Kimberley suppressed a smile; Leo, for the first time Al had known him, was without an immediate riposte. George wasn't finished.

"I was talking about expectation, not about critique." He sipped the Cab Sav he so liked. "But there are a few things also to be said about film reviews."

"Hee hah!" Ozzy Man said, whooping as he recognized the signs of a shit storm about to make landfall. Max recognised them too, and tried for a diversion: "Everyone have a full glass? Thomas, how's the wine?"

"Uh, it's nice," the podgy banker beamed nervously at his host, nodding like the little nodding man who always nods his head.

"He could have said," Ozzy Man said: "*The nose is intense plum and cedarwood, with an underlying promise of fruity fecundity. The palate is full-bodied and architecturally structured in layers of supporting synergy, intense with blackcurrant and a hint of wild bramble, delicately balanced on the whimsical correspondence between understated tannins and natural acidity.*"

"All of that"—Doppelgänger, tilted his head in complicit agreement—"in a Kalgoorlie accent." The two nodded together smugly—neither of them liked Thomas.

George looked happy to let it go, but Leo wasn't having any of it. "Film is barometric," he said, all but hissing. "A society's advancement and progress are measured by its artistic produce, in these modern times chief amongst them, Film. Those who analyse and interpret Film are the modern shamans, the shapers of the common destiny, the keepers of the collective ethos."

George chuckled indulgently, as if in discussion with an overly enthusiastic and ideological teenager. "You're a shaman? You kill chickens and dance with the spirit fathers?"

"Figuratively. Please don't let your infantility lead you into the trap of literal interpretation."

"Fair enough." George sipped his wine. "The finest achievement of Man is contained in a debate about how expressive Audrey Hepburn's eyes were."

"You undermine your own point when you deliberately understate the importance of literary criticism as a discipline." Leo's voice trembled. "And she was a *very* fine actress." He pulled himself up regally, turning an aristocratic profile to his detractor.

George was in his element: Had he scripted the evening he couldn't have done it better. Tessa was worried that there would be a scene at her table, but the core members of the gang waited eagerly for what their resident academic would say next.

"Acting," he said. "I have heard there is general agreement that Kirk Douglas can't act."

"Precisely," Leo said. "As wooden as a doorpost."

George smiled politely. "I don't actually know what that means: *He can't act*. It doesn't mean he forgets his words, or walks in the wrong direction, or cries when he should laugh, or in a fight he punches the wrong guy. I think it means he doesn't look like a real person—he looks like someone pretending to be someone he isn't."

"Precisely," Leo said, agreeing for a second time, happy how easily things were going his way.

"But here's the thing," George said. "When I watch a movie, I seldom get the impression that someone is *acting*. I just look at some guy doing things, and then I like him, or I don't. I usually just do what the director wants me to do—suspend my disbelief and go with the flow. It is, after all, not the reality that counts. Otherwise, no stage production could ever pass the most fundamental test. Does that mean I am better or worse than you at watching movies?"

"You have to distinguish between movies and Film," Leo said.

"Only if you are a wanker," George said. "I know Jim Carrey *always* irritates me, and I *always* like Jack Nicholson. But it's the type of movies they are in, The *Pet Detective* thing just isn't my cup of tea. And I like Jack's face."

"The Pet Detective is hardly *Film*," Leo said, offended to the core. It wasn't every day someone called him a wanker, *en passant*, before ignoring the very telling distinction he had made with such clarity. "If you are going to refer to *Star Wars* and teenage love dramas, this discussion is not worth pursuing." He turned the aristocratic profile again, like Caesar in an Asterix comic book.

"Metaphors be with you," Ozzy Man said.

"Truly." George was as dry as the scirocco sweeping across 9 million square kilometres of desert. "I also know there is consensus that *the* consummate actress is Meryl Streep. But *she* always behaves as if she knows she is *the* consummate actress; and when she was young, her face was slammed in a door. That's why it's so narrow now."

Leo affected a sharp intake of breath, like an elderly aunt.

"I think a book is your best friend." Tessa made her bid for harmony.

"Outside of a dog, a book is a man's best friend. Inside of a dog, it's too dark to read," Ozzy Man said. Everyone else ignored her.

"Why does Tom Hanks have two Oscars, but Matt Damon none?" George pushed on with his point. "Matt is a very convincing scary person. In fact, if the baddies went to movies once in a while, they would know not to look for trouble with him. And Tom looks as uninteresting as airline pilots always do."

"You are a barbarian," Leo said. "I see you alone are here without a partner." The *non-sequitur* obviously meant to wound deeply. On cue, Leo's partner, a beautiful young stud with a jet-black Mohican plume on top of his head, reached for his hand.

"I got divorced accidentally," George said agreeably.

"Accidentally?" Leo's upwardly rising alto inflection perfectly matched the cocked wrist and splayed fingertips he pressed to his chest.

"From my third wife, yes. I tripped and fell into a vagina."

Courtney spluttered; Leo was, again, without anything to say; and George looked pleased with himself. He continued from before Leo had interrupted: "Sly Stallone was convincing as an avenging Vietnam Vet with a grudge; and all the Spidermen have looked the same to me. Ben Affleck with an anti-aircraft gun in *The Accountant* looked the same as his brother in *Manchester by the Sea*—but the one was apparently good and the other not. Our Charlize always just looks like a pretty girl with nice boobies. Was she good as a Monster, but bad as She-Mad-Max? Or is she good as both? Or got the Oscar for the wrong one? Is Clint Eastwood good or bad? If he rode into a one-horse town where I was on holiday, I would behave respectfully. And if he is an ageing white American with a nice vintage car in a coloured suburb, I would do the same."

Leo huffed, pretended he wasn't listening anymore.

"I saw the film about Gandhi," Thomas said, trying to make his way into the conversation. "It was really good."

Leo ignored him because he had said *film* without the capital letter; and everybody else ignored him because his contribution was so facile. Except Ozzy Man, who said: "Gandhi walked miles and miles, was very thin and didn't brush his teeth. He was a super-calloused fragile mystic vexed by halitosis."

"So, what is a good actress; and what is a bad actor?" George asked. "Is it even possible to compare someone who plays a seventeen-year-old boy with Asperger's who loves opera and wears his grandmother's clothes, with someone who plays a forty-nine-year-old international assassin with a neurotic wife and a Jewish mistress who loves baseball? I just don't know. Maybe they should do the Academy awards like duplicate bridge? Everyone must act the same part in the same movie, and then you pick the best one. On the basis of facial expression, athleticism, accent, good looks and how tall he is."

"You misunderstand completely." Leo couldn't maintain his indifference. "You are so far off the point, it's not worth trying to have this discussion with you."

"Sure. Film critics are like the wine connoisseurs. They can't be wrong—it's a matter of opinion. They egg each other on and then say the same types of shite for each other to agree with, or to have little hissy fits of dispute over: The nose on this cheeky Brunello is leather and pinecone; and Lawrence Olivier is simply divine in *The Plight of Polonius*."

"You understand so little, you shouldn't ever go to the cinema," Leo said.

"But it's you, poor man, who hates the movies you are obliged to see. I read your reviews, and you never like anything. You should ask Edward to help you sue your employers for putting you through the trauma of having to watch all this stuff that offends your rarefied soul."

"We watched a show on TV," Courtney said, breaking her long silence, "where this interviewer has conversations with creatures from alternate universes. Every week there is a different universe, that has different rules and things work not as you would expect them to."

Al, who knew her better than the rest of the party, guessed that she intended to follow up by saying that the credibility of each imaginary universe was determined by the action in it, not by the actors' performance or ability. But George got in first: "I don't like reality TV."

Al saw the poor girl's face burn in embarrassment.

"I really like unreality in movies and shows; and I'm so uncritical." Max came to her defence. "I am disappointingly malleable in a cinema seat; I believe more or less everything that rolls up on screen. When I don't, I think it wasn't a good movie. I never think the acting was bad."

"You people *must* differentiate between movies and Film," Leo said, exasperated.

"As he said before: He never repeats himself," Ozzy Man said.

"There is a massive difference between the two." Leo, who couldn't hear Oz, started lecturing, closing his eyes. "Movies are for the entertainment of the masses and don't deserve serious consideration. Film is an art form, which is determinative of the social and moral progress of the world."

"Eish," George said, then completely disregarded the outburst. "All of it is just entertainment. It can be good entertainment, like Marvelous Marvin Hagler going toe-to-toe with Roberto Duran; or it can be bad entertainment, like WWB World Wrestling. The remedy, if you don't like it, is not to watch. Don't buy a ticket. Don't go. But if you go, see it for what it is—any truth that comes from Film is limited, incidental, superficial, and clichéd. If you rely on Film to interpret the universe for you, you are well and truly fucked." He looked experimentally at Leo to see how his correct differentiation between the sub-categories, coupled with his absolute dismissal of the smart one, had gone down.

"I agree," Kimberley said, before Leo had gathered himself together. "I loved *The Shape of Water*. It has a deliberately B grade Science Fiction feel about it; it deliberately has a very bad Cold War agent and his equally bad superior; it has a *wonderful* soundtrack; and it is shot convincingly, I think, in a no-time-and-place 1950s America where, particularly when it rains, it makes me feel a deep nostalgic loss for a place and time I've never known. I don't care if the girl who didn't speak or change her facial expression was good or bad as an actress. I loved the Film. I felt as if I had to get back there, to where I'd never been, where it's not possible to go. Because the director wanted me to do that. I was completely manipulated, and that's all right by me."

"Film is the reality we have lived in for all of our lives," Edward said. "No wonder you feel nostalgia. It's the place I love most. It's the closest thing I have to a home. I loved *Pan's Labyrinth* even more. And I must agree: It's what the director makes the camera do that has the biggest effect on me. I just dance to the tune he plays."

George looked at him in amazement, lifted his glass in a silent toast.

"Advancing age and red wine erase all memory of our troubles and turn long ago into a gentle haze," Max said. "That's the feeling best captured on the big screen while you sit in front of it with your popcorn."

"Shall we eat?" Tessa asked.

In the car on the way home, Kimberley was amused by George and his antics. She disliked Leo for his pomposity and overbearing confidence, and for having been so boring so often while she has had to listen. She loved the come-uppance he had got. After her chuckles subsided, she said sombrely: "Your little girlfriend was out of her depth." Then added with no humour in her voice: "It was funny how George put her in her place."

"She's not my girlfriend," Al said. *And she wouldn't be so bitchy about you*, he thought.

"And she will smile again," Doppelgänger said, "at the sound of a soft Spanish guitar."

They drove in silence from there.

23

"Oz, be respectful this morning," Doppelgänger said. "The shrink is trying to help."

"I am always respectful," Ozzy Man said. "Even at the dentist. He has fillings too."

Al stepped inside Missy's office, feeling as if he were a wayward schoolboy sent to the Headmaster to describe and explain his affront to the Math teacher.

"You'll be OK, Mate," Ozzy Man said. "She will tell you you're special. Just like everybody else."

When Al was sitting with the footrest up, Missy said: "You told me that your happiness was derivative; it depends on the happiness of other people. It doesn't exist independently. Why do you think that?"

"I think that because it is so. I can't be happy if the people around me aren't. That naturally leaves me with the obligation to make them happy, if only for my own purposes."

"Yeah, Mate," Ozzy Man told the psychologist, "that's what he said last time, and you wanted to know if it was love or if he just wanted to have his knob polished."

The doc didn't take notes as analysts on TV did. She spoke to Al, peering from under her fringe. "We need to unpack a few things you said. Let's begin by considering whether it may perhaps not be more important to make yourself happy, rather than everyone else."

"Told you, Mate," Ozzy Man said. "She's going to tell you to jump the Sheila."

"Oh, she's so not," Doppelgänger said.

The tabby cat Al had seen the week before hopped over the lowest strut of the burglar bars in front of an open window, landing gracefully on her forepaws on the windowsill inside the office, and announcing herself with a little salutatory chirrup.

"Hello, Tort," Missy said, then motioned for Al to answer.

"It's the same thing; there's no difference" Al said. "If I made Kimberley unhappy, I would be miserable—if I made her happy, I would be happy too."

Tort hopped lightly into Missy's lap, curled up and went to sleep. The doc's fingers ran softly through the fur on her back, and Al could hear the purring from where he sat.

"It's a difficult thing to do." Missy tried to reason with him. "Being responsible for someone else's happiness. It doesn't only depend on objective things. She could be unhappy because it's Tuesday, or because she was stuck in traffic, or her coffee was cold. Shouldn't you set your sights on something more attainable, something more useful? To repeat, like your own happiness?"

"Yeah, Mate," Ozzy Man said, "The Buddha says you yourself, as much as anybody in the entire universe, deserve your love and affection."

Al was silent for a while, thinking how best to explain why both Missy and the Buddha hadn't got what he meant. "Doc, I think you're missing the circularity, the equivalence of the cause and the effect: I want to be happy, but can only be if Kimberley is happy. If she isn't, it's literally impossible for me to be."

"You aren't often happy then, I take it? With the high bar you set for yourself?"

"On the contrary," Al said, slightly puzzled, "I'm happy most of the time. It's just when I am faced with an irresolvable conflict, that I don't know what to do. The issue, as I told you, is that I want both Kimberley and Courtney to be happy in their connection to me. I know that connection may be less important for them; but in the context of *my* life, it's pivotal. From my point of view, their contemporaneous happiness doesn't seem to be possible. And because they can't both be happy, neither can I. That's the problem in a nutshell."

In the thick greenery outside, a barbet was hiding. It soothed the afternoon with its high trilling song. *Don' cha worry*, it sang. *About a 'ting.*

"Yep," Ozzy Man said, reaching for authority from a different source of spiritual advice: "Behold the fowls of the air. For they sow not, neither do they reap, nor gather into barns; yet, your heavenly Father feeds them."

Missy's mobile phone buzzed—it was on silent but skittered noisily on the little table at her elbow. She silenced it without looking to see who was trying to talk to her. "But Alan, do you not think you should concentrate on yourself? What do *you* want? Make you the important person."

"I agree, Mate," Ozzy Man said, nodding enthusiastically. "You must not care so much what you are to others as you care what you are to yourself."

"Enough with de Montaigne," Doppelgänger said, wanting Al to take Missy seriously.

"I quote others only in order the better to express myself," Ozzy man said.

Dobby needn't have worried—Al agreed with Missy: "Yes, it would be a smart idea to concentrate on myself, to be my own number one, to rule my whole world. But do you think I choose to be the way I am? Do you think it's my idea never to be at peace, when the tides in the affairs of this one man turn out to be either flood or famine? I wish I could be different. I wish I could be *indifferent* to how the people around me are and behave, and whether they will think I'm nice or not. But I care. More deeply than I know why; more intimately than I can escape." He looked at the woman across the table. "Doc, am I just wasting my time here? Am I wasting yours?"

"Certainly not." Missy said, quietly, no smile. "I think you need to learn the virtue of selfishness."

"Mate! I hope she's not a closet Ayn Rand fan," Ozzy Man said. He didn't like either her financial theory or her elitist chauvinism, even though he did quite fancy the science fiction.

Missy, of course, paid no attention to the interruption, carried on speaking: "Winnie the Pooh said: *Some people care too much. I think it's called love.*"

"I can't believe she quoted Winnie the Pooh at you," Doppelgänger said.

"Same middle name as Vlad the Impaler," Ozzy Man said.

"Doc, I don't mind what you call it. I have a practical problem I need advice on. What do I do about Courtney?"

Tort lay curled up in the Doc's lap, fast asleep. On the wall, the red second hand of a clock ticked the seconds off one-by-one. Missy sounded almost impatient when she answered: "I can't tell you what to do, Al. That, you have to work out for yourself. I can only help you gain clarity on the context within which you should make your decision. You have to think it through for yourself."

"Yup," Ozzy Man said, "being emotionally disorderly means you can make new discoveries."

Al said nothing. In the ensuing silence Missy said: "You have to decide what about these two women complements the enjoyment of your own life."

"There is another, almost comical, side to it," Al said. "I can't properly enjoy anything unless I tell Kimberley about it. Until I do, it feels incomplete. But at the moment, even though I want to tell Kimberley of my conversations with Courtney, I can't. If anything in the world absolutely forbids me from having an affair, it's that. If I had a good time, I'd want to go straight home and tell Kimberley about it. Otherwise, it's only half done."

Missy made big eyes, made it her turn to say nothing.

"After years of therapy"—Ozzy Man smiled at them in the pause—"the shrink said to his patient, *No hablo Ingles.*"

"I feel worst when I can't make good on the promise I have made to someone: *I will take care of you,*" Al said. "If I then fail to take care of or to protect that person, from the random insults of life, I feel it intimately. It messes with my equilibrium."

"Did you promise Kimberley you will keep her happy always?" Missy asked.

"Oh absolutely," Al said without a second's hesitation. "I promised her that almost as soon as we met. I repeated the promise in front of a hall full of people, but that was just for form—my obligation comes from long before that."

While Missy was still thinking about that, Al thought to tell her more.

"You see, Missy, when a pretty young woman gets married to a young man, she is so vulnerable. She puts all her eggs in one basket, hands them over to the guy and hopes for the best—*please don't smash them*, she asks with all the hope of her being. Then she is duty bound to believe that he won't because she has no other option. She stands or falls by his integrity. If he treats her well, she has so much left to give: to him, to their life together, to their kids, to the world in general. If he turns out to be a selfish prick, she is so stymied. She has so little to start over with."

In the distance Al heard a saxophone playing a long wailing note. "It's a siren, silly arse," Ozzy Man said.

"You see it all the time," Al said. "Couples where the woman's career and interests take distant second place to her domestic obligations; and then her husband finds love in a fresh pair of legs under a much younger miniskirt. He moves on; but she is stuck. He's okay—he has a life and a big income, and looks ever so handsome, standing on his thick cheque book. He leaves his wife responsible for their children, compromised in finding a proper job, poor by comparison to him, and with little chance of starting again—certainly with no chance of a second family. The dice are so loaded. It's so unequal, so unfair. That's why I can't be that guy."

Missy listened, couldn't disagree. "Yes, you must take your responsibility seriously, I agree. And you must behave properly and honestly. But are you permanently responsible to make Kimberley happy, no matter what?"

"Pretty much, Doc," Doppelgänger said. He would know.

"Pretty much, Doc," Al replied. "She deserves the best I can give. Forever."

Silence slid down the wall, landed on the rug between them, while Missy thought what next to say to this old fella. Eventually, she murmured, making big eyes: "Wow. It again sounds a lot like love to me, but you don't want to get into a terminological debate. Tell me, though, what must you protect her from?"

"From everything," Al said without hesitation. "From the communist behind every bush; from myself; from when the world just capriciously decides to mess with her. Last year, for my birthday, she went to so much trouble, booking a restaurant on the crest of the Auckland Park ridge, where we would sit on the wide-open patio and see all the way to the Magaliesberg, over the heads and the noise of the city. We would be king and queen of the afternoon. But even though she had emails confirming the booking, when we got there, the place was closed; and she was so disappointed. I felt awful for her, felt I had failed her somehow."

"But, Alan," Missy said, "that is putting the standard way too high. You could never watch out for every little thing. You can never change the whole world, keep that sort of thing from happening. You have not a snowball's hope. Sometimes shit happens."

"Hee-hee," Ozzy Man said, laughing. "At last you get it. Numb Nuts here needs everything to go according to his personal script. Otherwise he thinks the world is a hat full of arseholes, and he's chief amongst them."

Al ignored the summary of his deficiencies. "I agree I can't change it or prevent it. But that doesn't keep me from wanting to. The point is that I want to keep her happy, and that includes saving her from disappointment."

"Disappointment is inevitable. Nobody dies from disappointment," Missy said.

"Ah, Missy," Ozzy Man said, disapproving—she'd been doing so well until then, he had thought. "There's a lot of things people don't die from but would avoid with dedication: Country music; volunteers who work for non-profit organisations; golfing stories, karaoke bars; herpes."

"There is more than one kind of disappointment," Al said. "There is disappointment that comes from an unfortunate confluence of random events. Nothing you can do about it. Irritating, but not a massive emotional drain. Then there is disappointment caused by third parties, strangers, who opportunistically or carelessly disappoint your expectations. They cheat you or they let you down. Emotionally there is a difference between the two—being let down isn't great, but it's better than being deliberately cheated. But you deal with it without feeling as if you have been fundamentally betrayed."

"Blessed is he who expects nothing," Ozzy Man said, "for he shall never be disappointed."

"The final category is the real bugger," Al said. "The one that really gets you down; Disappointment caused by someone you trust not to disappoint you. That's the one that wipes you out, puts you on the canvas for the full count of ten. You trusted the person implicitly not to let you down; you knew with certainty that he never would—and then he does. Missy, that's the one we are talking about. Except not talking as a victim. No. I am the villain—I am the one *causing* the disappointment. I am the person devastating the well held expectation, betraying the trust. And that, being the person causing such disappointment, is the worst position I can put myself in. I don't know if I can ever recover from that."

"Yeah, Doc," Ozzy Man said, adding his two cents, "get it now: Numb Nuts worries he will be that guy either with Kimberley or with Courtney or with both."

The doctor looked quietly at Al, thinking of what he had said.

"Let's approach this differently," she said. "Was there ever a time when you were completely happy?"

Al nodded. "Of course, yes. I'm happy often—just right at this moment I'm facing a crisis that is making me very unhappy."

The psychologist wrote a short note in her book, probably to remind herself to book a long series of appointments; perhaps making a note of her incipient frustration with Al's world view. "Let's talk about something else: You've said you weren't sure what love is?"

"Yes," Al said. "I think I know what it does; but what it is, I'm not sure."

"What does it do?" Missy asked.

"It creates the hopeless aspiration that I can shield someone from the deep sadness of daily existence," Al said.

"You can't say anything," Ozzy Man said, rolling his eyes, "in a straightforward way. Can you, mate?"

Al ignored him. "Take her back with me to a time and a place where it's safe and warm: Shelter her from the storm." Looking out the window he added, wary of incurring further scorn of the working man from Down Under: "As in DH Lawrence's poem: *If but I could have wrapped you in myself.*"

"That's not bad," Missy said, nodding. Then asked: "You feel that way about both Kimberley and Courtney?"

Outside, the shy fountain was singing its delicate trickle. Al thought how best to put the conundrum into words.

"In varying degrees, yes, I do. Kimberley ranks first, has always done; will always do. But that doesn't help me decide what I should do. Doesn't remotely begin to tell me how to reconcile the conflict between what I owe Kimberley and what I owe Courtney. Or what I should do next."

"We need to talk about this some more." Missy all but sighed. "Next time."

"Mate," Ozzy Man said, choosing this moment to test his semantic and logical conclusion, "if you are right about what love does, and that's exactly how you feel about Courtney, what the serious fuck are we arguing about? How is it that you don't love her?"

"Al loves Kimberley, you know that," Doppelgänger said.

"As an answer to my question, that's not right," Ozzy Man said. "It isn't even wrong."

The doc wrote a new appointment into her book and Tort woke up for long enough to stare at Al in an impenetrable yet insouciant dismissal.

"What you think?" Doppelgänger asked when the three of them had been driving for a while in brooding silence.

"I like that cat," Ozzy Man replied.

25

"**A** MAN LEAVES HIS OFFICE ONE evening, and heads for a wine bar around the corner for a drink," Doppelgänger said.

"Mate," Ozzy Man said, looking alarmed, "not another story?"

"No, not a story. This one is real."

Al pulled a shirt over his head, patted it down, asked: "Are you busy for lunch?"

Kimberley was lacing her sneakers—Air Jordans she had seen on a reality show. Two trendy presenters, pneumatic with toothy-white American smiles, find a frumpy slob, give her a haircut, clean up her teeth, pluck her eyebrows and put make-up on her, squeeze her into a dress with attitude and décolletage, and voilà! The new you. With much breathless gushing about there being no limit when you believe in yourself, actualise your potential, and reach for your dreams. Be who you are—you are a person, unique and special; and this is what you can do to change your ordinariness and be successful and glamourous like me. Sometimes that potential for self-actualisation is reached with the aid of a pair of colourful Air Jordans that look nice to an interested, if not committed, viewer.

"I've told you," she answered.

Al kept quiet, trying to remember what she'd told him about her day. He couldn't think of the conversation or when they had discussed it.

"It ain't that I don't hear." Ozzy Man added his voice to Kimberley's with a snatch from John Mayall. "I just don't listen no more."

Al could, accurately and effortlessly, remember the financial spreadsheets and corporate structuring of the stuff he did without noticeable passion or overt interest—but after thirty-plus years of being married, there were still distant relatives in Kimberley's family Sequoia he couldn't place. Her circle of acquaintances defeated him regularly.

"Hi, Al. Is Jesse back from his trip in Italy?" a complete stranger would ask. Al hoped that his friendly smile and slick second-person sincerity would get him out of the hole.

"Hi there! Yes, he's back, thanks. And how are *you*? And the family? Planning any trips?"

He suspected that he had offended a good many people over the years. The ones who didn't have a family; the ones who couldn't or didn't go on trips because of liquidity problems, incapacity, or psychosis. He had read with joy about Prosopagnosia, also called Face Blindness. Brad Pitt has it. Schalk Brinkman, his friend and doctor, declared that this is not what he had—he simply was a forgetful twit.

"Tell me again?" he asked Kimberley.

"Why would I bother? You're not interested." Kimberley was putting in earrings, tiny golden studs.

"The Auntie's in a mood, Mate," Ozzy Man said, rolling his eyes.

"She's just narked that Al doesn't remember what she tells him," Doppelgänger said.

"I'm just asking if you'll have lunch with me," Al said quietly, squashing the first tendril of irritation way down into the kitbag.

"Well, you know I can't." She flicked her hair haughtily.

"Okay," he said evenly, inclining his head, chin to the left. "How about tomorrow?"

"You *never* listen," she said, emphasising the adverb. Giving it status and reality, putting it out front. The correct word order in English, Mrs. Smart told them, writing it on the blackboard, is Manner, Place, Frequency and Time. *Rover waits patiently at the back door every morning before dawn.*

"I assume that means, No, Bud," Ozzy Man said. Doppelgänger kept quiet.

Adjectives are more complicated even. They go: Opinion, Size, Age, Shape, Colour, Origin, Material, and Purpose: *She had the figure of a beautiful, amply proportioned, mid-century, curvaceous, olive-brown, Spanish, lacquer wood, acoustic guitar.* Al arm-wrestled Mr. Irritation's red hair back down into the bottom of that bag, pulled the drawstring tight around the mouth.

"Come on," he said. "Let's have lunch. How about Thursday?"

"Oh, for God's sake," Kimberley snapped. "You know what happens on Thursday." She grabbed her bag and her keys and headed for the door. Al stood silently staring after her. She opened the door, turned back to him, and said, gimlet-eyed: "Just have lunch with your floozy."

Then she was gone.

"Well, at least *she'll* fucking say, Yes," Ozzy Man said.

Al stood in the hall, watched her on the security monitor. She walked down the steps; her car backed out the drive; the motor gate closed. He hadn't moved a muscle; had managed that elusive thing Holy Men spend many years meditating for—he hadn't allowed a single thought into or out of his head. Complete inner silence. Doppelgänger had put Ozzy Man in a headlock, whispered dire threats lest he should utter a syllable.

Without a word to himself or either of his companions, Al walked to the veranda, sat down, stared at the garden. His thoughts moved in languid shapes, a lava lamp of slowly rising and sinking synaesthesia. The calm, blue expanse of morning around a diffuse centre; a mild russet-orange border of other people and their issues; an indeterminable aloofness slowly expanding in cornfield-yellow, oval, and languid, repainting the morning and everything in it. Al closed his eyes, and, despite that he had only just got out of bed, fell into a light snooze.

Ten minutes later he woke. The cornfield was still there, in the background now, as the cosmic radiation of a Big Bang. He picked up his phone, dialled Courtney's number.

"Hey," she answered brightly. "I was just thinking of you."

"I can't complain about that," he said. "Fancy a bit of lunch?"

"That's why I was thinking of you; I'm hungry," she said, either teasing or answering sincerely, he never could tell.

"Already?" Al was amazed how healthy her appetite was and how slim she stayed. "Pick you up at 12:30? Where do you want to go?"

"Prizzy's?"

"Sounds good."

"12:30," she said and hung up.

Al kept his thoughts locked up, remained aloof; sat in vacant silence with no discernible thought in his head.

"Don't be aloof," Ozzy Man told him. "Too many of those. Be alert."

"Yeah, yeah." Doppelgänger closed him down, by his standards, rudely.

Al still hadn't entirely recovered his good mood when, a while later, Courtney bounced into the car, smiling. "I'm doing a piece," she said before the door closed, "on celery. It grows in a humid, warm climate; but if it gets above 25° C the whole crop gets bitter. Below 15° C, it dies. So much trouble for such a horrible plant. Who eats it, anyway?"

"I can't stand it," Al said. "Or coriander."

"They're from the same family. Same trouble to grow them both."

"Maybe my family is not so bad then after all. Why are you writing about it?"

"It's sort of an infomercial. It looks like objectively researched journalism, but it's an advert that says: *Eat lots of Celery!* I understand why people need to be encouraged."

"How do you avoid saying how awful it is and remain pretend-objective?"

"Some people actually like it." She looked at him, mock alarm in her dark eyes. "That's what the research says, anyhow. I'll say, *It may taste terrible, but it's healthy, won't make you fat; and it's better than coriander.*" She laughed. An icicle broke off Al's heart; and the morning felt better. At the table she ordered, with chilly on the side and sparkling water.

"I've got this new App that tracks your television watching and what you surf on the net. It syncs your phone to your TV."

"I changed my username to *Titanic*," Ozzy Man said, breaking one of the longest silences of his career. "My laptop is syncing now."

"The App collates the information it collects from your devices and directs your viewing. It loads shows for you, lines up sites for you to look at. It's so cool." She was genuinely stoked, excited at the prospect of so many undiscovered gems waiting for her.

"You're not concerned about privacy, and all that stuff?" Al asked.

"Perhaps. But it's *so* useful." Pragmatic Courtney, happy and up-beat.

"Have you seen the meme of Mark Zuckerberg sitting next to a kid who is on his laptop?" Al asked. "The kid turns to Zuck and says, *My dad says you spy on us.* MZ looks at him sidelong; says, *He's not your dad.*"

Courtney's throaty chuckle melted the last of the ice around his morning. Al gathered up his knife, his fork, and his mood.

"I started watching a new series last night, about these three guys who invented new technology for facial recognition. If you install it in a public place, you can program it to look for a particular person and track him throughout the whole day. They use it to track this billionaire to whom they want to sell the technology. They make a film of him, to show him in the sales pitch. But while he is being tracked and recorded without knowing it, he meets the head of a crime syndicate."

In the middle of her story of intrigue and deception, near-world sci-fi and pandemic crime, Al suddenly thought of Kimberley. She grabbed her bag and her keys and headed for the door, where she turned back. "*Just have lunch with your floozy,*" she had said. Al felt rushing anger, looking much as wide-eyed and wild-haired Michael Keaton in *Beetlejuice*, halfway out the kitbag. Like a cartoon burglar getting through a window.

"She didn't mean it," Doppelgänger said. Ozzy Man made no comment but silently underscored his deep annoyance with Kimberley in a reverberating Kalgoorlie accent.

Courtney's story had got to the point where the three young guys are fighting for their lives, by making a comprehensive video record of the gangster and his mob, but then the CIA appears on the scene, venal and corrupt. She hadn't noticed the shadow flit across his brow. When their coffee came, his a ristretto as strong as Mike Tyson, hers frivolous with foam, she was onto another topic:

"Jaguar has brought out an electric sedan, they call I-Pace. It looks great. It's fast and has a 400km range. Jaguar claims 480km, but the reviewer says that's an exaggeration."

"You fancy getting one?" he asked.

"They are expensive. You can get more for your money with conventional technology."

"And screw the planet?"

"And screw the planet," she said.

She bounced out the car with the same panache as she had bounced in. She hadn't said a thing all afternoon of her dreary life with the chubby banker. Al was thankful—he felt like a dreary banker himself. Kimberley was at home when he got there, but distant and withdrawn.

"What the fuck, Mate?" Ozzy Man exclaimed, hands spread in incredulity, like a carpet salesman in the Grand Bazaar.

"Everybody gets in a mood sometimes," Doppelgänger said.

"Yeah," Ozzy Man said. "She's waiting for an apology. Numb Nuts here always pops one out the bag sooner or later."

Al sat alone in the lounge long after Kimberley had claimed a tactical, if unspecific, ailment and had gone to bed. *I'm very tired*, was the usual formulation.

"Before you got married," Ozzy Man said, "you used to sit alone in the evenings with no one to talk to. Now that you are married, you sit alone in the evenings with no one to talk to—except that you aren't allowed to listen to music."

"Nonsense," Doppelgänger said. "She usually doesn't go to bed this early; and Al doesn't have to stay up until all hours—he chooses to. And he has earphones."

Night is when words fade and things come alive, Antoine de Saint-Exupery wrote. Al felt the shape of it but couldn't say it in words. He knew she wanted to hurt him because he had hurt her. He could no longer die before he fucked up because he had fucked up already. He drifted back to the memory of a cold linoleum floor and a candle in the bedroom in his grandma's house; two boys kneeling while the old girl listened to them say together:

"Now I lay me down to sleep,
I pray thee, Lord, my soul to keep.
If I should die before I wake,
I pray thee, Lord, my soul to take."

25

*H*EY THERE, GARY,
    *I'm delighted you eventually put a TV in the house.
I know you say Candice made you do it, but we are
a quarter way through the 21st century. A TV in the house is
principal amongst the stigmata of contemporaneity.*

*You're a screen writer, so I suppose it's a good thing to have.
Well done! It will put you in greater contact with the ethos and
social practices of the Now Generation. But lately I have gotten
so impatient with TV shows. Cantankerous and old, is maybe
the correct explanation, but I can hardly get myself to watch.
Kimberley watches any number of shows and programs. She and
everyone I know recommend lists of things I simply must watch.
I try, but I don't do well.*

*I recently read a letter written by Ernest Hemingway to
Scott Fitzgerald, who had asked him his view of his latest book,
one I hadn't heard of. Hemingway says: 'You write well, but your
characters are not believable, nor is what they do.' And there's the
essence of my complaint about TV show. I can't take the leap of
faith, can't make myself believe it's real.*

*Not that my threshold is high, I am prepared to believe any
number of things, provided that they are true in a context. When
Rutger Hauer, the icy-blue-eyed and blond cyborg warrior told
Harrison Ford, in Bladerunner, on a rainy rooftop in futuristic
San Francisco that he had seen attack ships on fire off the shoulder*

of Orion, and C-beams glitter in the dark near the Tannhäuser Gate: The moments that will be lost in time, like tears in rain, I believed. Man, did I believe. Because that's exactly how an icy-blue-eyed and blond cyborg warrior would behave and what he would say at the moment of his ultimate crisis. But what I can't get myself to believe is the abused wife and the crooked politician and dishonest cop and unscrupulous businessman who pollute a valley where the Methodists live, and they sell drugs to pre-pubescent handicapped kids who were sex-trafficked from their war-torn country (to get away from)/(by) Islamists/Racists/Russians/ Greedy Corporates. Them I don't believe. They just irritate me.

But nuff o' that.

More serious matters: I'm afraid the storm is breaking or may already have broken. Kimberley has become more and more tight lipped about Courtney, and my having lunch with her every day. I know it sounds weird, that every day part of that sentence. But I don't have many friends who are available during the week. Hell, I don't have many friends full stop. Kimberley flits around from arrangement to engagement to commitment to assignation; but I don't. I'm at heart a butterfly too, I just don't live where the flowers are. I miss the company, the interaction, if I just do nothing. The only person realistically available for me to have lunch with is… well, Courtney. When we do meet, it's light, it's easy, it's quick—we have lunch and that's it. Afterwards I come back home and think about the fate of Mankind and the struggle between Good and Evil. (I think Good is kicking ass, definitely getting ready for the final victory.)

I get Kimberley's beef. It looks as if I have more time for Courtney than for her (Defence: Kimberley is always busy, won't have lunch with me—figures we have breakfast and dinner to-gether already). Her circle of bitchy acquaintances see me with Courtney regularly—I don't try to hide—and they do the Steel Magnolia thing on Kimberley. They gossip behind her back; and in front of her back they sympathise (without appearing to ad-mit that they do—it's a female thing) about the other woman, and that makes Kimberley feel foolish. (Defence: They are such venomous life forms; she should wear PPE when they are near. But I know that is a male point of view. Aren't I sailing close to the heteronormatively patriarchal wind? And you thought I was a wuss.) She feels that she has lost her priority ranking in our nation of two. It used to be only her, and now it's her and Courtney (Defence: She's still, unquestionably, in pole position: I am friends with Courtney, I'm neither her paramour nor her sugar daddy. Nor am I her life-long companion, associate, part-ner, confederate, ally, confrère, consociate or husband. But I know emotion plays out better on a stolen guitar and isn't translatable to linear equations and precise formulation.)

You know, my distant and wise friend, I am well and truly fucked. The one thing in life I don't want to be, is a douche. I don't want to let anyone down. I know that sounds naïve and unachievably aspirational, but that's how it is. I just want to be nice and to be liked. Monica Lewinsky had it worse than me— she told the reporters all she ever wanted to be was world famous.

I have exactly two people in my daily face-to-face life (Jesse is far away, and I listen to his news, I don't make it) and I'm going to be a complete prick to one of them. Yup, inescapable is my future and inexorable is my fate: I'm going to be an unforgivable arsehole to Courtney—I'm going to say, Sorry, pal; our race is run; our days are done—So long, and thanks for all the fish. There's no way to avoid it, no way to escape it. I hate that I'm going to do it, hate that I have to do it, hate that I have gotten myself into a position where it's necessary to do. It snuck up on me—I didn't really do anything: One day we weren't friends, and the next day we were. I wasn't really in control, didn't think it through until it was too late. Even if I had tried to think it through, I'm not sure there was anything I could have done. My fault is in my stars, not in myself. Brutus. And yes, I shot the Sheriff.

The reason I'm telling you is to ask if you won't please come here and do it for me? I'll pay for your ticket and put you up in a hotel. You are so much more confident than me, better with words, and in social interactions. And you have experience—you've done this kind of thing before. If you come over, I'll just run away and hide. Then, I'll never have to look at Courtney and never see her disappointment that I turned out to be just another unreliable, fickle, bullshit artist, just another prick in the wall. And I also will never have to see the accusation in Kimberley's eye, or hear her ask: Lama Sabachthani? Which I fucking well haven't.

If you were a good friend … You know I would do it for you.

Well, OK. If you won't, you won't. But Gary, my friend, I hate what I'm about to do. And it's so much my own fault. And so not my own fault. Ah, Christ. I shouldn't have made friends—I should have been here to win.

Think of me now in my hour of need. And when I write again, I will still be

Yours without wax

Al

26

"ALI AND CARLA SAW YOU today," Kimberley said to Al over dinner.

"Yes, I saw them too," he said. "At Horatio's. They were just passing by, not eating. I think they said they were on their way to *Kaapse Draai*."

She wasn't interested in the detail: "They say you were looking very cosy."

"Mate." Ozzy Man's head came up in alarm. "What's going on?" He said: *gohwin awn*. Then he added a warning: "Watch out for that word *cosy*."

"Yes, it *is* a nice place," Al agreed amiably, his misunderstanding deliberate. But not effective. A silence settled that was more than just the absence of conversation.

"Jean-Paul Sartre distinguishes ontologically between absence and not being present," Doppelgänger said. "Or maybe not—philosophy isn't exactly my strong point."

"What'd he mean, Bud?"

"He says there's a difference between somebody not being in the room because he has nothing to do with it situationally; and not being there even though he is expected to be. Like if you go visit a married couple, but the wife isn't there and the guy jumps around serving tea without saying where she is. Or the same married couple in their executive apartment on the Atlantic seaboard in Mouillé Point, and John Brown, the bus driver from Essex, isn't there." Doppelgänger thought about that, added, "I think."

"Therefore, you are, Mate," Ozzy Man said. "So, there's a difference here and now between them not talking about the Large Hadron Collider and this awkward silence?"

"Zackly," Doppelgänger said, imitating his evil twin.

"Why do you have lunch with her every day?" Kimberley said, breaking the silence.

"What are you going to say now, Mate?" Ozzy Man raised both eyebrows. He said: *whatcha gowna say?*

"I had lunch with her today because you weren't available," Al said mildly.

"That's not what I asked. I said, *Every Day*. Why *Every Day?*"

"Well, there's no compelling reason. She is my friend. Neither of us have anything else to do at lunch, so we meet. All we do is eat, and then we go home again. It takes an hour; often less."

Kimberley left a long enough pause to let him know that his answer didn't remotely cut it. Then asked: "Why don't you have lunch with your other friends?"

Doppelgänger looked at Al steadily. Ozzy Man made big, round eyes, silently repeating his what-are-you-going-to-say-next line of inquiry. "Yeah, Bud. Why the fuck not?" He added for emphasis.

"I don't have many friends; and the ones I do have, work during the day. Henry is retired, but he is so obsessed with his troubles, I would shoot myself halfway through. Tim talks only about the stock exchange. Chico is a swimming coach, and I don't want to listen to how his twelve-year-old students are doing in age group competitions. And Gary is in Los Angeles. I'm not exactly spoilt for choices."

Silence flooded back into the room, not the Hadron Collider type.

"Sartre goes into a coffee shop and orders his without cream," Ozzy Man said. "*We're all out of cream, Sir*, the waitress says. *Can I give it to you without milk?*"

"Oz, give it a break," Doppelgänger said irritably.

"If you like her so much, why don't you just move in with her?" Kimberley said.

Al just looked at her, didn't reply. From the many things he wanted impulsively to say, none seemed likely to not blow the exchange into the stratosphere. Dinner heaved itself sluggishly to the point where Kimberley left for the television set.

"Ah fuck, man," Al thought, without elaborating.

"She's not being reasonable," Doppelgänger said, shaking his head.

Al shook his head too. "I'm not sure you're right, Dobby. If you see it from her point of view, what she says does make sense. No doubt those two poison arrows we saw at lunch couldn't wait to tell her they saw me with Courtney. They wouldn't have said anything directly but would have mixed up a thick paste of innuendo to smear on the very ordinary sandwich of their story. They have seen us before; and if they can't say anything nice about someone, someone like Courtney, they are ever so happy. It's what they live for: It's the one thing that still brings them orgasmic delight. Being a bitch is a calling—it takes both practice and dedication."

Al cleared away, put on the kettle. "If I go ask if she wants coffee, she will say, *No*. Without looking at me. If I don't ask, she will be furious."

"So, ask." Doppelgänger couldn't see the difficulty.

"Would you like a cup of coffee?" Al poked his head around the door.

"No," she said, monotone, keeping her eyes on the screen.

"And fuck you and the horse you rode in on." Ozzy Man completed her sentiment, just so Al wouldn't be in any doubt.

Al took the cat and his coffee outside to the veranda.

"Is an overview of other people's mistakes relevant?" Doppelgänger wanted to know. "Does it matter where on the spectrum you fit?"

"What are you banging on about?" Ozzy Man asked.

"Well, if we think of the people we know and what they have done, does that tell us what bad shape Al is in? Mario Romano took his secretary to Australia for the World Cup, and Fi didn't say she was following him, but knocked on the door of his hotel room at ten one night. He says he opened the door with his boner sticking through the slit in the gown he'd put on when there was someone at the door."

"Hee-Hee," Ozzy Man said, laughing. "It cost him a new BMW convertible, a cruise around the Bahamas, and several years of complete submission."

"Then there's Alec Thomas," Doppelgänger said, "whose missus had a son on a Wednesday; and whose girlfriend had a daughter, the next day, on Thursday."

"But, Mate," Ozzy Man said, "it's not his fault. His full names are Alec John Thomas."

"Hee-Hee." Doppelgänger laughed, as if he were the other. Then he said: "Anthony Newton has had several girlfriends. Louise has known about most of them, if not all. She even knows he takes them on his golfing trips with him."

"He's a stud, Mate," Ozzy Man said in awe.

"I don't know where you two are going with this," Al regarded them from under lidded eyes. "None of it is relevant. They're not me; what they do isn't what I do."

"I agree, of course, Alan." Doppelgänger immediately became more considered. "But seeing the thing in its context, in a continuum of possible offences, does allow you to form a view of how serious this is; how seriously you should take it."

"Aw, Bud." Ozzy Man turned in disbelief to Doppelgänger. "*Please. That's such* bullshit. Everything is contextual. You have to measure everything within its own set of circumstances and according to its own rules. You don't play chess by following the rules of Pokémon. Some people have such a fucked-up context, you can hardly credit it. But to them it's real—that's how they live their lives, and that's how they weigh things up. It's the same as how lethal bullets are in a movie. In some, thousands are fired, and one guy ends up with a scrape and a hole through his hat. In another, one is fired and it kills someone."

"It's seldom I agree with Oz," Al said warily. "But he's right. Yeats was in love for his whole life with Maud Gonne; but she wouldn't allow him anywhere near her because he wasn't fervent enough about the Irish cause. To them that was normal. He even defends it convincingly, and as if it were a good thing. Kimberley doesn't tell me to devote my life to Sinn Fein because that's not our thing."

"Yeah," Ozzy Man said. "They're such pussies."

Al opened his Kindle, read a story about a man who loves a woman, Beatriz, and, following her memory, finds an eyepiece from which to see all of existence—a place from which to perceive the entire Universe in one place and at one time. In an instant he saw millions of things happening and being done, some alluring for their beauty, others appalling for their cruelty; he saw all possible objects, not one of them in the same space as another, without overlap and without being crowded; he saw all of space, actual and undiminished; he saw the living oceans; he saw the break of day and the fall of night; he saw all the mirrors on earth and none of them reflected him. And in it all, he gets a greater understanding.

"I can't say I get it," Ozzy Man said, shaking his head.

"He means the great, consoling equanimity that comes from realising that tension amongst the parts is illusory. It's the wood, not the trees. It's the totality, not the detail. The final lesson of all religion," Doppelgänger explained, "is that our individuality, distinct and separate from the rest of existence, is incomplete. We are part of a greater whole. The Christians want to be one with God; the mystics look for enlightenment, achieving full understanding of Life."

"And that teaches us humility?" Ozzy Man looked for a hook from which to dangle his cynicism.

"Not necessarily. But it does put our actions into perspective: We can't fight the world, because we are part of it. We can't buck the trend, because we are the trend."

"Trend is your friend," Ozzy Man said.

"It is." Doppelgänger completed his train of thought, ignoring the interruption. "Fighting with the world is fighting with yourself, guaranteed to keep you from contentment. To stay in tune requires that you appreciate both your vanishing insignificance and your inextricable part of the harmonious, composite whole."

"I have to tell Courtney I can't see her again, I can't be her friend anymore," Al said, ignoring the esoteric debate. "I feel dreadful about it—I'm not sure how I'm going to do it." He sat in glum silence, staring at the dark garden.

"She thinks Kimberley likes her, is her pal," Doppelgänger said.

"Bud." Ozzy Man rolled his eyes. "Don't be so fucking naïve. These Sheilas are much smarter than you think. She tells Al shit about Kimberley to make him feel better. She knows it looks to everybody, except to Numb Nuts here, that she is trying to jump a claim."

"Oz, I just don't think that you are right," Al answered his Devil's Advocate. "Courtney doesn't think of me as a real man. I am an old fella who is kind and listens to her; and she is lonely. If we were the last two humans on earth, alone on a desert island, it would be bye-bye Human Race. I am her companion; her avuncular adviser; her confidant. Not her lover. That's just not how this thing goes."

"Nice speech, Bud." Ozzy Man hoisted his left eyebrow like the Marquis de Sade. "But are you stupid enough to think *that* is the issue? The Missus knows you can't leg anyone over if you tried. But that's not the point, is it?"

Far out in the night, a motorcycle dopplered down the highway, screaming through its gears, tearing at the world faster than any other boy had ever gone. Al listened, almost expecting to hear the crash. It didn't come before the speeding machine bansheed over the edge of the world.

"I suppose," he said, glum and defeated. "But the other charge, the real one, also isn't true—I'm not in love with Courtney."

"Tell it to the judge," Ozzy Man said. Doppelgänger looked away into the corner.

"And," Al went on, irritated by the interruption, "my affection for Kimberley is undiminished."

"Even," Ozzy Man asked, "when she behaves like a pork chop?"

"Haven't we just gone through the thing about context?" Al asked. "In the context of Kimberley's world, she's not behaving badly at all. She is preserving her position; she is reacting to an insult. She has been hurt—both privately, here at home; and publicly, when the vacuous little bitches like the ones this afternoon can't wait to tell her they saw her husband and his squeeze. That's got to hurt."

"And you want to fix it by recognising both your vanishing insignificance and your inextricable part of the harmonious, composite whole." Ozzy Man ridiculed Doppelgänger's You-are-a-Child-of-the-Universe line.

Doppelgänger didn't comment; Al didn't know; but he tried anyway. "I am not what determines how this thing should go. I need to find the balance, the tipping point where I am truest to myself and cause the least unhappiness and disruption to those around me."

"Okay then, Bud." Ozzy Man inclined a look by raising that same eyebrow, but only minimally. "It's time to get back into step with the Regiment. All you have to decide is what are you going to do?" He said: *watcha gawna do?*

Doppelgänger knew what Al should do; what he would do. But he didn't say.

The scroll behind the little window in Al's wristwatch, analogue and old-fashioned, clicked mechanically to its next number: Midnight. In bed down the passage, Kimberley lay sleeping. Al wondered at the gulf that had suddenly opened between here and there.

"I will try talking to her," he said. He believed in talking.

"Best of luck with that, Mate." Ozzy Man stuck out his chin like George Patton.

Doppelgänger kept his silence. He and Al both knew that plan wasn't up to much.

27

"CAN WE PLEASE TALK?" AL asked over the dead man's territory in the middle of the breakfast table. There was milk and toast and honey, and juice from oranges too. The sun streamed in like a golden blessing under the folds of cotton print blinds that stayed open except at night in the dead of winter.

"There's nothing to talk about." Kimberley avoided looking at him, her face set in a mask of disdainful apathy.

"Shut up, Oz," Doppelgänger said.

"Kimberley, there's lots to talk about. You are angry with me."

"So?" She bit the corner off her toast, chewed furiously, stared at the coffee machine or perhaps the filing tray beside it, with receipts and spare keys, rubber bands and empty pillboxes. When she turned to face him, deliberately, she asked, snapping: "Why don't you just spend the rest of your life with Courtney?"

Al's immediate response boiled up inside him, a geyser of hot anger: How unreasonable was that! But he held the lid firmly in place; he didn't know what to say and he couldn't very well pretend that he didn't know what the issue was, and his defence—*she's just a friend*—sounded lame even to himself. He finished his fruit salad, put down the spoon, asked into the silence that dragged around the room like Charles, the Lame King of Naples: "What do you want me to do?"

"You must do what you like," she said. No attempt to engage.

"Wrong, Bud," Ozzy Man said. "This is exactly how she engages."

What Al would like to do is to be friends with Courtney and be married to and happy with Kimberley. But that, he knew, and had known for some time, wouldn't work. Couldn't work.

"Do you want me to stop being friends with Courtney?"

"I don't care. Suit yourself."

Al's approach to disagreements and fights, if ever he could get it right, was to decide whether the point of contention was insuperable, truly insurmountable. If it was, cut your losses and walk away with minimal fuss. If it was not, make peace as soon as possible. Being angry is such a waste—a waste of time, a waste of emotion, a waste of opportunity, a waste of your days. Relationships and friendships are finite; you will die sooner or later—to drop weeks or months or years out the middle is such a profligate waste. This was perhaps the one lesson he had learned, if not from his father, then because of that intransigent old sod. If you don't use it, you lose it. It never comes back.

"Time watches from the shadow," Ozzy Man said, "and coughs when you would kiss."

"Kimberley," Al said, in his most reasonable voice, "you are angry with me because I have a friend you don't want me to have. If it bugs you this much, I will stop being her friend."

"Don't do me any favours." She clipped her vowels and shortened her consonants. She put down her coffee cup, half-full, grabbed her keys and bag, and headed for the door. The security camera above and outside showed the door opening, her leaving. She was crying.

"Ah Christ, Bud," Ozzy Man said. "You fucked that up neatly."

Doppelgänger said nothing; thought how to fix this. Wondered what lay ahead.

Al felt like shit.

"She is *so* unreasonable," he told the other two.

"*She* is unreasonable?" Ozzy Man asked, eyes open wide in mock astonishment. "I thought, Matey, that *you* are the one who is fucking around."

"He's not fucking around, you know that," Doppelgänger said.

"Maybe not with his dick, he isn't," Ozzy Man said.

Doppelgänger didn't answer immediately, then did an almost unheard-of thing, turned on Al: "She *does* have a point, Alan," he said. Bearing in mind who Doppelgänger was, that shook Al to his core.

Al now really felt like shit.

He took his coffee onto the veranda, sat watching the middle-distance and listening to the hypnotic click of the pool cleaner. A troupe of wood hoopoes flitted noisily from tree to tree, arguing like Italians in a coffee bar. The morning was bright and clear, no sympathetic meteorology. At funerals it should be cold and rainy, at weddings sunny and warm. Al needed the morning to diminish into misery, the sly slinking geese to shit on his grave in the rain.

Alfredo fell deeply in love with Violeta, a beautiful courtesan—which is a nice word for a hooker. Between them, alone and together, they sang several of the most beautiful arias ever written. Zeffirelli made the movie, shot those scenes through a pink filter, with Vaseline on the lens: Violeta singing about the madness of falling in love, Alfredo answering from outside her window in the rain. In a crowded, stylish parlour he proposes a toast, the Drinking Song everyone knows: Alfredo sings the exuberant ode of his love and her beauty, while she watches, sparkling eyes over the brim of a crystal goblet; and answers in a clear, ringing soprano. But what does Calvinism teach? Only this: When you are happy, you are riding for a fall. Alfredo's sister is engaged to an upper-class twit, whose sanctimony won't permit any association with a prostitute, however remote. Alfredo's father tells Violeta to break it off with Alfredo—to tell him she doesn't love him. Zeffirelli changes to a cold-blue, razor-edged lens for the misery and heartache that follow.

"Not exactly in her shoes, Bud," Ozzy Man said, "but I can see the similarities." He said: *seemalaridies*.

They sat in the courtyard of a newly built office block—only two floors and a tiny rectangular footprint. Unpainted orange brick with small-paned large-scale windows, like an upgraded schoolroom, and deliberately raw finishes; bare concrete floors, exposed structural steel and plumbing, no ceilings, painted bare steel staircases.

Counter-corporate 21st century office accommodation for hip kids. Dappled shadow from a tree that had stood many decades before the careful architect planned and executed his ecologically savvy version of a relaxed, understated, undemanding shared workspace. In the offices were graphic designers, web developers, social consultants—young people in trendy outfits, modern hairstyles, and tattoos.

Their table was square, metal, unadorned, except for tiny leaves and twigs that fell unchecked from over their heads, reminding everyone of the tree's eminence.

"What is it?" Courtney asked, having tried, unsuccessfully, for twenty minutes to do her usual one-woman show.

"It's a fuck up," Al answered, avoiding her eyes.

"What is?"

"Ah, Christ, Courtney. Kimberley thinks I like you more than I like her."

She did a double take, frowned, and said: "That's ridiculous. We are friends."

"Ridiculous?" Ozzy Man said. "That's a bit bloody hurtful."

"I know," Al muttered, glancing at her, looking away smartly. He didn't want to see those dark eyes.

"This would be the wrong time, Alan," Doppelgänger said softly, "to answer Missy's question about whether you love her."

"So, what are you telling me?" Courtney asked, no longer smiling, but not angry. Sad was what she already appeared to be, guessing what was coming.

Al squeezed his eyes closed, sighed. "She doesn't want me to see you."

Courtney just kept quiet.

Al felt like shit.

"I'm sorry," he said.

"Numb Nuts," Ozzy Man said.

Courtney looked at him steadily. "What do *you* want, Al?" She never used his name; never asked him a direct question; never wanted to analyse what they had between them.

"Christ, Bud," Ozzy Man said. "Why do all the Sheilas ask the same question?"

"Courtney." Al sighed again; he eventually looked at her.

"Not now, Bud." Ozzy Man added his warning to Doppelgänger's, aware of the emotional impact the scene was having on Al.

"You don't want me to answer that question," he said quietly, shaking his head minimally.

"*You* don't want to answer that question, Mate," Doppelgänger responded, trying to sound like his counterpart.

"A heart that cared; that went unshared; until it died within his silence," Ozzy Man crooned like white shoes Pat Boone.

"You are just going to let her tell you what to do?" Courtney's question flashed in her eyes, her dark, vulnerable eyes. Then she looked down in mute apology.

Al felt like shit, more so by the minute. He shifted heavily, looked at her. "What are my options, Little One? I am in my mid-sixties, set in selfish, comfortable ways. Not much of a catch. Not much of a companion. I have shared a life with Kimberley for the past thirty-five years; and all my eggs are in that basket—my son, my memories, my photograph album, my life as I know it." He was quiet for a moment. "My life. That's a hell of a weight on one side of the scale. On the other side is a dear friend, with coffee and lunch dates I enjoy and look forward to more than you can know. Will miss like part of my soul."

"In a different universe, you are twenty-five years younger, and you meet at university," Doppelgänger said.

"He'll still go for Kimberley, Bud," Ozzy Man said. "She's got his number. And his balls in the palm of her hand."

"You leave me alone with Thomas," Courtney asked softly, the accusation written plain in the space between her hands.

Al didn't answer; reached across and squeezed her hand. They hadn't touched, he realised, since the Springsteen concert. She turned her hand over, returned the pressure; and they both let go at the same time.

He stopped in front of the complex where she stayed. She looked at him quietly before undoing her seatbelt.

"Don't say it, Alan," Doppelgänger said.

"Bye. Thanks for everything," she said. And then she was gone.

Al felt like shit. Really felt like shit.

He drove home, put the car away, went outside to sit on the veranda; didn't want to see Kimberley.

Felt like shit.

The afternoon wasn't made for brooding, but he managed anyway. The angry conversation he rehearsed went something like this: *I have one friend. ONE friend. And I'm not allowed to see her. You have many friends, and you flit about all day long. I say nothing about that.*

"Ah, but, Mate." Ozzy Man interrupted his self-righteous tirade. "She's not trying to screw any of her friends."

"You *know*, Oz," Doppelgänger said, "Al isn't trying to do that either."

"Oh, isn't he?" Ozzy Man sniggered. He said: *eezzenee?*

Much later, when he went back inside, she was in front of the TV. They didn't speak to each other, not even to say *Hi*. Al felt really angry, righteously indignant, badly treated. His anger worked on itself, pulling itself up by the bootstraps, replicating like a viral load, wanting a *Corona Muralis*.

"She has been very unfair," Doppelgänger said.

"Yeah, Mate," Ozzy Man said to Al. "You can do whatever the fuck you please. She must fit in."

Al noticed how Doppelgänger didn't jump to his defence.

They didn't have supper together. He lay on the couch, blasting his ears off with the Bose headphones, while she went to bed.

He woke with a start. Anouar Brahem and Jan Garbarek were playing a wild, disassociated, syncopated, middle eastern duet, it felt like between his eyeballs. He pulled the earphones off, clumsy, and thick with sleep, turned off the music. He sat up, rubbed his face in the palms of his hands and thought: "What the fuck are you doing?"

It was quiet, quarter-to three. Beyond the garden walls, the suburb lay asleep. The house was as a grave. A lonely dog barked twice from his vigil a few houses down the block.

"You really hurt Kimberley, you know," Doppelgänger said, not reproachfully. Just stating a fact.

"Yes, I know," Al said.

"Didn't do so great with Courtney either, did you, Mate." Ozzy Man tied together the loose ends of Al's soul, leaving him wound up like a pretzel. "The end of a perfect day for you."

"Oz, just stop," Doppelgänger said.

Al brushed his teeth, slunk silently into bed next to his One-and-Only. She was fast asleep, without a sound, as always. In their younger years, he often worried that she was still alive—watched for long stretches until she moved or twitched an eyelid. Only then would he relax, go to sleep himself. Later, when Jesse was born, he realised it was his own neurosis—he would watch baby Jesse as well, anxious to know that he was still breathing.

Now, he tried to look at Kimberley, but her head was turned away, her face in the shadow.

"I'll try tomorrow," he told the other two. "I will try to say sorry."

"Ah Christ, Mate." Ozzy Man chose his special way to say good night. "Stop being so tediously fucking predictable."

28

"ADVICE IS THE PRODUCT OF the man who gives it." George, med-school prof, nodded for emphasis: A slight, under-stated nod; a George-Clooney-handsome nod; and nod from under half raised left eyebrow; a complicit nod; a nod that signalled at least half-way through a bottle of Cab Sav on the table at his elbow.

"You can drink too much," Ozzy Man said, "but you can never drink enough."

"Alan." George directed his disconcerting intellect across the table straight at Al. "You know me. I *never* give advice. I am con-temptuous of advice. I am dismissive of advice. Advice is for Agony Aunts, for women's magazines. For psychologists and other pseudo scientists. It was invented in the feel-good part of the 20th century, and now follows us as an inevitable consequence of our cultural dis-array." Realising that he may be dissing all professions in one broad stroke, he added: "*Life Advice*, I mean." And took another slurp of wine; the restaurant noisy behind him.

"But, Bud," Ozzy Man said, "what you don't sow, cannot grow."

"If you look at who gives advice, you will weep," George said. "Oprah Winfrey, Prince Charles, Kim Kardashian, Jay-Z, Cosmopolitan Magazine, talk-show hosts. I can be accused of many things, but not of being approachable. I set myself high standards of aloofness and intellectual snobbery, and I show in word and deed that I think I'm better than other people, and they must leave me alone."

"It's really good that poor Edward isn't here," Doppelgänger said, "to slide an equal-opportunities comment chin-first into this moment."

"Which leaves me without any understanding." George rounded on his point. "Why my students—not stupid people let me assure you: They are at *med school*. I know everyone is equal and we can all realise our dreams, *yada-yada*; but only the smart kids get there—*they*, the *smart* ones, line up at my door to ask me advice. *Me!* As if I've ever attempted to answer any of their questions seriously. Surely word has got around by now?" He shook his head in amazement.

A waiter put down their food; they picked up their cutlery.

"What do you tell them?" Al asked, bemused at the thought of a sincere and impressionable young person standing in front of George, asking him what to do with his life.

"Float with the tide or swim for a goal," the man answered, prompt and direct. "It covers more or less everything. But then the little whining sods want me to elaborate—*I always wanted to be a proctologist, but now the thought bums me out.* And they want me to resolve their tedious attacks of existential *angst*. Wait fifteen years, I want to say. It will resolve itself."

Al refilled their glasses.

"I had a young man in my office this afternoon," George told him. "He said he may be changing his mind about whether he should be at med school at all. *Wishes change, man*, I told him. *You used to want to be a pirate when you were five, but not anymore. It's not because pirates changed. It's because you changed.* Why would it be so surprising for him that the same thing happens when it's a more realistic job?"

"Every person is the product of his own reactions to personal experience," Doppelgänger said. "That product changes with differing inputs and subjective processes. Which bring about a new set of priorities."

"The Dalai fucking Lama," Ozzy Man said, rolling his eyes, "needs you like a brother."

"It's another way of saying," Doppelgänger explained, "that everyone who walks a mile in a set of moccasins will have calluses and blisters in different places and will have different things he wants to do next and different ways in which he wants to go about them."

"It can be said even more simply." Ozzy Man stared at his counterpart. "Don't substitute anybody's advice for your own. Make up your own mind and tell everyone else to fuck off."

"What did you tell the poor kid?" Al asked George.

"I told him that if he trusts blindly in a predetermined goal, he is being, at best, unwise. I said, don't set your heart on being a copy typist or an arboreal ecologist. What you have to do is be the thing you are, inherently, by nature. Be that which is part of you, and then it will be naturally what you become. If being a sushi chef is inherent in your make up, by being yourself, that's what you will become."

"Farkenhell, Mate." Ozzy Man made big eyes. "If you had a column in Woman's Weekly, the Sheilas would line up to hear you say shit like that." He thought about it, and added: "Did the kid have any idea what the fuck you had said to him? And is he going to become a sushi chef?"

"Make the dream conform to the person, rather than the person to the dream?" Al restated. "You and Oprah are like this." He held up the index finger of his right hand, with the middle finger curled around it like an overly eager much taller ballroom dancing companion.

George crinkled his forehead, looked puzzled, took a little sip. "Fuck," he said, drawing it out and one long vowel. "I accidentally *have* been giving New-Age advice. I suppose *that's* why the little snots come stand at my door—it's bullshit but sounds insightful. I don't know what else to say to them. I can't very well say: *Fuck Off, why don't you?*"

"You could say," Al said, "do that which is meaningful to yourself, and allow the sum total of your abilities to deliver the greatest possible fulfilment of that persona."

"You think they would get that?" George frowned.

"I don't know." Al shook his head, then said wistfully: "Jesus, I wish I could manage to do that myself."

"Me too, me too." George rolled his head, side-to-side like a prize fighter; took another sip. "It's a con-job. Your entrance ticket allows you to play the game once only. The odds are stacked against you; and when you are halfway through, they, the ones who were so happy to give you advice at the beginning, look at you with big eyes and say: *Well, you are fucking that up, aren't you?* The best intentions behind advice given, do not keep it from being insidiously destructive."

Al nodded. "Maybe put a sign on your door that says: *Make up your mind how you want to live. Then find a way to survive while you are doing so.*"

"That should be all the advice they need." George chuckled. "And it'll save me a lot of time."

In the silence that followed, Doppelgänger said: "This is kind of the crux of what Missy says, Al. If you say: *I don't know what to do next*, the question becomes whether it is worth giving up what you have, to look for something better. And only you can make that decision."

"Yeah, Bud," Ozzy Man said. "She also says you don't have to do spend the rest of your life doing something you don't want to; but if you do end up doing that, try to convince yourself that you had no choice."

Al knew exactly what his choice had been; as he knew exactly why he made it. Because he still felt like Judas about it didn't make him doubt that he had been right.

On their way out of the restaurant, George tripped over the single step at the front door, fell flat on his back. He lay completely still, like a pole-axed starfish.

"Don't worry, Bud," Ozzy Man said. "You're not that drunk if you can lie on the floor without holding on."

George sat up, smiled at the concerned manager as if he had stage-managed the entire scene, hopped nimbly to vertical, and called an Uber: He had suspected that he might not be able to drive home.

Watching him disappear into the night, Doppelgänger, unusually judgmental, commented: "George only drinks for two reasons: When he is happy; and when he is not."

When Al got home, the lights were off, Kimberley was sleeping.

"Kimberley is in her bedroom, Mate," Ozzy Man said, "with the lights turned off. Writing shit about you on social media under the covers."

The night was cool and pleasant. He and the cat carried his Kindle to the veranda to read. Technology made things simple: It was too dark outside for him to read a paper book, but the Kindle was back-lit. Going on holiday, he took only this little device; and Kimberley a crate of books—she wanted, she said, the tactile experience, feeling and smelling the paper, the satisfying sound of turning a page, the weight of the words different in every edition. But the days of paper are numbered, as surely as chipping texts into the granite pillars of Thebes passed into yesterdays immemorial along with the centuries ruled by Akhenaten and Amenhotep.

Al sat without reading.

"She won't speak to me," he said.

"Can't blame her," Ozzy Man said.

"Oz," Doppelgänger said

"Well, he did fuck her around, didn't he?" He said: *deedenee*.

"I don't agree," the more reasonable of the two exclaimed. "But she has won the battle and the war. Al hasn't spoken to Courtney in weeks."

"Yes, but he likes the young Sheila. That's why Kimberley won't speak to him," Ozzy Man explained.

"That's not a reasonable position."

"Oh," Ozzy Man said. "Now you want reasonable? OK for Al to be a dick, but she must be reasonable."

"I'm not a dick," Al said miserably. "I'm just not as in charge as I'm expected to be. I'm the Steadfast Tin Soldier. Is all. I have fuck-all control over where this went or will go."

The Tin Soldier stood on his only leg, fell in love with the ballerina who also stood so. He tumbled off the windowsill, was put in a paper boat, sailed down a gutter, was swallowed by a fish, got back to the house where his love, the ballerina, still stood on one leg waiting. Through all of it he couldn't do a thing. For his final act of invalidation, he fell off the mantelpiece into the fire, and melted into the shape of a little tin heart.

"Treat me like you really should." Ozzy Man crooned like Elvis "Coz I'm not made of wood, and I don't have a wooden heart."

29

"How long is now?" Doppelgänger asked. "Have you ever thought of that: How long is the moving edge of time on which we live?"

"Some of the shit you worry about, Mate," Ozzy Man said, shaking his head, "will stiffen the wombats."

"No, seriously; the popcorn philosophers tell us to live in the moment; live for today."

"Real philosophers too," Ozzy Man said. "Janis Joplin said: *If you've got it today, man, you don't wear it tomorrow. It's all the same fucking day, man.*"

"Not exactly what I'm talking about." Doppelgänger waggled a downward open palm, thumb, and little finger like the wingtips of a gull, semaphoring the need subtly to redefine.

"Oh," Ozzy Man said. "Like Mother Teresa then? *Yesterday is gone. Tomorrow has not yet come. We have only today.*"

"Closer, but not quite." Doppelgänger wanted to recover the conversational lead.

Ozzy Man made big eyes. "*How did it get so late so soon? It's night before it's afternoon. December is here before it's June. My goodness how the time has flewn,*" he said dramatically, with expository hands.

"No, no, no." Doppelgänger tried to stop his flow. "It's more like when you say *That's how I feel right now.* When is *right now;* how long does it last? It's not very long, is it? When you said the thing about wombats, is that *now* or is that in the past?"

195

"Oh, I get it. Deep intellectual point, Mate. The only existence we have is in the present, and that, of necessity, is fleeting; and therefore, our existence too is ephemeral, founded on a fairy's wing?"

"Well, yes, but without the fleeting existence thing. Just how long is the moment in which we live? Before it's gone, before it too, is history. How long have we got? How long does the present last?"

"Not very long." Ozzy Man shook his head once to go with his disinterested monotone.

"We read that science-made-easy thing," Doppelgänger said, "that said, now is about four seconds. Anything that happened more than four seconds ago, is in the past."

"If a clock is hungry, it goes back four seconds," Ozzy Man said. "Why is this significant, Bud?" He said: *seegneefeecand*.

"Well think about it: The present is like a bright cursor, skipping endlessly along the axis of time. To the left, we have all of time that has already passed …"

"13.787 billion years."

"Yes, thanks. And to the right, all the time still to come. And what we pay attention to as a species, what occupies our entire focus and energy, is four seconds in the middle."

"A lot can happen in four seconds."

"Sure," Doppelgänger said. "A barista can put down your ristretto in front of you on the counter; the US president can push the button for global nuclear destruction; Al and Kimberley can have a fight."

"Yeah," Ozzy Man said, "but it takes her longer than four seconds to forgive him again."

Al met Meg in their usual spot—the coffee shop that did light lunches, had tables inside and under three oak trees; and a section for smokers next to the deliveries load-bay of a large supermarket. Al liked his sister's company more than he disliked where they sat. The game Jesse had played with his dad while he was growing up, had prepared him for such choices. "Dad." Jesse would begin his inquiry with an inflection that warned Al of what was coming.

"Would you prefer to wake up with spiders on your eyeballs, or snakes around your neck?"

"What's eating you?" Meg asked, squinting through a haze of cigarette smoke. Her explanation for their delegation to the worst table, not even in the house, was that the Minister of Health was funded by a cigarette-smuggling cartel, whose boss had aspirations of being a modern-day Al Capone. Apart from her nicotine-fuelled blind spot, Meg's opinions were rational.

Al looked put-upon, seemed not to see the bright blessed day, the dark sacred night. "Meg," he said, "Kimberley hasn't spoken to me in three weeks."

"She's giving you the Silent Treatment?"

"It's more than a treatment. She doesn't engage, she doesn't respond, she doesn't change her expression. She just doesn't behave as if I exist."

"The Silent Treatment. Platinum-edged diamond class."

Al was unsure. It looked hell-of convincing from where he stood. "You think it's a tactic?"

"Without a shadow of a doubt." Meg fixed him with her no-bullshit stare. "What do you think she's after?"

"I don't know," Al said miserably. "She wanted me not to see Courtney, and I don't—I broke my friendship off with her. I haven't seen her or spoken to her since I last saw her, at the beginning of Kimberley's silent spell. The beginning of the Cold War."

"But you miss her?"

"Of course."

"Well there's your problem then."

"How do you mean?"

"You really don't get it, do you?" Meg shook her head, amazed. *Men*, her expression surmised. "It's never enough to comply—you must be seen to comply happily, willingly, enthusiastically. It's like German High Command and what it wanted from Hansel and Gretel. You couldn't just put a swastika on your arm and carry on as before. No. You had to sing the Horst Wessel Song, do the stiff-armed salute, inform on your neighbour, love the Führer. That way you stayed alive long enough to die on the Eastern Front."

"Ah," Ozzy Man said, "the *Reductio ad Hitlerum*."

"I thought you don't do Latin?" Doppelgänger raised an eyebrow.

"Meg," Al said. "It's a bit heavy to compare Kimberley with the Nazis."

"Same tactics," she said, drawing another toxic draught into her lungs. Then she relented: "Alan, see it from her point of view. Or, maybe we can do this Socratically: Why was Kimberley angry with you."

"Not was. *Is*."

"Why was she originally angry with you?"

"She said I hurt her."

"And you did, Mate," Al's ever supportive Antipodean passenger said. Doppelgänger, more diplomatically, let silence speak for itself.

"How did you do that?" Meg asked, as if interrogating a toddler.

"I spent too much time with Courtney."

"Yes, but *why*?" Meg asked, edging closer to irritation.

"I like her."

"There you go," she said, as if having revealed the big secret. Al looked at her uncertainly.

"Al." Doppelgänger offered an explanation of the exchange. "I think what Meg means is that, because you don't see or speak to Courtney anymore, it doesn't fix the problem. The problem is that you liked her, and you still do."

"Oh," Al said, looking properly put-upon.

"The loneliest moment in someone's life," Ozzy Man said, "is when he is watching his whole world fall apart and all he can do is stare blankly."

"Oz," Doppelgänger said. "Keep your folksy wisdom out of it. He's feeling shit enough as it is."

"Folksy? Bud," Ozzy Man said, "that's Scott fucking Fitzgerald. The man's a genius."

Meg, unaware of the bickering, helped her brother to the depressing conclusion. "You mustn't just be *seen* to comply. You must *actually* comply."

"But how can I do that? I feel so guilty about Courtney. I treated her so badly. To get Kimberley talking to me again, you say I must *actually* stop liking Courtney? Even if I don't see her, I must somehow manage to undo something over which I have no control? I must convince myself somehow that I don't like her and that I'm indifferent to her?"

"Yep." Meg looked at Al, no discernible expression on her face, like the dealer in a high-stakes Texas hold 'em game when the chips lie waiting in an untidy stack in the middle of the table.

"Hee-hee." Ozzy Man laughed. "On ya *bike*, Mate. You fucked this up like a genius."

"But Meg, how can I? I mean, how could I even begin?"

His sister watched him critically. "You married her, not me." Then she felt sorry for him. "You could lie about it? Tell Kimberley you really don't like Courtney."

"I can't see where the opportunity for saying such a thing presents itself, when she won't even look at me. Besides, she's not stupid. She won't believe me. In fact, it will piss her off even more, if I try such transparent child psychology on her."

"Then I don't know what you're going to do. Maybe you should get divorced." This had been Meg's advice for years, following hot on the heels of her initial advice not to marry Kimberley.

For maybe the first time ever, Al wondered whether there was merit in his sister's suggestion.

"No, Mate." Ozzy Man helped him out of his immediate quandary. "Not before you give it a fair shake of the sauce bottle."

In the car on the way back home, Al, still thinking of what Meg had said, mulled over the circularity of salvation. "Christians worry their whole lives about being properly respectful to and of God—to ensure their own salvation. But that is just a metaphor for how people act in relation to each other."

"For sure," Doppelgänger said. "You tell God you love him, but in reality, you are scared silly by what he will do to you if you don't."

"Yes, if you love Him enough," Ozzy Man said, getting down to the essence of the thing, "He will *save* you from all the things He will do to you, if you don't."

"Well," Al said, "I didn't mean it to be as harsh as that but look at my position now with Kimberley. She holds the power both of disapproval and of forgiveness. I must find her salvation or stay in misery."

"Yes, that's right," Doppelgänger said. "Kimberley is both the problem and the solution, the question and the answer, the damnation, and the salvation. *In loco Dei*: She is the reason you need salvation; and she is the only one who can give it to you. Your only choice becomes whether to cut and run, or to grovel."

"Leave or beg, Mate." Ozzy Man grinned at the dichotomy.

Doppelgänger nodded. "So, what do we do now?"

What they did was make tea, carry it out to Al's chair on the veranda. With the book, an actual paper book, he had been dipping into from time to time.

"Mate," Ozzy Man asked, "you don't think it's a bit dorky to read Julius Caesar's Gallic Wars for *enjoyment*? In the original."

"It's not the original." Doppelgänger revelled in a bit of pedantry. "It's an English translation."

"Aw, Bud." Ozzy Man rolled his eyes. "A translation *is* the bloody original, close enough."

Al read in silence and with attention, not thinking about his troubles.

"Fuck me," Ozzy Man decried when Al later put the book down. "Those Romans were hard core."

Caesar mentioned, in one simple line of his memoir, all of fifteen words, that after the battle against a tribe that had pissed him off by not wanting him as their owner, he had sold the *plunder* as a job lot to a single trader. He was later told, he added, that there were 79,000 heads. The footnote explained, because Caesar didn't bother, that 79,000 captives were sold into slavery in one mighty pada-boom. Al had nearly fallen out of his chair when he understood what the Roman hero had said, sort of, in passing. He had killed everyone he could and sold the rest as slaves.

"Long live Caesar," Ozzy Man said. "And, Mate, it puts your own problems into perspective, doesn't it?" He said: *pirspecdif.*

"Makes you wonder about famous people," Doppelgänger said. "If you want to be famous, it's not essential to be a megalomaniacal solipsist, but it helps."

"Like John Wilkes Booth, Leonardo da Vinci, Vincent Van Gogh, Malcolm X, Patrice Lumumba, Chico Marx, Muhammad Ali, Mahatma Gandhi, Christopher Columbus, Rosa Parks, Eva Peron, George Orwell, Haile Selassie, Fidel Castro, Coco Chanel, and Amelia Earhart," Ozzy Man suggested.

"Yes, all of them," Doppelgänger said.

"And Mozart, Elvis, Beethoven, Stalin, Tolstoy, Picasso, Plato, Sting, Cleopatra, and Pele," Ozzy Man added.

Nobody answered.

"And Miou-Miou?" Ozzy Man said.

"You have the emotional quotient of a three-year old." Doppelgänger shook his head sadly.

"The police were called in," Ozzy Man said. "There was a three-year old resisting a rest."

But Al wasn't resisting. His eyelids drooped and he slipped into a slow slumber. Because during sleep, your body repairs itself: muscle, organs, cells. Your immune system boosts up, you grow; you regenerate. The older you are the less it works, though. By the time you're in your mid-sixties, it probably doesn't work at all anymore. For which, in this sad circumstance, Al was probably just wasting time—a series of little four second snatches, stretching without hesitation, repetition or deviation to his inscrutable final hurrah.

30

"JUST A LITTLE BIT LONELY; just a little bit sad," sang the girl from inside the Bluetooth speaker. Wispy and seductive, inimitably Summer-of-Love, the voice belonged to a singer with long straight blonde hair and the tallest legs you ever saw. The hot pants and micro minis she habitually wore, had made them look even taller. Al picked up his phone and poked at the screen: Trying to find out how sixties pop had followed immediately after a parade of jazz players, lined up by agents of the ether and set in a playlist for people like Al. The slim device in his hand combined, in equal proportions, high-tech electronics and magic; and just then its screen lit up: Jesse on FaceTime.

"Hi, Al," the young man, curtain of curly hair and pencil moustache, bright smile, and perfect teeth, deep dimples, and eyes bluer than robin's eggs, said. The eyes had skipped two generations, came straight from Al's grandfather to his son. The old guy had used his see out his life of *Sturm und Drang*. Al hoped Jesse would be more circumspect in how he used his own set of piercing blue.

"Biggest," Al said. "So good to see you." He spoke to and saw his son on the video link probably three times a week, not short conversations; and every time was a treat.

"It's a bit late, Pops. You aren't on your way to bed?" Jesse asked, more for the sake of form than as a real question: It was quarter to midnight, well before Al's bedtime.

"Things okay?" Al asked.

"We were on site today," Jesse said, a project site in rural Spain. "They are drilling for water, and there was this guy, this water diviner, standing around."

"Hah!" Al barked a laugh. "With a dowsing rod and everything?"

"Absolutely. And just about everybody was respectful. Everybody, except the hydrologists. They could hardly contain their irritation."

"Did anyone listen to him?" Al asked, amused.

"No, the engineers were in charge, and had told the drill rig where to set up. But the old guy was there to check—make sure that the scientists don't get it wrong. Magic is alive and well."

Al laughed. "I was just thinking the same about my mobile phone. Sufficiently advanced technology is indistinguishable from magic."

Jesse grinned, moved the conversation on: He expected to be back home, his home, on Friday. "*The Drakes* are playing at a pub not far from me. I think I'll go."

"Lucky bugger." Al sighed with real envy. In his younger days, Johannesburg had had two strikes against it as a venue for international musicians: It was remote; and it was on a performers' blacklist. It's still remote.

"Are you and Kimberley OK?" Jesse asked.

Al liked his son too much not to be direct and honest. "Not really, but we're working on it."

"What's the issue?" If Jesse had an issue, Al would ask. No reason why the other way round was different.

"Kimberley thinks I was seeing too much of Courtney."

"Were you?"

"Probably, yes. I was having lunch with her every day; and when Kimberley didn't want to see a film, I went with Courtney."

"Are you having an affair?"

Al heard the incredulity in Jesse's voice. "No, Bossy. I'm not."

Of course not, implied his son's tone: "Why were you seeing her so often?"

"Jess, no real reason. I haven't got other friends who are available for lunch; and we got into a kind of a routine—we were lunch buddies. Looking back, I can see why Kimberley got upset, but it didn't feel anything other than ordinary: We just had lunch, chatted while we did, and then carried on with our own days. Once it became a routine, I didn't really think about it that much—it's just what I did."

Jesse was silent while he thought that through. "What you going to do?" he asked.

"I have told Courtney I can't see her."

Jesse thought again. "Isn't that a bit drastic?"

"Kimberley is really pissed. In her circle of friends there is a bunch of snide, menopausal cows who love telling her when they see us together, and they ham the story up for her: She has become the woman whose husband *may be having an affair*. Which, when you say it with the correct level of false confidence, that it's not so, and combine that with just enough fake lack of sympathy because there's no need for sympathy, it nails Kimberley to the mast of the Ship of Fools."

"I see. You put her in a shit position, Al." He stated rather than accused.

"I did. But that's not all, really. Kimberley is also upset that I like Courtney. She wants me to like only her."

"You always have." Jesse was thoughtful, testing out the idea that a fundamental building block of his life may have shifted. "Do you like Courtney that much?"

"I like her a lot, Jess. But as a mate. We don't have a physical thing. I like her, I like talking to her, I like spending time with her, I like her energy. But she isn't realistic competition for Kimberley. We aren't the same age, we don't have the same conversation, we don't have a history. In any event, she's looking for a substitute father—that's how she treats me. She wants to tell me her stuff and I must listen and help her if she asks—which she really doesn't do very often. She just wants unthreatening company, but from someone she trusts and likes. She's far more competition for you than for Kimberley."

"Huh-huh," he said chuckling. "I don't mind if you have lunch with her."

They said bye, hung up; and Al sat staring at the garden. In the city and its tree-lined suburbs, it never got dark. Even with the outside lights off, the horror of Gothic short stories had been moved along, away to the country where it could find gloomy spaces to make eerie noises and be spectrally scary. The ghosts were missing, but the cricket somewhere in the lawn, quite close to Al's chair, never went to sleep—he had read that a cricket was as loud as a lawnmower—it wasn't. It sounded way louder.

"The truth," Ozzy Man declared, "the whole truth and nothing but the truth, so help me God."

"What are you talking about?" Doppelgänger asked.

"Just reminding some of us, Bud, about the oath you take before you do the perp walk; when the eyes of justice are on you."

"Any reason for you to tell us?"

"Funny you should ask, Mate. Our brother in Christ bore witness to the state of mind of the female protagonist; she said she wants a father, but the aforementioned witness was silent about his own state of mind; didn't say if he wanted a daughter. The set-up rings to me as if the truth, but not the whole of it, has been told." Into the silence that followed, he added: "So help me, God."

"You are saying Al lied to Jesse?" Doppelgänger asked, to be sure.

"It's definitional, Mate," Ozzy Man answered. "He told the truth, but only the bit he can live with."

"Al did say he liked Courtney, liked spending time with her."

"If you're happy with that, Bud, we're all good."

Al shut the debate down, kept both of them quiet. When Jesse had been a little tyke, he had, on an occasion, taken offence at something his dad did—Al never worked out exactly what. He wouldn't speak to Al or listen to him, and on the third day of their silence, Al wrote him, his very best young friend, a letter, put it on his pillow and never mentioned it again. Nor did Jesse, until the end of their call just now.

"Al, remember the letter you wrote me when I was cross with you? I don't know if, even then, I knew what you had done to get yourself in trouble. I think I was just testing to see if I could make you jump. But in your letter, you were so kind and asked so nicely that I speak to you again and be your friend. I did immediately. So now, I'm not saying there's any similarity between the situations, but have you written to Kimberley? It does have weight and permanence, an apology on paper."

Al sat down and this is what he wrote:

My dearest Kimberley,
   I read Wallace Stevens say:
      A man and a woman and a blackbird
      Are one.
   I am so sorry. And I have thought, there are many things recently unsaid between us that need saying. Many of them have always been said; yet need repeating:
      and it is you are whatever a moon has always meant
      e.e. cummings
   I am so sorry. You haven't spoken to or looked at me in weeks.
      I hunger for your sleek laugh
      Pablo Neruda
   I am so sorry. Yet, you are, have always been, will always be, the queen, undisputed ruler, sole possessor of the innermost sanctum of what I call my heart.
      all that's best of dark and bright
      Meet in your aspect and your eyes
      Lord Byron
   I am so sorry. I have put you in a position of personal hurt and public embarrassment. I did this stupidly, not maliciously. If you could think me a fool, not a brute.
      Again and again the two of us walk out together under the ancient trees
      Rainer Maria Rilke
   I am so sorry. But you, you alone, are the one I hold so dear. There is no other, never has there been. Nor will there be.

Yours is the name the leaves chatter
at the edge of the unrabbited woods
Lisa Olstein

I am so sorry. I spent so much time with someone else, I know it looks as if I formed an attachment at odds with my love for and friendship with you. But that is not so, emphatically not. It was a friendship, nothing more. I have left it behind me.

And I will luve thee still, my dear,
Till a' the seas gang dry
Robert Burns

I am so sorry, my chummy, my heart, my friend, my dear. Please forgive me for making you sad; for making you doubt my devotion and my loyalty; for letting you appear less than you are. I will love you now and forever.

I love your style
I love your grace
I love your smile
I love your face

Al

Please be happy again and let me out of this dark misery?
Come. And be my baby.
Maya Angelou

Al

He folded the letter into an envelope, wrote her name on it and left it on her laptop. She would find it in the morning, after he had already gone.

31

Missy watched Tort hop onto Al's lap, landing so gracefully and softly, it was almost magic. She settled into a pose, mysterious and inscrutable as the Oracle of Delphi, and stared unhurried and languid at Al, giving him permission to caress her back. When his fingers found the thick fur and he ran his fingernails up her spine, she purred like a cat.

"How are things?" Missy asked.

"I'm still not sure, but I hope better. Kimberley and I are almost back speaking to each other."

"Almost?"

"She acknowledges I exist; and she says where she's going and when she'll be back."

"And you?"

"He snivels like a little girl," Ozzy Man answered.

"I do my best to get things back on track," Al said. He hadn't told her about the letter because she would have asked what it said; and that was between him and Kimberley.

"And Courtney?"

Al looked miserable. "I haven't spoken to her since we last saw each other."

"How does that make you feel?"

"Christ, Mate," Ozzy Man said. "Is she trying to sound like a cliché?"

"Not great," Al said.

Missy sized him up from under her fringe that was getting longer with each of his visits.

"If you simply suppress what you want to do, it is likely to go wrong somewhere down the track. You have to pay attention to what you want."

"Yeah, Buddy." Ozzy Man was at it again. "If your Ego suppresses its desires, pushes them into the personal and collective unconscious, they will bounce back up much harder than ever, with renewed vigour and energy. Your Self is not to be denied."

"Oz," Doppelgänger said, "that's such old-fashioned nonsense."

"But do I really have to?" Al asked. "If Kimberley is happy again, isn't that enough?"

"Only you will know what importance to attach to each issue. If Courtney isn't important enough. Only you can tell," Missy said, professionally non-committal.

"Yeah, that's great." Ozzy Man shook his head. "If it works out right, Missy did it. If it doesn't, you fucked it up for yourself."

"Let's talk about something else for a while. What else in your life, apart from Kimberley, is important to you?"

Al tickled Tort behind her ears, and she head-butted his hand when she thought he would stop.

"Well, there's Jesse," he said.

"Yes?"

"It's the cruellest trick evolution pulled on us, Missy," he told the analyst who had let slip previously that she had no desire to have children, "It's the one you are lucky enough not to have to experience first-hand. It's this: We are genetically predisposed to love our children without reserve, as they are predisposed to love theirs. Just that."

"I don't understand?" she asked, proving him right about her not having to experience that exquisite little agony.

"My Jesse, when he was at university overseas, had to come home for the summer vacation. Something to do with his visa.

Every year he spent two glorious months here, at home. Glorious for me. He was so solid and present: Noisy and immediate and un-kempt. He filled the house and his room and our lives."

Al stared out the window at the green entanglement of Missy's garden. He had to give himself time to regain his composure, be-cause, deep into his sixties, he suddenly realised he was about to cry.

"Alan," Doppelgänger said. "He's well and he loves you dearly."

"And then, inevitably, the evening would come when he was back on a plane to the other side of the world. He is kind and em-pathetic; and saw how far I slithered down into the dumps because he was leaving. He was gracious, and sat with me for hours, and chatted, and showed me stuff on his phone, and played me new songs, and told me his secrets. Then, when I hugged him goodbye at the airport, and I was desperate, he saw that as well; and was even kinder. And at the same time ever so keen to get back to his own life of high-tech and new friends in the Big City."

Missy saw that tears lay shallow under his brim. She pretended to make a note in her book, to give him time—she seldom wrote down anything for real.

"Missy, I used to think that *heart ache* was just a metaphor, But it's not. I used to get an actual low-grade ache in my chest before he went. It started a few days before he would go; and lasted a few days after. Whenever I think of him, it comes right back."

"Ah fuck, Mate," Ozzy Man said. "What a hopeless wuss you are." But he couldn't manage to convince even himself.

"And now?"

"Now." Al looked at the cat on his lap. "Now I count up the weeks before I see him again. Halfway through December he comes back. That's still so far away. And then it's for eleven days."

Sometimes Missy wondered how it had become her lot in life to listen to the things she couldn't change; things that broke her heart under its professional suit of armour.

"The one bright point," Al said, "is that this silliness isn't recip-rocal. He is sad that I feel the way I do; but he leaves with a song in his heart. He's too nice to say: *Dry up, won't you.* But he doesn't really get it. It's the beginning of the year! Stuff to do; stuff to see! Worlds to conquer."

"It's not really like that," Doppelgänger said.

"But if he has children ever," Al said, "he will unfortunately know this devastation one day: He will understand that I loved him as he will love his own children. When you are the recipient of unquestioning, unqualified love, you are incapable of understanding it. When one day you feel that love for your own child, it's too late."

Al had forgotten about Tort, who jumped off his lap in dudgeon, strolled across the gap and hopped into Missy's lap.

"Did your father feel the same way?" Missy asked.

"Ah Christ, Missy!" Ozzy Man exclaimed. "Just kick him in the nuts, why don't you?"

Al didn't answer.

"Did he?" the doc insisted.

"No."

"Al, I'm not just trying to be a bitch. I'm trying to show you that there is always another way. It doesn't have to be so hard. There is always an alternative."

"Only if you're a cunt, Missy," Ozzy Man said. "Only if you're a complete cunt."

Al didn't say anything.

"What I'm trying to tell you, is that if you are fixated simply on other people, you can't achieve your own happiness. You've *got* to take account of yourself as well." Missy tried to establish eye contact with him; failed. "If you do things simply because Kimberley wants you to, to keep the peace, your solution won't last. The least you have to do is speak to her about it."

"Follow the ribbon of your own highway, Mate," Ozzy Man said. "Fire all of your guns at once and explode into space."

Al sat quietly, made no attempt to answer. It was too obvious, too immutable, too in-your-face: Where leviathans walk, the grass gets trampled. Al was the grass.

"To start again: Do you love Courtney?" Missy asked.

"Missy." Al sighed, suddenly tired of the conversation. "We've been through this. I liked spending time with her, I liked her company, I felt responsible for her."

"And now that you don't see her you don't feel so great," Missy said. "Why would that be?"

"Because I was such a prick to her," Al said, feeling, unusually and from nowhere, aggressive. "Because I treated her so badly. She needed a friend, and I let her down. She was kind to me; I was an arsehole in return. That's not who I want to be. Few enough people in the course of my life have invited me in to be close friends. And this is how I treated the one who did. If she thinks the worst of me, then that is her right, good entitlement. I agree with her: I was so unkind; I was so inadequate. I abandoned her. And she certainly didn't deserve that."

Al drove away, thinking about duty.

"Being dutiful," Ozzy Man said, "requires you to pretend that the inconsequential is vital."

"Very helpful, Oz," Doppelgänger replied, "but not that kind of duty."

"Yeah, right. Do you mean determinist or epistemic duty? Or maybe deontological? Are you wondering whether morality is determined by the consequence of your action or your intention?"

"No." Doppelgänger shook his head. "Neither. The question is how your duty to one person affects your duty to another."

"Oh, I get it, Mate" Ozzy Man said. "The trolley bus: About to wipe out five kids in pyjamas: They have big, cute eyes and freckles, and each one is holding a baby koala bear. You can pull the switch to redirect the trolleybus, but then you will kill a Republican lobbyist who disses global climate change. Otherwise, you can just do nothing, which allows you to say you didn't kill anyone; but then the five cuties get squashed in the mangle. What do you do? Where lies your duty to act, or not to act? Wherein lies the moral imperative?"

"Maybe," Doppelgänger answered. "But this is more like the trolleybus is going to hit either Kimberley or Courtney, and you must decide. If you pull the switch down, the train hits Kimberley; if you push it up, the train hits Courtney; if you do nothing, it hits them both."

"Well, Bud." Ozzy Man rolled his eyes. "Al found a second alternative, didn't he? He let the train sideswipe both of them before he put his grubby little paws on the lever." When neither Doppelgänger nor Al said anything, he added: "And then he threw Courtney straight under it."

"Yes," Al agreed miserably. "I did exactly that. How do I square it with myself now?"

"Dunno." Ozzy Man shook his head. "But you dithered for fucking ages! That's why the missus won't speak to you."

"We need an artificial intelligence computer or something," Doppelgänger said, cutting in over Ozzy Man, "to give us that answer."

"Yeah, Bud. But artificial intelligence is no match for natural stupidity."

Al put the car away, his keys on the counter in the kitchen. Kimberley was there. She hadn't said a word about the letter, but her whole being was different—as she had always been, except with a tiny sliver of lingering reserve.

"I'm making tea," he said. "Want?"

"Yes please." She smiled. Actually smiled, "Where have you been?"

"I've been to see Missy," He put the kettle on. She had sent him there in the first place—had insisted he ask Schalk Brinkman for a referral. "I think for the last time," he said.

"Oh, why?" She was interested. Kimberley divided the world into two parts, not equal. The one part, far smaller than the other, held what the world was, how it was put together, where tax returns came from and went to, why the sea is boiling hot, and whether pigs have wings. The other, more important part concerned emotions and relationships. How the divorcee husband messed his ex and her children around; why the spinster alone in her apartment was so quick to pick a fight; whether the self-confidant young man would behave properly when he married the vulnerable young girl whose parents wanted her to snaffle him.

"I think we have worked through the issues," Al said vaguely. Fortunately, the circles in which Kimberley moved were hot on doctor/patient confidentiality. She didn't push the subject; would no doubt later tell her mates that Missy had resolved Al's conflicts for him.

"You're not going to say, Mate," Ozzy Man asked, "that it has been worth tits on a bull, to coin a euphemism?"

"Oz," Doppelgänger said. "Don't be obtuse. If Kimberley likes the idea that matters psychological have run their course, how can you think it wasn't useful?"

"As fair as these green foreign hills may be," Ozzy Man said, "they are not the hills of home."

"What have you been up to?" Al put down two mugs of tea, sat down opposite his wife.

"I've been to meet the councillor," she said. "He is going to support our initiative with Inner Bertrams. The old gas works is being turned into a space for artists and crafts people, and the municipality will grant us a long-term lease for no rent."

"That's great!" he said, smiling encouragingly.

"Erica Holshausen is coordinating the finance. People say she's outstanding."

"When I was a scarecrow," Ozzy Man said, "people said I was outstanding in my field. But hay, it's in my jeans."

"Some of your puns are so convoluted," Doppelgänger said, rolling his eyes.

"Shall we go to movies on Thursday?" Kimberley announced the end of the war. "There's a film about widows in the displaced communities of Iraq."

"Ah, Christ, Mate." Ozzy Man groaned. "Maybe fight with her some more?"

"That sounds great," Al said, smiling. "Shall I book?"

32

"HOW WAS THE INTERVIEW"? AL asked. It was two days after the Iraqi widows had driven Ozzy Man into eye-rolling despair that he could ever leave the cinema again. Doppelgänger had bravely maintained that hundred-and-fifty-five minutes may feel long, but really weren't.

"The author was interesting and well spoken. He's an eccentric Scot, so well informed and funny, and with such a lovely accent. But the interviewer was a pain." Kimberley put down her bag, sat down at the table while he poured her a glass of wine.

"How so?"

Kimberley smiled over the crystal rim. This is what she was looking for—someone to listen and be interested. An ally against the world and its petty irritations. Going to talks and interviews was her thing, but her standards were exacting, and she needed an Ombudsman to whom she could detail her complaints. Al was perfect for the job.

Later, when she went to bed, he fired up his laptop. Here's what he wrote:

> *Hi there Gary,*
> *I have big news: Kimberley is speaking to me again; and I'm at the end of my dalliance, as I told you last time. My extra-marital deception lies scattered behind me in broken pieces, trodden into tiny shards and dust. And a hell of an Affaire de Coeur it was:*

Let me list for you the indelible taints of my infidelity: Once, when I became feeble about Jesse being far away, she squeezed my hand at table. At the Springsteen concert, when Kimberley and her husband had gone home, and we were wet and cold, and He was right there, weaving together His blend of magic and music, she leaned back against me and I put my arms around her, oh, for all of five seconds. And when I was saying to her 'I can't see you ever again,' and no doubt looked as if I were facing a firing squad, she squeezed my hand again. One, two, three strikes you're out, at the old ball game. I think Jane Austin would have wanted me to grow a pair.

The shrink I'm seeing, because Kimberley thinks I have father issues, wants me to follow my own destiny, look for my own happiness. It's not derivative, she says. It comes from within. I don't actually know what she means me to do: Perhaps she means me to have wild sex with Courtney; perhaps she wants me to tell Kimberley to fuck off and stop being so bossy; perhaps she doesn't know what she means.

But she's wrong, and so am I. I really did hurt Kimberley, albeit not intentionally. There is something deeply hurtful about your spouse really enjoying another person's company. Why? I don't really know, but I'm no different. Kimberley flirts with a wide array of hopeless and hapless admirers, sort of like her party game. A retired judge, the dean of music at Uni, a sincere old man (although not as old as me) who has a poetry reading circle, and anybody within range of her magnetic personality. It's never anything other than pure banter, a game, a light-hearted teasing. But I know it gets me down. I don't say so, but it does.

I haven't seen or spoken to Courtney since we said goodbye, and I feel like shit about it. I haven't behaved like a dick to many people, but I really pulled out the stops for her: I was a true-blue arsehole. And my shrink is wrong, about this as well: Happiness IS derivative. I'm only as happy as the people close to me. If Jesse has an issue, I want to tear the world down brick by brick to fix it. If Kimberley is miserable, I can't function properly. What

I need to manage now, is to stop caring about Courtney. I can't make her happy (in relation to me) and the only thing that will fix this is if she's no longer around—AND I forget about her. The second thing there being the difficult bit.

What shall we do with the drunken sailor? We'll put him in the long boat until he's sober. I don't know when that will be. But if it's early in the morning, I'll have a good breakfast.

A boiled egg is hard to beat.

How did I score with my affaire, do you think? When you had your fling, the one I know about, at least it was with an actress with screen presence. Sure, you got divorced because of it, but first you had the days of love and exhilaration, the nights of Rock 'n Roll. And now you've become such a smooth operator. So, my Bud, where did I screw up best of all? Did I jerk Kimberley or Courtney around most? Or myself? And how could/should I have avoided it? Please tell your parochial pal and motivate your answer in not fewer than 350 words.

I need every one of them.

Now, I put my tweezers away, until my eyebrows meet again.

Al

The night slid smoothly on towards its middle—when the ghosts come out and haunt everyone who is still awake. It's the witching hour because no one is praying: The monks and the nuns and the priests are all asleep. And if you are reading this late at night, you don't know what's creeping up behind you. Al made jasmine tea in the little cast iron pot, and sat with his cat out in the garden, together to interrogate the silence. A late-night flight rushed noisily overhead but didn't disturb the cricket that kept up its monotonous high-intensity screeching. Al finished his tea, went inside, locked up, turned out the lights.

He was happy that Kimberley was happy again.

That leaves only one thing then, in this part of Al's story.

33

EUROPE CLOSES DOWN IN AUGUST: Sends its people on holiday. South Africa does the same in mid-December. The curfew that tolls the knell of the dying year, is the 16th: The day on which the pioneers, the *Voortrekkers*, squared off against the *Zulu*, at the battle of Bloodriver. The Boers, presumptuously, promised God that if they won, they and their descendants would keep that day holy. Forever. Which became a problem when the side that won, lost political power in 1994. Nobody felt comfortable asking God for a dispensation, but fortunately, there always is the obfuscating combination of politics and PR. Between them, they rebranded the promise as *The Day of Reconciliation*, a masterstroke of equivocation, and the day became a secular holiday: You can choose for yourself what you want to do on it. The three weeks from then is Christmas holiday: Season of good cheer, commercial excess, and indulgence.

Before their set would disappear on holiday to warm African beaches and cold European ski-slopes, they got together at Max and Tessa's for a meal they all contributed to. It was the kind of evening every year where people say in amazement: *Where did the time go?*

At table, Al was seated next to an empty seat on his left. There was a matching gap at the other end of the table.

"I'm reading a book," Jenny Cartwright on his right said, "on the devastating effects of capitalism in developing countries. It's fascinating."

"I am reading a book on antigravity," Ozzy Man said. "I can't put it down."

Over the starter she kept up an haranguing monologue about all the stuff she reads: Three books a week, she said. While she told him, she poured several elegant glasses of chilled white wine, carefully chosen and curated by Max, straight down her gullet. Her pronunciation and articulation loosened a notch or two, and the narrow focus of her reason broadened substantially.

"Harper Lee's sister was a heavy drinker," Ozzy Man said. "She wrote *Tequila Mockingbird*."

Al heard Thomas first—out in the hall, explaining exuberantly: "So sorry we're late. We're doing an initial public offering for The Squintillion Fund, and my conference call ran late. Is everybody here? Have you started? That's a 2008 Dom Perignon—I got it in London yesterday. Have we disrupted your arrangements? Is the Judge here?"

The chair next to Al was for her. "Hi, Courtney," he smiled politely while adrenalin hollowed out his stomach.

"Hi," she said, looking searchingly into his eyes, then presenting her cheekbone to be kissed, as all couples did in this circle. Except that he hadn't ever kissed her cheek before. She sat down, but before Al could say a word, the Judge bellowed from the far end, where Kimberley was sitting: "We have an historian here! Say there, Clive my boy, where does Christmas come from?"

Clive was a bachelor, five-foot tall; and never bothered the scale in his bathroom to bring up the sixty-kilogram mark. His hair was sandy, short and conservatively fringed to the right; his eyes were attentive behind metal frames and lenses tinted faintly yellow; his expression was inclusive and conspiratorial; and his title was Professor, Dean of History.

"Heh-heh." He chuckled coyly, flattered that everyone should have focussed their attention on him. "The name, *Christmas*, is obvious: It comes from the Mass of Christ, said between sunset on the 24th of December and sunrise on the 25th. Midnight Mass, as it became."

"It wasn't always Christian though, was it?" Sy asked, business-man extraordinaire.

"No," Clive said. "The first official Christmas was during Constantine's reign. He was the first Christian emperor of Rome. It was a mass, a church service."

"But what is the history of Christmas?" Courtney asked, keen, as always, for the detail. She looked at Clive and Al looked at the side of her face. Doppelgänger and Ozzy Man were quiet as mice.

"There were many festivals at that time of year," Clive said. "The Romans had a festival called *Saturnalia*, with lots of food and drink; and they gave each other gifts. On December 25, they had the celebration of *Sol Invictus*, the *Unconquered Sun*. It was when the sun started coming back and the days started getting longer again."

"More wine?" Max asked, like the generous Paterfamilias during Saturnalia: Let the wine flow, let the band play, let friends gather—the end of the year was nigh.

"The Bible says nothing about when Jesus was born," Clive said. "But the theory goes that spring equinox is when the world was created; and on the fourth day there was light, which, of course, was the day of Jesus' conception. That would then be March 25; and December 25 is nine months later."

"That scientific, huh?" George, med school professor, said, taking a deep draught from his glass.

"Exactly." Clive nodded in amused agreement. Courtney's eyes flicked in Al's direction, caught him looking at her. He almost whipped his gaze away, like a guilty thief; but didn't. She held his gaze for an instant, crinkled her eyes in the tiniest of smiles, looked back at Clive.

"Where does Father Christmas come from?" Lewis Wilkins, nice guy and wine snob, asked.

"He comes from a poem," Clive said, looking impish and enjoying himself. "'*Twas The Night Before Christmas*. It describes Santa Claus as a jolly old elf, with a big stomach and the ability to get down a chimney by nodding his head. The public loved that. Christmas had become secular—the religious thing was still there, but most of it had run a full circle back to just a feast."

"In Aussie," Ozzy Man said, "they party on the beach; and Santa wears a white beard and a red budgie smuggler." He said: *pah-dy*.

"And the stuff about you had to behave otherwise you wouldn't get any presents?" Tracy Moore, owner of an HR recruitment agency, asked. "Used to scare me stupid every year."

Clive laughed shyly. "From a song. One you all know: *Santa Claus is coming to Town.*"

"*He's making a list, he's checking it twice; Gonna find out who's naughty and nice,*" George sang in a clear tenor.

"*Santa Claus is coming to town!*" the whole table responded. The intellectual cream of Johannesburg. Courtney laughed along with the rest.

"It was a mid-winter holiday that started simply as a feast, circled through a period of religious austerity, and is back to where it came from—just an excuse for a party. The only imposter, really, is Christ."

A few pairs of eyes widened at the kindly Professor's closing remark, but no one commented right away.

"Have you been well?" Al asked Courtney the most banal of all questions. Her eyes said: *If you were interested, you could have phoned.*

From the middle of the table, thankfully interrupting their awkward attempt at conversation, George was in full flow, in response to Edward's cautiously downplayed remark that Christ actually was the essence of Christmas.

"When you say you don't care for religion but believe in God, you are entirely incorrect. About both things." Edward, acting judge and AIDS activist, wilted in anticipation of the lesson he was about to receive. "God, as a concept that expresses your need to be noticed by the Universe, is wishful. Existence, in its many facets, doesn't give a fuck about you, wouldn't help you out of a tight spot even if it was aware of you, even if it could. God is simply a fiction that serves no useful purpose, other than dream fulfilment."

Courtney looked at Al, a smile riding as passenger in her eye. She had missed this stuff.

"But, by contrast," George said, "religion, the holy mashup, it works. There's the soul thing, so you have a tangible moral point of no-return. There's the congregation, so even the socially inept can have mates. And there's the charity business, to keep everyone busy. It all serves a purpose. Doing for others what they can't do for themselves, and not asking anything in return. Except the admiration of your fellow congregants and a shoo-in past the Big Gate in the Sky. It's the retired aunties and uncles and fresh-faced young priests and overweight spinsters with bushy hairdos and sensitive skin who, together, do all those things that need to be done: Being nice to the old and abandoned; keeping track of the feckless; feeding the hopeless; collecting blankets every year for the homeless. *Well done*, I say, to the Pentecostals, the Presbyterians, the Methodists and the Adventists. *Well done* to St Martins in the Veldt and in the 'Hood.''

Main course was on the table and the conversation fractured into several one-on-ones. Courtney and Al spoke in a narrow corridor. She dropped her voice, locked her gaze on Al. Like those many months ago, tiny magnets clicked together.

"Do you love me?" she asked. She kept those dark eyes on him while he squirmed. She wouldn't look away; he couldn't.

"Courtney," he said. Doppelgänger and Ozzy Man both silent. On a lonely mountain somewhere in California, the SETI telescope array scoured the forlorn icy vacuum of forever, looking for an answer. Down the other end of the table, Kimberley sat between the retired Judge and Ronald Kahn, Professor of music. She was the centre of their concentrated attention; she tossed her head, laughed—the sound Al loved best.

"How many loved your moments of glad grace and loved your beauty with love false or true," Doppelgänger murmured, watching her.

"Do you?" Courtney asked, insisting.

He held her gaze quietly, compressed his lips into a thin, unforgiving line; nodded almost imperceptibly. "You know I do," he said.

Across the table Kimberley laughed.

But one man loved the Pilgrim soul in you and loved the sorrows of your changing face.

About the Author

GERRY SHELDON is a retired attorney, living in Johannesburg. He started school in Afrikaans and, in high school, swapped to English. He qualified as a lawyer at Wits University in Johannesburg, studying six languages as an undergrad. He spent 40 years in city law firms specialising in commercial drafting; and has been married for more than 30. His children have left home, one to Australia, the other to the USA. Both dogs and his cat are still at home. Gerry is a secular humanist who regards morality as a product of evolution. This is his first novel.

Printed by Imprimerie Gauvin
Gatineau, Québec